THE ECHOING STRANGERS

Gladys Maude Winifred Mitchell – or 'The Great Gladys' as Philip Larkin called her – was born in 1901, in Cowley in Oxfordshire. She graduated in history from University College London and in 1921 began her long career as a teacher. She studied the works of Sigmund Freud and attributed her interest in witchcraft to the influence of her friend, the detective novelist Helen Simpson.

Her first novel, *Speedy Death*, was published in 1929 and introduced readers to Beatrice Adela Lestrange Bradley, the heroine of a further sixty six crime novels. She wrote at least one novel a year throughout her career and was an early member of the Detection Club, alongside Agatha Christie, G.K Chesterton and Dorothy Sayers. In 1961 she retired from teaching and, from her home in Dorset, continued to write, receiving the Crime Writers' Association Silver Dagger in 1976. Gladys Mitchell died in 1983.

T0314588

ALSO BY GLADYS MITCHELL

Speedy Death
The Mystery of a Butcher's Shop
The Longer Bodies
The Saltmarsh Murders
Death and the Opera
The Devil at Saxon Wall
Dead Men's Morris
Come Away, Death
St Peter's Finger
Printer's Error
Hangman's Curfew
When Last I Died
Laurels Are Poison
The Worsted Viper
Sunset Over Soho
My Father Sleeps
The Rising of the Moon
Here Comes a Chopper
Death and the Maiden
Tom Brown's Body
Groaning Spinney
The Devil's Elbow
The Echoing Strangers
Merlin's Furlong
Watson's Choice
Faintley Speaking
Twelve Horses and the Hangman's Noose
The Twenty-Third Man
Spotted Hemlock
The Man Who Grew Tomatoes
Say It With Flowers
The Nodding Canaries

My Bones Will Keep
Adders on the Heath
Death of the Delft Blue
Pageant of a Murder
The Croaking Raven
Skeleton Island
Three Quick and Five Dead
Dance to Your Daddy
Gory Dew
Lament for Leto
A Hearse on May-Day
The Murder of Busy Lizzie
Winking at the Brim
A Javelin for Jonah
Convent on Styx
Late, Late in the Evening
Noonday and Night
Fault in the Structure
Wraiths and Changelings
Mingled With Venom
The Mudflats of the Dead
Nest of Vipers
Uncoffin'd Clay
The Whispering Knights
Lovers, Make Moan
The Death-Cap Dancers
The Death of a Burrowing Mole
Here Lies Gloria Mundy
Cold, Lone and Still
The Greenstone Griffins
The Crozier Pharaohs
No Winding-Sheet

VINTAGE MURDER MYSTERIES

With the sign of a human skull upon its back and a melancholy shriek emitted when disturbed, the Death's Head Hawkmoth has for centuries been a bringer of doom and an omen of death - which is why we chose it as the emblem for our Vintage Murder Mysteries.

Some say that its appearance in King George III's bedchamber pushed him into madness. Others believe that should its wings extinguish a candle by night, those nearby will be cursed with blindness. Indeed its very name, *Acherontia atropos*, delves into the most sinister realms of Greek mythology: Acheron, the River of Pain in the underworld, and Atropos, the Fate charged with severing the thread of life.

The perfect companion, then, for our Vintage Murder Mysteries sleuths, for whom sinister occurrences are never far away and murder is always just around the corner …

GLADYS MITCHELL

The Echoing Strangers

VINTAGE BOOKS
London

Published by Vintage 2014

2 4 6 8 10 9 7 5 3 1

Copyright © The Executors of the Estate of Gladys Mitchell 1952

Gladys Mitchell has asserted her right under the Copyright, Designs
and Patents Act 1988 to be identified as the author of this work

This book is sold subject to the condition that it shall not,
by way of trade or otherwise, be lent, resold, hired out,
or otherwise circulated without the publisher's prior
consent in any form of binding or cover other than that
in which it is published and without a similar condition,
including this condition, being imposed
on the subsequent purchaser

First published in Great Britain by
Michael Joseph Ltd in 1952

Vintage
Random House, 20 Vauxhall Bridge Road,
London SW1V 2SA

www.vintage-books.co.uk

Addresses for companies within The Random House Group Limited
can be found at: www.randomhouse.co.uk/offices.htm

The Random House Group Limited Reg. No. 954009

A CIP catalogue record for this book
is available from the British Library

ISBN 9780099583882

The Random House Group Limited supports The Forest Stewardship
Council® (FSC®), the leading international forest-certification organisation.
Our books carrying the FSC label are printed on FSC®-certified paper.
FSC is the only forest-certification scheme supported by the leading
environmental organisations, including Greenpeace. Our
paper procurement policy can be found at
www.randomhouse.co.uk/environment

Printed and bound in Great Britain by Clays Ltd, St Ives plc

CHAPTER ONE

Deaf and Dumb Alphabet

*

*'Either the attention was allowed to dwell upon the
ruins . . . or else the intervening layers were impatiently
broken through for the purpose of arriving at the oldest
and most primitive evidences of human life.'*

A History of Greek Religion
by Martin P. Nilsson translated by F. J. Fielden

*

IF THERE is one morbid phenomenon of civilized existence
to which scant justice has been done in English fiction, it
is the devastating re-discovery in later life of the old
school chum. The supreme examples, in Mrs. Bradley's
opinion, were couched in the language of comedy and farce
respectively: the visit of Cissie Crabbe to the Provincial
Lady and the agonising eruption into the married bliss of
Richard (Bingo) Little of the egregious Laura Pyke.

'. . . he returns with Cissie Crabbe, who has put on
weight, and says several times that we have both *changed* a
good deal . . .'

Mrs. Bradley sighed. The letter she had just laid down
could have been, she reflected resignedly, from Cissie
Crabbe in person. The world, it seemed, abounded in Cissie
Crabbes.

'Now that you're this way for a spell, I do wish you would
come and see me. No doubt we have both changed a good
deal, but Auld Lang Syne still counts for something. Shall
expect you some time next week. No need to let me know
which day, as I am always in and there's quite a good hotel
in the village where I always lunch people. It saves so much
trouble, and as I myself am on a diet . . .'

9

These diets, thought Mrs. Bradley dispiritedly. 'Utter impossibility of obtaining lentils or lemons at short notice . . .' So much for the diet of Cissie Crabbe; and in the case of Laura Pyke, 'She spoke freely of proteins, carbohydrates and the physiological requirements of the average individual. She was not a girl who believed in mincing her words, and a racy little anecdote she told about a man who refused to eat prunes . . .'

Mrs. Bradley shook her head. She had last met Mabel Parkinson in the year 1922 or thereabouts, and she could not imagine what they could still have in common except, needless to say, that curse of Auld Lang Syne to which Mabel had already paid tribute. If proof were needed of its power, Mrs. Bradley found herself, a quarter of an hour later, writing to accept the invitation.

Mabel Parkinson lived in the village of Wetwode, a hybrid little place on the River Burwater. At one end was the village proper with its one hotel kept alive by motor traffic and river trippers, and at the other end was the new but not particularly objectionable housing estate on which Mabel had chosen to live. Along the river frontage were a couple of boat-builders' yards, a timber store, a kiosk which sold picture postcards, cigarettes, Ordnance Survey maps, newspapers and jig-saw puzzles, and on the opposite bank, over the bridge and about a couple of miles down-river, were a few sodden-looking holiday bungalows, each with its boathouse and tiny staithe.

Mabel Parkinson's house happened to be the first one on the new estate, as the car came out from the village, and Mrs. Bradley's chauffeur found it without difficulty. There was a notice on the gate.

So sorry. Sister suddenly taken ill in Gateshead. Do come another day.

Mrs. Bradley, mentally paying the usual automatic homage to illness, at the same time felt relief at the prospect of not being obliged to pay the prearranged visit. The car had passed the hotel on the way out. She proposed to return there for lunch, potter about the village and its environs, have tea at her favourite hotel in Norwich, and return to friends in Kings Lynn (where she was staying) in time for a bath and dinner.

The date was towards the end of June, the weather discreetly perfect. Lunch at the hotel was good, and when it was over she had coffee in the riverside garden. There was a large tree for those who preferred the shade. It was set in a long, smooth, lawn broken here and there by circular flower-beds in which roses were freely blooming. For entertainment there were the coming and going of boats, a friendly cat, and the hotel boatman who suggested, when the maid collected Mrs. Bradley's tray, that it was a nice afternoon for the river. Mrs. Bradley glanced at two small motor-launches. Their gleaming brass and highly-polished mahogany had already produced a seductive and weakening effect upon her determination to have nothing whatever to do with aquatics that afternoon. She gave in almost immediately.

'Self-drive, madam, or man to accompany?'

'Oh, there will most likely be two of us. We shall be all right,' said Mrs. Bradley, who could imagine few things more uninteresting than a launch trip with man to accompany.

'I'll get her out for you, then, madam. Which one would you prefer?'

Out of the corner of her eye Mrs. Bradley could see her chauffeur. He was talking to the gardener, and they began to turn away towards the shrubs which screened the hotel's lock-up garages. She called her man by name.

'George!'

'Yes, madam?' George came over to her. He was a stocky fellow, friendly, obliging and discreet.

'Which of these boats do I want?'

'The Thornycroft, madam. I inspected both motor-launches whilst you were finishing lunch. It is a better engine than the other, is suited to the construction of the launch, and is nicely bedded.'

'Ah,' said Mrs. Bradley, looking at him with the reserved

admiration which she retained for all persons who understood petrol or diesel engines. 'Are you coming, George?
Don't, unless you like. I can manage the boat quite well so
long as nothing but starting, stopping and steering are
involved.'

'If not obtruding myself, I should be very happy to
accompany you, madam.'

'Good. Then I'll tie my scarf over my head and we can
be off.'

She produced a witch-like effect by dealing with the first
item on this agenda and grinned amiably as she watched the
boatman untie the launch. In less than five minutes, with
George lounging in the back and herself at the simple
controls, the launch was purring upstream at about four
knots, this modest speed being maintained out of deference
for the oozy banks of the river.

'Not much further this way, madam,' said George, at the
end of three-quarters of an hour. 'Our draught won't
permit. We're getting into shoal water.'

'All right,' agreed his employer. 'Let's go back. *You'd*
better turn the boat round.' She cut out the engine and
moved over. When they got back to the hotel it was barely
three o'clock.

'Should we not go downstream for a bit, madam? You
will like to see what lies beyond the bridge.'

'Shall I? All right, then. We have plenty of time.'

The boatman, seeing their intention, called out from the
bank:

'Keep well over to starboard, and give a touch on the
horn. And don't forget all moorings is private until you get
to the Broad.'

Under the centre arch of the ancient bridge drifted the
launch, with her engine barely ticking over. Then George
accelerated. They passed the kiosk, the timber-store and
the boat-builders' yards, and at the end of twenty minutes
or so they found themselves approaching the first of the
riverside bungalows. In front of it was a small lawn, chopped
into to provide a mooring space for a yacht or a cruiser. On

the lawn were a middle-aged woman and a slender, hand-some youth. The river made a pronounced bend where the bungalows began, so that, although there were numbers of boats on the river that afternoon, it chanced that, as it came into the bend, Mrs. Bradley's launch had the short reach to itself.

The middle-aged woman was looking downstream and the youth was standing close to and a little behind her. As Mrs. Bradley watched, he suddenly extended both arms and pushed the woman into the river.

George gave a smothered exclamation. The youth turned and cantered towards the bungalow, leaving the woman to struggle. It was soon obvious that she could swim, and was in no immediate danger, but, encumbered by water-clogged clothing, she was not able to get back on to the bank with-out assistance. George cut out the engine and brought the launch up to the lawn. He leapt ashore with the mooring rope, took a couple of twists round a post, lay on his stomach, extended his arm to the woman and soon had her safely on the lawn.

Mrs. Bradley, meanwhile, had also stepped ashore. The woman was sitting on the grass squeezing water out of her skirt. She coughed, spat, and gratefully accepted a dry handkerchief on which to blow her nose.

'Thanks,' she said. 'Well, he's never done *that* before.'

Mrs. Bradley could not sufficiently admire this philo-sophic handling of the situation. George withdrew to a respectful distance, ready to unhitch the launch when this seemed to be required. In a few moments the youth came up to the woman, looked at her, then sauntered towards the water. He was a tall boy of about seventeen, with a thin face and remarkably large eyes. These accorded to his countenance a saintly expression which did not seem to coincide with his actions and intentions. George kept a wary eye on him but, looking down at the launch and presenting to George a thin profile as stern as that of a Red Indian, the boy added nothing to anybody's knowledge of his mind.

The woman, declining further assistance, went into the bungalow, presumably to dry her hair and change her clothes. Mrs. Bradley returned to the launch and the youth removed himself to the far side of the lawn.

'I don't like leaving them together after what we saw, George,' said Mrs. Bradley, 'but the woman insists that what happened was an accident. There seems nothing for us to do except to take ourselves off.'

George untied the launch, and the next minute they were moving gently upstream towards the hotel.

'Those bungalows,' said Mrs. Bradley, when she had paid the hotel boatman and tipped him. 'Who lives in them?'

'Oh, most of them only let for about three months in the summer, madam. The first one this way, that's let permanent, though. A deaf and dumb young fellow and a lady named Higgs that look after him, they have it. He come from a very good family, so I hear, but his friends don't want him.'

'How long have they been there?'

'A matter of ten year or more.'

'Do you see them about much?'

'Pretty fairly. She shop in the village mostly, and sometimes they drop in here for lunch or tea. And the boy, he's solitary. That do go about by himself a good deal.'

'Is the boy a mental case?'

'No. That seem intelligent enough, except he can't hear or talk proper.'

'Oh? We met them. The woman fell into the river and my man got her out.'

'Wasn't this young Mr. Caux handy, then? Fine swimmer, he is. We have a regatta and swimming races on the Broad here, and that win every race he go in for.'

'Interesting. How does he know when to start if he's as deaf as you say?'

'He watch Miss Higgs. She drop a handkerchief.'

'I see. She's fond of him, I take it? Apart from just looking after him, I mean.'

'Oh, yes. Proud of him, too. They get on a treat together.'

'What do you make of it, George?' asked Mrs. Bradley,

for her man had been standing within earshot. George shook his head.

'Extremely odd, madam. The young fellow certainly pushed her in. Maybe something she did exasperated him and he acted hastily.'

'That seems to be the most reasonable explanation. But I don't like it much, because he certainly wasn't going to attempt to get her out.'

'He may not have realized how great an encumbrance a lady's skirt can be, madam.'

'True. Oh, well, we can't do anything more.'

She was wrong about that, however. She told the story at dinner to her host.

'Caux? Caux? Oh, yes, there was a shocking scandal about fourteen years ago. I forget the details, but the father was had up for manslaughter. He was lucky not to have been charged with murder, I believe.'

'Really?'

'Yes. Oh, I remember now. It was something to do with one of the women servants, and a manservant got to know about it. He tried to blackmail Caux, and Caux lost his temper and banged him over the head with a decanter of port. It was a very heavy cut-glass thing and it smashed the fellow's skull. It was proved by the defence that the skull was thin and that the blow wouldn't have killed the average person.'

'So Mr. Caux went to prison, I take it?'

'Only for a year. Then he was killed in a car crash three or four years later. His wife, too. He left two boys, one of whom, I believe, was in the car at the time of the accident. I heard some rumour that the shock had left him deaf and dumb. Anyway, the grandfather got rid of this poor lad and is bringing up the other to be his heir. The property is entailed and the boys are twins, and there are dark rumours that the thrown-out one, Francis, is the older twin, but I know nothing about that.'

'How do you come to know what you do know?'

'Oh, the estate is in Hampshire. I used to live in the next

village and we shared the pub. You get lots of gossip in a
pub, some of it fact, some not. And, of course, we used to
play them at cricket.'

'It is such a coincidence that you used to live in that
village, and such another coincidence that I should have
witnessed what certainly looked like an attempt at murder,
that I don't feel inclined to leave matters as they are,' said
Mrs. Bradley thoughtfully. 'I wonder how I can manage
to . . .'

Her host caught his wife's eye, and winked at her.

'You'd better rent the bungalow next door,' he suggested
facetiously; but Mrs. Bradley, who had intercepted the
wink, nodded vigoously.

'The very thing!' she said. 'I wonder who the agents are?
Oh, well, the people at the hotel are certain to know. I'll
go over there to-morrow and enquire. I don't remember
seeing a board out, though.'

Her luck, as usual, was in. The people who had hired a
bungalow for July had been prevented from coming, and
Mrs. Bradley made a satisfactory bargain for tenancy. She
moved in on the Saturday. Rather to her surprise the
woman in the first bungalow welcomed her warmly, made
her a cup of tea and suddenly unburdened herself.

'I know you saw what Francis did the other day. It
wasn't a bit like him. There's something on his mind. It's to
do with the river, but, of course, he can't tell me what it is.
He can't speak properly, you see.'

'Can't he read and write?'

The woman's face darkened.

'That old brute, his grandfather, wouldn't have anything
done for him at all, and I can't afford to, on the money I'm
paid. I've tried to teach him, but I haven't the knack. All I
can do is to love him and try to understand him.'

'He looks remarkably intelligent.'

'Oh, he is. I'm sure he is. But it's so difficult, you know,
when there's no communication in words and when he
can't hear anything, either. I've tried to teach him to lip-
read, but it means nothing to him at all.'

'I should be interested to get to know him. Is he very shy?'

'I think he knows he's under some serious disability, and of course he knows he wasn't wanted at home. It makes him a bit . . . queer. I don't know what or how he thinks. But do make friends with him. If only you or somebody . . . anybody . . . could manage to find out what's troubling him. I know it must be the river, because he won't take out the dinghy and he won't go swimming any more.'

'I'm a psychiatrist. I should be most interested to make his acquaintance. Was he born deaf and dumb?'

'No, he wasn't. He had a terrible shock when he was a little boy. He saw his father and mother both killed. It dates from then. I'm always hoping something may put things right, but he's almost a man, and, so far . . .'

'So far nothing has happened . . . or, rather, no miracle has happened. He is in a state of trauma. It should be possible . . .' She pursed up her beaky little mouth. 'Tell me more about him.'

'There isn't much more to tell. He's moody, of course, and his appetite varies very much. For days at a time he'll hardly eat a thing, and then he becomes quite hungry. Sometimes . . . I'm speaking of the time before all this worry began about the boat and the river . . . he won't be persuaded to swim at all, and at other times he revels in the water. It's most peculiar.'

'Does he take any other form of exercise?'

'He played cricket one year for the village, and did very well, but they couldn't get him to play again, not even in the return match. He just turned completely obstinate.'

'Does he show any sign of being interested in girls?'

'No girl would want him, would she? There was trouble once, though, about a year ago. The father came here and wanted to thrash him. I threatened to call the police. I was terribly frightened, and so was Francis. He ran away and hid, and I had great difficulty in getting him to come back when the man had gone. I believe he did behave disgracefully, but fortunately there were no consequences, and the girl got married a month ago and went to live in Norwich, so that was a very good thing. I think Francis learnt his lesson, but I was terribly worried for a long time. I'd never thought of him as a *bad* boy, and it doesn't seem as though he is. He just forgot himself, I suppose, or perhaps the girl tempted him. She was nineteen to his sixteen, and ought to have known better, but she complained that he was violent and took her by surprise. Of course, some boys are lustful. It's nature coming out, I suppose, but it's very inconvenient. I wrote to Sir Adrian . . . that's his grandfather, you know . . . about it, not mincing my words, and suggested that perhaps it was time a man took Francis over, but I got no reply except an addition to my usual cheque. It was welcome, but I'd rather have had it for some other reason.'

'What about pocket-money? Does the boy's grandfather supply any?'

'Oh, yes. Sometimes I've wondered . . .' she hesitated, and then added, 'I might as well say it, as I've begun . . . sometimes I've wondered how Francis gets as much money as he seems to possess. Sir Adrian sends it to him once a quarter, and he always hands me the cheque to cash for him, so I know how much he has. Yet sometimes I've suspected that he must have some other source of supply.'

'His twin brother, do you think?'

'Oh, no. The envelope containing the cheque is the only one he ever receives, and the cheque is always signed *Adrian Caux*. There is no letter inside . . . at least, I don't think there can be because he would have to give it to me to read if there were, and, in any case, he wouldn't be able to learn the contents, as he can't hear.'

'You have a difficult task. I don't envy you.'

'It's a living,' said Miss Higgs, 'and I'm fond of the boy, you know.'

CHAPTER TWO

Amateur Status

★

'They are depicted as the eye of imagination sees them.'
Nilsson

★

A FEW DAYS after Mrs. Bradley had gone to live in the village of Wetwode, a young schoolmaster named Tom Donagh was glancing at the advertisements in an educational weekly when he chanced to read one which interested him very much.

'I say, Bishop,' he said to the only other master in the Common Room, 'what do you make of this? *Holiday Tutor required for one boy, slightly backward, during Mede Cricket Week. Opening batsman and slip fielder preferred. Public school and University essential. Give last season's batting average, state whether Blue, bring pyjamas and black tie if called for interview. Apply Sir Adrian Caux, Mede, Hants.'*

'Questionable way of getting a bit more class into a village team,' said Bishop.

'I shall apply, I think.'

'What on earth for?'

'I don't know. I wouldn't mind being paid for a week's cricket, and that's obviously what it comes to.'

'It doesn't give the date, and we've still a week of term.'

'Don't I know it! I haven't finished my reports yet and the Old Man has still to sign the beastly things. I've done Masters' three times. What can you say about a harmless half-wit without giving offence to his parents?'

'I always put *Tries* for Masters, and leave it at that. After all, he *may* try. We've no evidence that he doesn't. The boy who worries me is Gregory. He's a brilliant mathematician but not a word of English literature will enter his head, let alone stay there long enough for the examiners to rake it out again. I'm afraid he'll fail Common Entrance.'

'I'd better make a special study of both lads if I'm to take on tutoring a backward boy. I wonder what the pay will be?'

'Dash it, you haven't *got* the job yet!'

'I've got a feeling I'm going to apply for it, anyway. There's a smack of bare-faced jiggery-pokery about it which fascinates me. I'm very anxious to meet this shifty and snobbish baronet. I'm not sure I won't apply to-night, as soon as I get to my digs. This paper only came out to-day, and I might be first in the field.'

He did apply and received a telegram in the following week which read: *Waterloo four-thirty Saturday meet car Brockenhurst the very man Caux.*

The train was packed, but Donagh had booked a corner seat and the journey was not a long one. Waiting for him at Brockenhurst were a large car and a small, ferrety-looking chauffeur.

'Mr. Donagh, sir?'

'Yes.'

'Any other luggage, sir?'

'No.'

'Very good, sir.'

'Is it far?'

'Matter of nine miles, sir.' And with this they drove through an open stretch of the New Forest, through a village, past inviting lanes and so to a short, squat, gloomy house.

Tom's first sensation was one of slight deflation. The place certainly did not give an impression of the wealth that he had anticipated. There was no suggestion of ease and comfort about it, and his entry into a dim hall lighted only by a hideous stained-glass window at the further end through which a defeated late-afternoon sun seemed disinclined to attempt to penetrate, gave no more promise of what he had expected than had the unimposing first sight of the house itself.

A manservant had opened the door. He led Tom through the hall and up to the stained-glass window. This he put down Tom's bag to open. The scene changed with some abruptness. The unprepossessing window looked on to an enormous green field golden with the late afternoon light. It was bounded by heavy elm trees on one side and on the other three by a tall fence painted primrose colour and broken only by a large pavilion which backed on to the house. Batting screens, a motor mower, an enormous roller and a stretch of tarpaulin laid in the centre of the ground left nothing to Tom's imagination.

'Yes, sir, that's our cricket field,' remarked the man-servant. 'We thought you'd like to see it before you went to your room, as that does not overlook the back of the house.'

'We? Then you're in the team?'

'Oh, yes, sir. We're all in the team, sir. That's how we keep our positions here, and obtain our gratuities.'

'All amateurs, I take it?' said Tom, ironically.

'Oh, yes, but keen, sir. Very keen indeed, if I may say so. Oh, we shan't disgrace you with our company.'

He turned away from the window, leaving it open, and picked up Tom's suitcase. Tom, carrying his cricket bag, followed him to the left and up a dark staircase. At the top was an equally gloomy landing. The bedroom doors were named. The man stopped at one marked Neville Cardus, opened the door and stood aside to let Tom pass.

The window was heavily curtained, giving the impression of a death in the house. The man put Tom's suitcase on a wide wooden stool, went across to the window and disclosed it.

'The sun can do little harm now, sir.'

'I shouldn't suppose so.'

'The master has a theory, sir, that a cricketer's eyes should not be unnecessarily exposed to a bright light. You will, in consequence, discover this to be a restful house, sir.'

Tom had already come to the conclusion that it would probably drive him mad, but both courtesy and policy made him disinclined to say this, so he nodded and asked:

'Where do I aim for when I've changed?'

'I will personally conduct you, sir. Should you care to give me your clothes, sir, I will press them whilst you bathe.'

'Oh, they'll be all right. I'm a careful packer.'

'Very good, sir. Would you be so good as to ring bell number four when you require me? Bell number one is for drinks, bell number two is connected with the garage, bell number three is for the housemaid and bell number four is my own personal bell, sir.'

He departed, closing the door noiselessly. Tom looked at his watch, gave the man a couple of minutes, and then experimented with bell number one. It was answered immediately by a tall young fellow who carried a slate and chalk.

'Something after your journey, sir?'

'Yes, please.'

'Brandy and splash, sir?'

'No. A longer drink than that.'

'John Collins, sir?'

'Yes, please.' It came in five minutes' time. 'Where's the bathroom? I forgot to ask.'

By the time he was ready to ring bell number four it was half-past seven and he was extremely hungry. The man-servant, whose name turned out to be Walters, conducted him downstairs and to the right and so to a large, depressing dining-room. It was decorated in sage green, and the portraits on the walls were all of cricketers. Tom had no difficulty in recognizing Hutton, Hendren, Sutcliffe and Hobbs, but was defeated, until he appealed to his host, by one or two others whom he felt he should have known by sight but did not.

His host turned out to be a man in what appeared to be the middle of middle age, although it turned out later that he was sixty-three. He was stoutish and florid, with the profile of a cruel man and the full face of a self-indulgent one. Tom immediately took a deep dislike to him.

'I see you're looking at our family portraits,' said Sir Adrian. Tom agreed, and added that he was sorry not to see Larwood among them. 'Oh, but he is,' Sir Adrian declared. 'You haven't looked in the window alcove.'

Tom repaired this omission and then asked, 'Does your cricket week begin on Monday, sir?'

'Here, here! None of that *Sir* business! I'm not as old as all that! How old are *you*?'

'Twenty-four.'

'Correct. I've looked you up, you know.'

'I should hardly have thought you'd had time.'

'Oh, I keep the tabs on you fellows. You're the T. P. St. X. Donagh who scored fifty-seven not out in the Winchester match in 1945 and had a batting average of forty-three point nought six recurring in the season of 1948. Not all that good, mind you. You should never have attempted to hook Chaveley. Chaveley should never be rashly handled. His length is perfect.'

'It pays to take a chance sometimes.'

'Ha! You can take chances, young fellow, but you can't take criticism, eh?'

'Not when I know I did the only thing I could.'

'Good. Splendid. Well, our week begins on Monday, a friendly against Lord Averdon's team. That doesn't matter a bit. On Tuesday—well, more about that later. Just two innings apiece on Monday, you understand. If the second innings by any chance shouldn't be concluded, we draw, of course. Now Thursday really is important. On Thursday and Saturday we play the next village, Bruke. Last year they beat us. That's why I advertised. There's no residence qualification or any nonsense of that sort. It's like professional soccer. What you can get hold of is what you play in your eleven. Well, I've got hold of *you*, and God help you if you don't earn your keep!'

'What is my keep, by the way?'

'Oh, as to that, yes. You'd better meet Derek. We are a strictly amateur side, Mr. Donagh. I want no question raised about that. You are here to tutor my grandson. The cricket is by the way . . . officially, I mean, of course. You will like Derry.'

'You mentioned in the advertisement that he was backward.'

'Don't be an ass, man. If he weren't backward he wouldn't need a holiday tutor. But you don't want to hear about that. He'll be down in a minute. You want to know what I'm going to pay you. Well, what do you say to free board and lodging for a week, a tenner, and, if we beat Bruke, another twenty pounds?'

'Am I up for interview, Sir Adrian, or have I got the job?'

'Oh, you've got it, of course. I thought you understood that.'

'Then I'll take the ten pounds for tutoring your grandson, but I don't care, otherwise, whether we win or lose, provided it's a fairly decent game.'

'Done,' said Sir Adrian immediately. 'Although the twenty pounds wouldn't prejudice your amateur status, you know. It would only be an honorarium.'

Before Donagh could argue this point the door opened and in came the most beautiful youth he had ever seen. He was tall and graceful, had a noble profile, golden hair, a short Greek mouth and large brown eyes. He smiled at Sir Adrian and came straight up to Tom.

'How do you do, Mr. Donagh? How decent of you to come, sir. Did you have a good journey?' His voice was as exquisite and, somehow, as unreal as his appearance.

'Yes,' said Tom puzzled, for if this were a backward pupil then he himself was a moron. 'You are not my baby bear, are you?'

'And you my bear leader? Oh, yes, of course. I say, sir, the bowlers must have been glad to see the back of you when you got that one hundred and twenty-one at Lords last season!'

Tom, who had found himself wondering what effect a swift kick would have upon the Dresden china lad, politely smiled, for open admiration is disarming.

'Oh, I don't know,' he said, deprecatingly. 'I rather think I had an awful lot of luck. I was missed at second slip when I'd made two.'

'That was an impossible catch, sir. You didn't really give away a chance there. *You* might have taken that ball, but I don't know of anyone else who could have held it. You agree, Grand? You know, we said at the time . . .'

'Now don't go puffing him up, Derry,' said Sir Adrian. 'His cricket isn't at all bad, but there's no need to hero-worship him. Let's just hope he makes one hundred and twenty-one for *us* on Thursday, and gives no chances of any kind, and leave it at that.' The words were harsh enough, but the look which accompanied them was so dotingly affectionate that it transfigured Sir Adrian's fleshy face and bulbous little eyes to such an extent that Tom could suddenly see a family resemblance between the Narcissus of a youth and his beefish grandfather. It was fleeting, however. The gong sounded. Sir Adrian, rubbing the side of his jowl, observed that he was famished, seized a glass of sherry from a tray brought in by bell number one, waved to Tom to help himself, gulped down the drink, seized another, gulped that, blew out his cheeks, smacked his lips, and led the way to table.

The dinner was a good one, but there was nothing else to drink, not even coffee at the end. Sir Adrian ate heartily; so did Tom; but Derek took only a small amount of soup and a morsel of sole and refused the roast. Tom saw his grandfather look anxiously at him once or twice, but no comment was made. Nuts, preserved ginger and *marrons* appeared on the table together with grapes and peaches, and at this stage Derek ate avidly and his grandfather looked a little happier.

'What's the St. X. in your name stand for?' he suddenly demanded of Tom.

'St. Xavier.'

'R.C. name.'

'Yes, I'm an Irishman.'

'Oh, yes, of course. They're not much good at cricket as a rule.'

'It is not a game that appeals to them very much, Grand,' said Derek, looking up from peeling a peach and smiling very confidingly at Tom. 'It doesn't accord very well with their national temperament.'

'Too crude and impatient,' said Sir Adrian, 'to do anything really well except fox-hunting and fighting. What do *you* say, Donagh?'

'I've not lived in Ireland since I was six,' replied Tom, who found himself, to his own rueful annoyance, becoming extremely angry.

'Well, you're entitled to an opinion, surely?'

'It's this, then: I don't think Irishmen are a particularly patient race, and this particular Irishman isn't patient at all except with animals and very small prep-school boys. As for cricket——'

'I wish I'd gone to a public school,' said Derek, displaying social tact in changing the conversation. 'It's always been a bone of contention between Grand and me. I was educated privately. It makes me feel out of things.'

'You weren't tough enough for an English public school,' said his grandfather, looking at him fondly. 'You shall go to Oxford, though, when you are a couple of years older. You'd like that, wouldn't you?'

'Very much, Grand. Thank you. You are very good to me.' He wiped his lips and fingers on his table napkin, laid it on the table, went round to his grandfather, and, to Tom's horror, kissed him on the forehead and ruffled his stiff dark hair with a hand as slender as a girl's.

Tom was glad, when dinner was over, to be told abruptly by Sir Adrian that he could come into the library if he chose, but that he was free to do exactly as he liked provided that he got enough sleep to keep himself fit for Monday's game.

Tom said he would write some letters and stretch his legs by going out to post them.

'Good idea,' said Sir Adrian. 'Turn right at the gates. Post office is the other end of the village. About a mile and a half from here. Exercise will do you a world of good. I like a man who doesn't need a car to take him half a mile.'

'I wish I could go with you, Mr. Donagh,' said Derek, 'but I want to get on with my Chinese.'

'Chinese?'

'Yes. I am teaching myself Chinese. I prefer it, I think, to Russian, although, of course, that is fascinating, too.'

Tom, rather staggered by this further evidence of backwardness in his pupil, went up to his room, wrote a letter to his mother and went out, with it and a pipe, towards the village. His objective was not so much the post office as the pub.

CHAPTER THREE

Dead Man's Keel

★

'. . . and deeds beyond remedy been wrought.'
      Iliad—Homer (Lang, Leaf and Myers)

★

MRS. BRADLEY, unaware that her path would so soon cross that of Tom Donagh, was very slowly gaining a little ground at Wetwode. Having taken up her tenancy of the riverside bungalow, she had begun by sending for a grand-nephew, Godfrey Lestrange, a mechanically-minded boy of eighteen, telling his parents over the telephone of the task she proposed to set him if he were permitted to join her.

Godfrey turned up next day on his elder brother's motor-cycle and when he had had a meal he brought the machine on to the riverside lawn and proceeded to take it to pieces. (Mrs. Bradley had guaranteed to its owner a new contraption if disaster overtook this one.)

Francis Caux, mooning about the next-door lawn, strolled over to see what was happening. Two hours later Godfrey came in for some food, two tall glasses and a jugful of shandy-gaff. He went outside again, and by five o'clock was able to report progress.

'He doesn't know the first thing about bikes, but he's frightfully keen. He watches everything I do, and when I want a bit of the bike or a tool I point and then say its name. We're not doing too badly, on the whole.'

Mrs. Bradley, who had kept surreptitious watch on the proceedings, had come to the conclusion that her grand-nephew was managing to communicate with Francis with a considerable degree of success. She did not say this, but she

27

commended her relative for his patience and good-nature and adjured him to continue the work on the morrow.

'Oh, I'd like to. It's quite interesting,' he said. 'Of course, one can't tell what sort of bloke he would have been if he'd been all right, but——'

By the time the motor-cycle was re-assembled he and Francis were strolling in and out of both bungalows and obtaining food from both larders.

The immediate problem, however, was no nearer to being solved. In spite of Godfrey's example and persuasions, Francis would neither swim in the river nor take out the dinghy, so one wet morning Mrs. Bradley unwrapped a large and chunky parcel which George had brought in the car from Norwich, another large flat one and a small, more intimate-looking affair.

Both boys were in her bungalow seated at a small table playing chess. That is to say, Godfrey was teaching Francis by moving both sets of pieces himself, beginning from the king's gambit, and then moving Francis' piece back each time so that he could play the move himself.

Mrs. Bradley, taking no notice of the boys, leisurely unwrapped her parcels on the large dining table and disclosed a wooden board, a chunk of plasticene and some modelling tools. Francis had his back to her, but Godfrey could see what she was doing. The game of chess continued for some time, and then Godfrey, who had been primed, looked up and asked:

'What are you doing, Aunt Adela?'

Mrs. Bradley, smirking horribly, displayed a coal-scuttle, a small fish of indeterminate species, an oar and a rabbit, all fashioned in the childish medium of plasticene. Francis put out his hand to the fish, looked at Mrs. Bradley, received an encouraging nod, squeezed it up in his hand and then swiftly fashioned a pike, using the modelling tools with obvious artistry and skill.

He stayed to lunch, over which Mrs. Bradley presided. Miss Higgs, delighted to be relieved of her charge, was spending the day with relatives in the village. When lunch was over Mrs. Bradley remarked that Miss Higgs had disclosed that Francis, as a little boy, had been fond of modelling. Godfrey, recognizing his cue, put the board back on the table, seized a piece of plasticene and began to fashion a primitive shape vaguely reminiscent of a horse. Francis watched closely, and Mrs. Bradley watched Francis.

Godfrey put down his embryonic figure, looked at Francis, and laughed. Francis picked up the model and with long fingers transformed it into the perfect representation of a man, but with the arms curving outwards and slightly upwards as though he was clasping a barrel. Godfrey laughed and began to fashion one.

Mrs. Bradley left them to it. The rain was over and the unmatched odour of an unspoiled rural river filled the green of the woodland air. She untied a canoe which was hitched to the edge of her staithe and paddled gently downstream with the current. She was gone for about two hours. When she got back the boys were still at the table. Francis was making a plasticene model of a dinghy. It was almost complete. As Mrs. Bradley watched, he finished the second oar and gently laid it along the thwarts. The little man he had previously modelled was still on the table. He picked it up, looked uncertainly from her to Godfrey, and then did a very strange thing.

He stuck a raised centre-board on to the model of the dinghy, and then stuck the plasticene man underneath the bottom of the boat. He put the horrid conclusion on the table, so that the plasticene man was hidden, and then looked at Mrs. Bradley, his eyes blinking and his mouth beginning to quiver. He scrambled the model together into a shapeless mass, made a sound between a snort and a sob, and galloped out of the room.

'Good Lord!' said Godfrey. 'What on earth's up with *him?*'

'He's told us what has been troubling him,' Mrs. Bradley replied.

'You don't mean he's seen . . . *that?*' Godfrey pointed to the scrambled-up mess.

'At any rate he's seen something which gave the impression of that. I want you to do something more to help me. Please behave naturally and, if you don't mind, take him for dinner this evening into Norwich and put in a couple of hours at a cinema. He won't embarrass you there. The dinner you may find a little difficult.'

'Oh, no, I shan't. It only needs one to do the ordering. I'll go and help him shove out some clothes. By the way, we played chess again for a bit when you'd gone. We haven't been using the plasticene all the time. Have a look at the board. And I thought I was teaching him to play!'

Mrs. Bradley had already noticed the chess board. She went over to it, however, and inspected it closely.

'Quite a tricky proposition,' she remarked.

'I should just about think so. I retired, as you can see, my position being absolutely hopeless.'

'Not absolutely,' said Mrs. Bradley pensively. She stretched out a yellow claw. 'There is the answer.' She moved her grand-nephew's pieces. 'And if that doesn't warn him he's very foolish indeed.'

'Warn him? What do you want to warn him about?'

Mrs. Bradley cackled, and did not reply. Godfrey looked at her thoughtfully and then went off to dress. Both boys presented themselves for her inspection about half an hour later, Francis as golden as a girl and Godfrey with the saturnine good looks of all the Bradley men. Both were wearing dinner jackets and both had the newly-scrubbed appearance which allies itself with black jackets and newly-ironed shirts. Mrs. Bradley took an affectionate farewell of both. Godfrey sized her up, kissed her, held her at arm's length for a moment and then said with apparent inconsequence:

'And a smile on the face of the tiger.'

'How did you get Francis dressed?' Mrs. Bradley asked.

'Just by pantomime. He cottoned on as soon as he saw my dress trousers, and looked quite bucked. I then gave a masterly imitation of a man eating a large, rich dinner, and his grin widened. Handsome and dashing, ain't he? All we need now is a couple of beautiful girls.'

'Francis doesn't behave very nicely with beautiful girls.'

'Oh? That's very tactless of him. Right. I will bear it in mind. Beautiful girls are out. Keeping 'em at bay is the trouble.' He laughed happily, took Francis by the coat-sleeve and led him away. They borrowed Mrs. Bradley's car for their expedition, so that she had to choose between using the motor-cycle or going on foot to the village. She proposed to pay a visit to Mabel Parkinson, for old school-fellows have at least one virtue: they can provide one with a back-ground and with references—in short, with the warm cloak of respectability. She knew that Mabel was back in Wet-wode, for George had reported her return, having gained this information in the post-office.

She strolled by back lanes to the village, crossed the bridge and came to Mabel's neat villa. After the exchange of false compliments and ancient memories was completed, Mabel Parkinson suggested that they might dine together at the hotel.

'Later, perhaps. Don't you want to come and see my corpse?' asked Mrs. Bradley briskly.

She thought it was unlikely that Mabel would take this invitation seriously, and she was right. Mabel was, however, interested in the riverside bungalows.

'I've always wanted to visit one of those,' she said. 'Are they really as tiny as they look?'

Mrs. Bradley replied that they were even tinier, and added that she had had to bed George down in the village but that the bungalow most fortunately was on the telephone so that she could call him when she wanted him.

'He is enjoying the fishing,' she said. They reached the bungalow at seven in the evening. The river was very quiet, for most of the yachts and cruisers had found their night moorings. There was no wind. The woods behind the bungalow were still, the tree-roots deep in the ooze and the branches sleeping.

George put the car away and then joined the two elderly women at the boathouse. He had with him a village youth of about twenty.

'All set, George?' Mrs. Bradley enquired.

'If you please, madam. Malachi here will dive. He knows what to expect.'

'Good.'

The boathouse ran alongside the bungalow but was separated from it by a strip of lawn about twelve feet wide. The next-door bungalow had its boathouse similarly placed and it was to this one, not to her own, that Mrs. Bradley directed Malachi's attention. Her own boathouse held nothing except for the canoe, but the neighbouring one held a broad sailing-dinghy.

'There it is, Malachi,' said George. 'Not scared, are you, lad?'

'No,' replied the youth. 'I reckon I've fetched up two drownded uns already, so I'm used to it, and there in't any weed in these staithes. Father keep 'em cut clean.'

He stripped off jacket, shirt and trousers to display a fine young body clad neatly and attractively in a pair of diminutive bathing trunks coloured, very choicely, chocolate brown. He walked to the moorings-edge of the staithe, studied the dark water, wriggled strong, long toes on the woodwork, inflated his lungs and went in with the sinuous self-confidence of an eel.

To the watchers he seemed to stay under for a very long time. When he surfaced he pushed back his hair, spat water and then looked up and nodded.

'He be there all right, I reckon. I could feel him. What do you want I should do now?'

'Nothing more, Malachi, at present. Come out and get dressed. I'll ring up the police, and you'd better stay here as a witness,' said Mrs. Bradley.

She went into the bungalow. Malachi picked up his towel and, with an apologetic look at Miss Parkinson, began to rub his hair, arms and shoulders. Miss Parkinson took the hint and followed Mrs. Bradley indoors. A few minutes later male voices from the kitchen and the clink of glasses proclaimed that the diver was dry and dressed and was now receiving some compensation for his experiences.

The police arrived in the form and person of Constable Tutt from the village, who, as soon as he had taken statements from everybody, rang up Norwich and gave a laconic, correct account of what he had been told.

Miss Higgs arrived home at ten to find her bungalow in the possession of the police, who had made a thorough investigation by the time she got back. As it was unreasonable to suppose that a woman of her age and stature had been able to fasten a dead body to the bottom of the dinghy, they questioned her gently and elicited one important fact. Her bungalow had been empty for a week at the beginning of June, when, out of what she had managed to save from her salary for looking after Francis, she had taken the youth to Great Yarmouth.

'It will require the doctor to tell us whether that's when the murder took place,' said the inspector, 'but it's a pointer, anyway, madam.'

'Whatever it is, nothing will induce me to stay here,' said Miss Higgs.

'I'd like you to, madam. I can leave a man on guard, you know. There'd be no objection to that on my part. I quite understand you feel nervous.'

'You mean I'm under suspicion,' said Miss Higgs shrewdly. 'Well, I can't blame you. But I'm only a very moderate swimmer, you know.'

'The job wasn't done under water, madam, and, for your information, it isn't the kind of job a lady could very well do. Whoever secured the body in the way it *was* secured is either a very handy man indeed, or else he knew exactly what he wanted and got somebody else to make the tackle to his instructions.'

'Oh, I see. Well, I don't suppose I shall get another wink of sleep while I stay here. And there's my boy to consider.'

Francis had returned with Godfrey at just after eleven, but long before that time the body had been removed from its extraordinary hiding-place and, after the doctor had made his examination, and the police had concluded their measurements and photography, it had been conveyed to a

B

mortuary. The dinghy was on the lawn under guard, and the boathouse in which it had lain had been cordoned off. A patient policeman, accommodated with a deck chair and a rug by the thoughtful Miss Higgs, kept watch and ward all night over both exhibits.

In the morning there was further questioning. The police found it impossible to accept the fact that Francis had discovered the body and yet had found no means of communicating this fact to Miss Higgs, but they could get nothing out of the boy. Godfrey had taken him to the dinghy, which was now upturned, but beyond making some inarticulate sounds and giving the boat a look of extreme horror, Francis had made no contribution.

The police took his fingerprints, and also those of Miss Higgs. Both sets and some other (so far unidentified) prints, together with those of the dead man himself, were found on the mast and on the oars. Miss Higgs was able to supply the date on which Francis had first refused to use the dinghy or to swim in the river, and this corresponded nearly enough with the doctor's estimate of the time of the death, allowing for the week during which Francis and Miss Higgs had been on holiday. It was fairly clear that the boy must have discovered the body as soon as they got back from Yarmouth.

'There's not much doubt about when it happened,' said Godfrey to Mrs. Bradley, 'but I wish they'd let Miss Higgs take Francis out of it all. It's too much for the chap. After all, he's told all he knows by making that plasticene model. He looks just about finished off. Isn't there anything you can do to get him away? Surely the police aren't such bone-heads as to think he did it?'

'It is not unlikely that he did it, and poor Miss Higgs is nearly out of her mind, too. I have advised her to send for Francis' relatives, but it seems that she does not like to make demands on them.'

'You'd think they'd have shown up before this. After all, the thing is in all the papers.'

This was true. Reporters had swarmed in by land and river to interview Miss Higgs, the occupants of the neighbouring bungalows, the agent who handled the letting, and anybody else who might conceivably have any kind of story to tell. Before they could waylay Mrs. Bradley or Godfrey they had been fobbed off by the police with the promise of a fuller report as soon as this could be furnished. The inquest was over so far as the preliminary findings were concerned, and it had, as usual, been adjourned after formal evidence had been taken. It had proved to be of exceptional interest, nevertheless, for not only was the cause of death known, but also the identity of the murdered man.

The medical evidence made it clear that the man had been hit on the head with some heavy object and had never recovered consciousness. What the heavy object might have been the doctors did not state, and the police were far too canny to put ideas into anybody's head at so early a stage in the proceedings.

The coupling of the corpse to the bottom of the dinghy was likewise not described in any kind of detail, for the police believed that in the method used they might have a valuable clue.

The identity of the corpse was disclosed by two persons who had good reason to know what they were talking about. One was the agent for the letting of the bungalows; the other was the dead man's sister, a letter from whom had been found among his papers. It appeared that he was a misanthropic naturalist named Campbell, who, for the major part of the year, tenanted the bungalow which Mrs. Bradley had rented.

When Mrs. Bradley heard this she was visited with a sudden inspiration which caused her to seek out Miss Higgs at the conclusion of the adjourned inquest and ask her what proved to be an important question.

'I suppose the dinghy to which the body was attached was really *your* dinghy?'

'Well, yes and no,' Miss Higgs replied. 'It was supposed to go with the bungalow *you've* rented, but ever since we've been here Francis and I have had the use of it during the summer while Mr. Campbell—you know——?'

'The murdered man.'

'Yes—while he was on holiday, and, of course, at other times, too. He was very good about it. Sometimes he and Francis would go out in it together.'

Mrs. Bradley was sufficiently intrigued to continue investigations on her own account, for she had been impressed by a fact which had also interested the police, namely, that somebody had possessed sufficient knowledge of local affairs to realize that the bungalow would be empty and the dinghy available during the week in which the murder had been committed.

'How many people *could* have known, do you think?' she enquired of Miss Higgs. The number was disconcertingly unguessable, for it included not only the village shop-keepers, who would have had no reason for keeping the news secret, but anybody else that they might have chosen to tell.

'I think I might go to Mede. It is not so very far from my own house,' said Mrs. Bradley to Godfrey. 'I should like to see this unnatural grandfather for myself. What would *you* like to do?'

'Stay here with old Francis. He's getting over the shock and he said my name this morning. It was a funny, croaking kind of noise, but it was my name all right. Miss Higgs says she'll cook for me and see that the place is kept clean, so would it be all right if I stayed on?'

Mrs. Bradley pursed up her beaky little mouth into a non-committal shape and looked at her grand-nephew with affection. She had no intention whatsoever of involving him in what promised to be an unrewarding and dangerous business. She knew better, at this juncture, however, than to say this to a high-spirited youth. She said, instead, that she was giving up her tenancy of the bungalow, rewarded the boy generously, and sent him off home.

CHAPTER FOUR

Bowler's Wicket

★

'. . . of his own self he challenged to combat all our best.'
Iliad—Homer (Lang, Leaf and Myers)

★

O N THE Sunday morning Tom Donagh was aroused at
half-past six by the drinks footman who came in with
early tea and two slices of thin bread and butter.

'Good morning, sir. Sir Adrian's compliments and he
expects you at the nets in half an hour. Breakfast at nine,
sir, church at eleven, lunch at a quarter past one, and the
rest of the day is free.'

'Oh, thanks,' said Tom, sitting up. 'Two hours at the
nets, eh?'

'That is the usual arrangement for Sunday, sir. We all
turn out except for the vicar, who has early service and
whose views on Sunday cricket Sir Adrian has not attempted
to ascertain.'

'I see. So *you're* in the team, too?'

'Yes, sir. I keep wicket.'

'What's your name?'

'Henry, sir.'

'Tell me, then, Henry—this match on Thursday and
Saturday. What's so important about it?'

'It's an annual fixture and it is Sir Adrian's way of dealing
with an ancient feud, sir. At one time, I believe, the two
villages had an annual football match, but it caused so
much bad feeling, and so many people got hurt that Sir
Adrian thought cricket might be preferable.'

'What about body-line?—or isn't that in the local
répétoire?'

37

'It's been known, sir. But two can play at that game. Parrish got old Wheeler, their star batsman, with one in the ribs and a split thumb the year before last, after their Bill Burt had laid out Tripp.'

'Who's Tripp?'

'The chauffeur, sir.'

'Good Lord! Is *he* a cricketer?'

'He collected seven catches at silly mid-off last year, sir. He isn't much of a batsman, but he could field a .22 bullet if it came his way. Quick as a cat, he is, and as nippy as a weasel. You're going to like playing with Tripp, sir. Pity you ain't a bowler. That's when you'd find what Tripp was worth.'

'Who else is in the team?'

'Well, let's see. There's me and you and Tripp, and Sir Adrian and Mr. Derek and Walters (that's him as you see here first, sir) and the vicar. You know about all of them. Then there's John, the knives, shoes and wood, and there's Inch—he's ploughman to Farmer Somers—Cotton, what keeps the village shop, and Parrish, our second gardener. Then there's Cornish, the landlord of the *Frenchman's Inn* . . .'

'Oh, yes. I met him last night. He told me he was twelfth man. Seemed a bit surly about it—or is that his usual style?'

'He umpires if we don't need him in the team. If he has to play, then Doctor Bazil umpires, and if the doctor has to play, then any of us as is out puts the long white coat on, and carries on giving no-balls against the visiting side.'

'You seem to have it all weighed up.'

'Bound to, sir. The other lot, they bring an umpire of their own. Nobody wouldn't stand for nothing different.'

He departed, and Tom ate the bread and butter and poured himself a second cup of tea. Then he got up, plunged in and out of a tepid bath and presented himself at the nets at seven thirty-three. Sir Adrian was looking at his watch.

Tom had expected to be able to dodge church, but his employer proved obdurate over this. He was verbally sympathetic, mentally rigorous.

'I know what you fellows feel about church-going, but I can't afford to offend the vicar. He's the best bat I've got, bar none (unless you can fill the bill) and I'm not going to put him off his stroke.'

There were three practice nets. Tom, Tripp, Sir Adrian and the youth John were assigned to the first one, Derek, Walters, Inch and Cotton to the second, whilst the third went to Parrish and Henry. No batting was done at this third net. Henry kept wicket, and Parrish, relieved at intervals by John and Sir Adrian, bowled yorkers, googlies and in-swingers at the undefended stumps until he was called upon to go to one of the other nets to face a batsman, or was given an occasional rest.

There was no doubt of two things. One was that Sir Adrian had built up an eleven that could have given a fair account of itself in minor county cricket. He himself was a sound, forcing batsman and a crafty slow bowler. In Parrish he had one of the most devastating fast bowlers that Tom had ever seen; a man who seemed capable of keeping a perfect length, too, and one who varied his bowling in the most bewildering and intelligent way. (Tom learned later that Parrish would certainly have become a professional cricketer but for the fanatical objections of his mother, who believed that to play games for money was a sin.)

Derek, although he lacked his grandfather's weight and strength, was a stylish and graceful batsman with an excellent variety of strokes and an intelligent sense of when to use them. He stood up manfully, too, to the rather terrifying bowling of Parrish. Young John, who could make the ball break both ways, had him guessing a good many times, but Derek, in playing him, was more times right than wrong.

The other point observed by Tom was that Sir Adrian, if the luck of the game went against him, was not going to be a good loser, but this did not particularly worry Tom. He proved this when he accepted in good part Sir Adrian's morose and jaundiced comments when, off John, he put up what would have been a sitter to first slip, and again when a ball from John which broke back caught him with a divided mind. It struck him that Sir Adrian was rather suspicious of his apparent lack of interest in the cursing he got each time.

Breakfast and the after-breakfast pipe were more than welcome when practice was over, but at twenty minutes to eleven precisely he was collected by Sir Adrian and ordered to go to church. He allowed himself to be pushed off with Derek in the direction from which the bells were jangling.

The congregation was conspicuously large for a village church. The vicar looked athletic and scholarly, Tom thought. Keen eyes gleamed in a thin, ascetic face, and the lean hands holding the outstretched wings of the lectern were obviously large and strong. The vicar moved, too, with a kind of soldierly grace, and the shoulders which showed off the surplice were more than ordinarily wide.

'Good for a couple of centuries,' muttered Tom, when Derek demanded of him half-way through the service and in a whisper what he thought of 'Bonzer' Black.

'Of course, sir,' murmured Derek, smiling with pleasure at this answer, 'everybody comes to church on this particular Sunday to pray for the team. So nice of them, sir, don't you think?' He continued to smile his girlish smile, and joined in the offertory hymn in a thin, sweet counter-tenor which Tom found rather embarrassing. However, in friendly spirit they returned to the house for lunch. Once lunch was over Tom was reminded by Sir Adrian that he had the rest of the day to himself.

'Tea, if you want it, at any time and in any place,' said Sir Adrian. 'Just ring Walters' bell. Dinner at nine on Sundays in summer. Get to bed in good time. We're playing Lord Averdon's eleven at ten o'clock to-morrow morning. A one-day game. Just a friendly. Win, draw or lose—it doesn't much matter. If a ball looks very fast or dangerous, don't go anywhere near it. I don't want bruised ribs or hands or anything like that for Thursday.'

Tom thoroughly enjoyed the game next day, although he earned a glare of fury from his difficult and single-minded host for holding a catch which shot into his left hand when he had expected the batsman to loft the ball into the deep.

'Hm!' said Sir Adrian, as they crossed at the end of the over. 'Not bad at all. Hurt you?' This question was added suspiciously, for he strongly suspected Tom of having disobeyed orders.

'Yes,' said Tom. Sir Adrian again glared at him.

'No impudence,' he said.

'None intended,' said Tom, giving him a broad smile of complete dislike and irreverence. Sir Adrian snorted and passed on, but Derek, who was playing at mid-on, asked anxiously:

'I hope it didn't really damage your hand, sir. I say, though, it was a jolly good catch.'

The match resulted in a draw, which apparently satisfied everybody.

'Mistake to beat Lord Averdon's eleven, sir,' said Henry when he brought Tom a long drink at half-past seven that same evening. 'A pleasant game, sir, I thought.'

'Very pleasant indeed,' agreed Tom. 'Why a mistake to win, though?'

'It might upset the master's annual invitation to shoot over Lord Averdon's coverts, sir. Sir Adrian has not yet put it to the proof.'

'Oh, I see,' said Tom, who was beginning to appreciate wryly his employer's mentality. 'And what about the match to-morrow?'

'Sir Adrian will inform you at dinner, sir. Allow me to congratulate you on catching out Mr. Devizes.'

'I'm not sure I was meant to.'

'It was not altogether an injudicious move, sir. Sir Adrian was undoubtedly impressed.'

Tom felt that it was undignified to make a *confidant* of Henry, but he could not resist adding:

'Well, I should scarcely have guessed it, especially after what you've just told me.'

'Blimey, I could tell you a lot more than that,' said Henry, reverting to type.

At dinner that evening Sir Adrian burst a mild bombshell. Tom, gazing out of the dining-room window at a green and peaceful sky, was suddenly brought back to a different kind of reality by his host, who suddenly remarked:

'Ah-ha! Colney Hatch to-morrow. Remember that fellow who tried to murder Tripp, Derry?'

'Yes, indeed, Grand. I wonder whether he's still in the eleven?' Derek hastily swallowed a forkful of salmon mayonnaise in order not to delay his reply to his grandfather. Sir Adrian laughed heartily.

'Sure to be. A fellow like that is worth thirty runs an innings before he's batted or bowled or fielded or even barracked,' he replied.

Tom asked for further information.

'You don't really mean we play a team of lunatics, sir?'

'Annual fixture, my boy.' The thought seemed to give Sir Adrian joy. 'Big mental hospital about twenty miles from here. The eleven come in motor coaches with about fifty supporters and half-a-dozen keepers . . . only they call them patients and nurses nowadays. Their umpire's a loony, too, so if he comes sneaking up behind you just as their bowler starts his run, tear down the pitch like hell. He had a silk stocking last year and nearly strangled Henry. They're all homicidal, of course. It's a sort of second-class Broadmoor.'

Tom decided that Sir Adrian was exercising what he probably thought was his sense of humour. He grinned, but offered no comment. Sir Adrian chuckled, and then looked at his grandson's empty plate.

'Try just a morsel of the chicken, Derry,' he said. 'You've picked up quite an appetite.'

'I think I will, Grand. Thank you for noticing I was eating more than I usually do. You are terribly good to me, always.'

Tom, who had begun to have a sneaking sort of liking for his charge, was put off again by these remarks. He scowled at his plate, but the two relatives had no eyes except for one another, and completely disregarded him.

The match next day, although neither as dangerous nor as strange as Sir Adrian's words had suggested, nevertheless had its own peculiarities. The eleven looked normal enough . . . in fact, a man in the foremost coach whom Tom mentally classed as the silk-stocking umpire turned out to be the alienist in charge of the party . . . and when they had changed it was seen that they were beautifully dressed in excellently-tailored flannels and sported very natty caps with resplendent scarlet peaks lined with green.

Sir Adrian and their captain tossed up, and, after one man had been discovered crying because the field had no daisies, the match began with Sir Adrian carting their fast bowler for six into the adjoining paddock. The umpire came up and warned him not to do it again. To Tom's astonishment Sir Adrian took this advice and blocked and spooned for the rest of the over.

When Tom's turn came to bat the score stood at twenty-three for three. Sir Adrian was still in, but the vicar had been caught at mid-off by the daisy-chain expert, and Derek, who was obviously very nervous, had lost his wicket to a long hop which an eleven-year-old would have walloped.

'We're doing fine,' said Sir Adrian, walking a little way to meet Tom. 'I'm sorry I forgot myself with that opening ball. Just remember that you'll be out as soon as the score reaches sixty. I always declare at sixty, otherwise these fellows get disheartened.'

'Oh, it's understood that they win, then?' Tom understood, at this, Sir Adrian's meekness when the umpire had admonished him for scoring a six.

'Of course, of course! Mustn't let them down, poor chaps.'

Tom, asking the silk-stocking umpire for middle and leg, decided, not for the first time, that he would never even begin to understand the workings of Sir Adrian's mind, although he could sometimes perceive what these were.

The visitors, all ecstatic smiles except for one who said he had not had his hit yet and who had to be taken back on to the field to be bowled at by John and fielded for by the vicar, Tom and Derek, at last were seen off amid cheers. Sir Adrian, with a sigh of relief, announced that next day no cricket would be played, and that Tom might do as he pleased provided that he did not tire himself, injure himself, drink too much, eat too much, or go to bed with a girl.

'I don't know any girls who would be obliging enough for

that, sir,' Tom said pleasantly. The match had amused him, but the tidings of a cricketless day were decidedly welcome. He felt at peace with everybody, even with his not very lovable employer.

'What shall we do?' he asked Derek.

'Steady, now, Derry,' said his grandfather. 'Nothing too strenuous, mind! I want you in the pink for Thursday.'

'I would like to swing in the hammock in the paddock and eat raspberries,' said Derek. 'And perhaps you could read to me while I eat,' he added, turning to Tom. 'I'm sure you read beautifully, sir.'

'All right,' agreed Tom, whose conscience was beginning to smite him because of their mutual neglect of Derek's studies. 'But I'm not going to read you a blood or any of that sort of tripe. It'll have to be something to do with your work . . . at any rate for part of the time.'

'Oh, yes. Let's have some Herodotus. I adore that old man, don't you? Or would you think history too light a subject if we are supposed to be working?'

Tom suspected the youth of irony, but Derek's beautiful, girlish face was innocent and enquiring, so he laughed and replied that Herodotus would do perfectly well if that was what Derek would like, although he did not particularly endorse his own ability to read him aloud.

'I shall tell you at once if I don't understand you,' said Derek. Tom aimed a playful smack at him—and then caught the red gleam of an almost maniac fury in Sir Adrian's fishy little eye.

'Good heavens! I know another madman besides those who came for the match,' thought Tom.

As it happened, Herodotus came to nothing. The next day was wet. Tom woke at six, got out of bed and went to the window. The sky was an uncompromising, flat, steely grey, and the rain was pouring down.

He stood there in his pyjamas and stared gloomily out. He had a batsman's horror of rain in summer. He did not hear Walters come in, and turned with a start at the sound of the manservant's smooth voice.

'A bowler's wicket to-morrow, sir. John is delighted. He has been dancing on the lawn since five o'clock. The sound of the rain woke him and he has been morrising it in the nude as though demented. An enthusiastic lad, sir, for a sticky wicket.'

'Let's hope he catches cold,' said Tom morosely. Walters gave him a sympathetic glance and put down the tray on a bedside table. Tom got back into bed and helped himself to a cup of tea. At seven Derek came in.

'Grand is delighted to see the rain,' he said, seating himself on the counterpane and taking a piece of bread and butter. 'I am delighted that he is delighted, but my personal disappointment is profound. I had hoped to make a century to-morrow.'

'Spoken like a man,' said Tom. 'What shall we do to-day?'

'The pub, I think, sir, don't you?'

'You can't be served. You're too young. Besides, your grandfather would fire me at once, and quite rightly, if I took you to any such place.'

'Oh, no, he wouldn't. Besides, I need not have anything to drink. We could play darts and mess about with those slot machines Cornish installed last winter. What did you think of Cornish as an umpire?'

'Oh, all right. There's nothing special about him, is there?'

'He's what I call a rather sinister man.'

'Rot. He's quite a good chap. Rough, ready and so forth.'

'Oh, yes, *outwardly*.'

'Go on with you! You talk like a girl!'

'I was meant to be a girl. My parents prayed for a girl. Literally, I mean. It wasn't very good luck on me to be born a boy. Besides, I miss my twin. Twins do, you know.'

'Your twin?'

'Yes, of course. I had a twin brother. I remember him quite well. We were seven years old when he was taken away from me.'

'How do you mean?'

'I don't know. I was too young to know. All I remember is his name. He was called Francis. I've mentioned him to

Grand, several times, but I only get fobbed off. Yet Grand must know all about it.'

'Maybe he'll tell you when you're twenty-one,' said Tom, speaking in a facetious tone because he found himself oddly sympathetic towards the impossible youth. Derek sighed, ran a hand through his shining hair, turned away from the window, and then asked childishly:

'Well, pub or no pub? I suppose it's no?'

'It's no.'

'All right, then. *You* think of something to do.'

'We could still read Herodotus.'

'*In the rain?*'

Tom laughed. A line from an old story by Lord Dunsany came into his mind and he quoted it aloud.

'I want a little god to worship when it is wet.'

Derek gave a high, falsetto shriek of laughter.

'Oh, so do I! So do I!' he cried. 'I'll tell you what! Let's make one! Oh, do let's make one, shall we?'

It seemed to Tom, no devotee of the Ten Commandments, as good a way as any of passing the time.

'What shall we make him of?' he asked.

'First of clay, then, if we like him, of wood. If he is especially good we might send him to an exhibition of sculpture. In Switzerland the men were always whittling things out of wood and I was quite good at it, too. We had an instructor who made more money that way out of the summer visitors than out of his salary. The only thing was that he used to sell our stuff as well as his own, which I always thought not quite fair, as he never even bought us chocolate out of the money.'

So, when breakfast was over and a beaming Sir Adrian had held a sort of board meeting with the eleven and with Cornish the Mede umpire (who did not Open until eleven), Tom and Derek settled down with some billets of wood from the woodshed and a mess of artist's modelling clay to fashion their little god.

The rain continued during the whole of Wednesday. Decency (the ethic of English cricket) impelled Sir Adrian to

have the wicket covered with tarpaulins from mid-day onwards, but up to that time the weather was allowed to do its
worst. Thursday, however, dawned fair, for the rain ceased
at four in the morning, and by seven a jubilant Sir Adrian
had the tarpaulins taken away to give the pitch (such was his
explanation) a chance to dry, but actually to make quite certain that the pitch would be implacably sticky for the batsmen.

'We win the toss and put them in first,' he said.

'But we may not win the toss, sir,' objected Tom.

'I am using my new lucky florin,' said Sir Adrian. 'And as
Witt, their captain, will undoubtedly want to use his, the
one he had last year, we are *certain* of winning the toss.'

Apart from a feeling that there was going to be dirty work
at the crossroads, Tom could make nothing of this prophecy
and did not pursue the subject. He was privileged, however,
to see what obtained when the toss for innings was made.

Witt, the opposing captain, a large, blond, red-faced
person whom Tom immediately and irrevocably wrote off
mentally as a bounder, produced a silver coin from his
blazer pocket and spun it tentatively.

'No,' said Sir Adrian. 'It's my turn to do the tossing. You
tossed and I called last year.'

'Oh, as you like,' said Witt, handing over the coin. Sir
Adrian looked at it.

'A lucky one, eh?' he said. He laughed pleasantly and
showed it (before Witt could prevent him) to Tom. 'Don't
you wish *we'd* got something like this, Donagh? Quite an
heirloom, isn't it?'

Witt seized it, scowled, thrust it back into his pocket,
snatched at the coin Sir Adrian held out to him and spun it
as high in the air as he could.

'Heads!' cried Sir Adrian. Heads it was. Sir Adrian
grabbed back the coin, thrust it into his pocket, and said,
in a growl, 'We'll field, and you can't grumble. I did let you
toss, after all.'

'You were right, then, sir,' said Tom, with grudging
admiration of his employer's unsporting forethought. 'I
suppose *your* coin was two-headed as well?'

'What do *you* think, my boy?' responded Sir Adrian genially. 'That . . . needn't think he can pull off that rotten dodge of his two years running!'

The game was therefrom carried on in a spirit of animosity and cussedness to which Tom was entirely a stranger. The Bruke umpire no-balled the bowlers whenever he was in a position to do so, but, on the whole, quite fairly, and the Mede umpire, landlord Cornish, rightly interpreting certain signals from Sir Adrian, gave some l.b.w. decisions which made Tom gasp. There was argument and counter-argument, too, between the two umpires and between the umpires and the players.

In spite of landlord Cornish's best endeavours, at lunch the score was eighty-three. During lunch the rain began again.

Sir Adrian had provided a noble meal to which both teams, dining at separate tables in the interests of peace and their digestive juices, were only too willing to do justice. Sir Adrian kept a watchful eye on the weather, and as soon as he could he rose from the table and gathered his men around him out of earshot of the men of Bruke.

'Now, you fellows,' he said, 'we shall have to do better. There are more wickets to fall, but we don't want 'em falling just yet. The pitch is nicely treacherous by now. They can't score on it, but we couldn't, either, so my orders to you are that you are to keep their last men in as long as you can, provided they don't score runs. We want the pitch thoroughly wet before we put ourselves in. Now, you fielders, you are not to take any catches until I tell you. Stop the runs, but nothing more. No fancy throwing-in to bust the wicket, or any nonsense of that kind. And you, Parrish, just see whether you can't contrive a respectable slide of mud at the paddock end. You know where their fast bowler likes to take his run, and it needn't interfere with yours if you're reasonably intelligent about it. You, Derry, my boy, are not to come out in the wet. It might bring on your chest. Go and lie on your bed for a bit. It won't do you any harm at all to have a rest.

'Now, you battin' fellows, once we get going I shall look

to you to knock off the runs. Eighty-three ain't much of a score. If only we can keep 'em in until the wicket is really wet, it ought to be child's play to wipe them off the earth on Saturday. This pitch is dead when it gets properly soaked. Their slow and medium-pace fellows won't be able to get up to tricks, and with any luck their fast bowler may break his neck. All right, Walters. Tell the vicar he can come back now. It's no good telling *him* anything about the strategy of the game,' he added in an aside to Tom. 'He just don't understand the finer points. But *you* will do as you're told. None of that clever business with left-handed catches we had from you the other day, young fellow. *I'm* captain, and what I say goes.'

Ten minutes later the game . . . or, rather, battle—was resumed. Witt, the opposing captain, had gone in at second wicket down and was still in. He had given no chances, and by dint of displaying the remarkable agility of a *prima ballerina* he had, so far, made it impossible even for Cornish to agree to some painfully vociferous appeals for l.b.w. from the wicket-keeper. He also had his eye on the weather, and less than ten minutes after the resumption of the game he skied up a soft ball which caught in the neck of Henry's shirt.

'*Out!*' said the Bruke umpire uncompromisingly; and Witt, who was a strategist, too, had walked away from the wicket before the indignant Henry had had time to disengage the treacherous ball and hastily drop it on the grass.

'*Not* out!' bellowed Sir Adrian, ably seconded by umpire Cornish. But it was too late. The incoming batsman was sprinting towards the wicket. Sir Adrian spent a good three minutes in re-arranging his field, and Cornish used another minute and a half in stamping on two imaginary bumps . . . an extraneous duty for which there was no warrant. The game had to be resumed, however, and there was no doubt of the remaining batsmen's intentions. They did their very best to be caught, bowled, or run out. To counter this the bowlers bowled well off the wicket, but not sufficiently wide to add to the score, and if the batsmen offered up catches, no matter how cleverly or discreetly, the fielders moved aside or put their hands in their pockets. And still the rain poured down. Tom began to envy Derek Caux.

Suddenly, at the end of three-quarters of an hour of these farcical proceedings, Sir Adrian semaphored to his bowlers. The wicket was wet enough. Parrish, at the risk of his neck . . . a risk negligible to Sir Adrian since Parrish was no sort of batsman . . . braced himself up, sent down unplayable balls, and the Bruke innings was over.

'But why on earth didn't their captain declare when he found out what our lot were playing at?' Tom demanded of Walters as they walked towards the pavilion.

'It's been agreed not to declare in this match, sir,' Walters replied. 'Bruke once scored four hundred and ten for six, and Sir Adrian, well, sir, he nearly went out of his mind. Us didn't get a chance, in that match, to bat until late on the Saturday, and as we don't, against Bruke, recognize a draw but only the number of runs we each scores in the two days' play, it had to be reckoned Bruke's match. We never heard the last of that for a long time. Oh, the gov'nor, he didn't half create. I thought at first he was going to give us all the sack, but I suppose he thought better o' that. Anyway, looks like he'll have his revenge to-day. Seems a pity us can't play proper. I don't belong to Mede *or* Bruke meself, so it wouldn't trouble *me* who wins. But we got our jobs to think of, don't you see, and Sir Adrian won't be beat . . . not if *he* knows it, he won't.'

During the interval, during which the teams changed over, the umpires remained on the field. Ostensibly their object was to inspect the pitch, but there was no doubt that in reality they were keeping close watch on one another to prevent any jiggery-pokery with the wicket.

It was while Sir Adrian (who, with Tom, would go in first) was seated at the front of the pavilion blissfully putting on his pads, that a black-avised man from the Bruke eleven came striding up to him.

'I be sendin' for constable,' said he, his face contorted with fury. 'Mr. Witt be layin' there dead. One of your b——s 'ave killed en.' He then hit Sir Adrian in the eye.

CHAPTER FIVE

Wetwode

★

*'Where all have been candid, communicative, and
courteous, it may be a difficult and invidious task to
distinguish the different degrees of obligation.'*

James Ingram, D.D.: *Memorials of Oxford*

★

A T WETWODE, in Norfolk, Mrs. Bradley, irrespective of
what was planned by the police, was still occupied in
making her own investigation. It was possible, from
what was shown at the inquest, that neither Francis nor his
guardian (if Miss Higgs merited that title) had been concerned in the murder of the naturalist Campbell whose body
had been fastened to the bottom of the dinghy, as they had
been away from Wetwode at the time when the death had
taken place. That they had actually spent the week at Great
Yarmouth on the dates which Miss Higgs had specified,
there was not a shadow of doubt.

On the other hand, there was the patent, inescapable fact
that from Great Yarmouth to Wetwode the bus service was
frequent and the buses usually crowded. It would have been
quite possible for Miss Higgs or Francis (or both, if they had
happened to be in collusion) to chance their luck in escaping
notice if they had decided to return to Wetwode and murder
their neighbour.

Besides, it need not have been a bus, Mrs. Bradley
reflected. A hired car, self-driven, would have been even
more to the purpose, especially if Miss Higgs had hired it . . .
an unnoticeable, mouse-like woman . . . and had picked
Francis up *en route*. A hired taxi was scarcely a likely means

of conveyance. The driver might not remember the middle-aged spinster, but he could scarcely fail to recollect the beautiful, handicapped youth.

Her more definite enquiries had resulted in some interesting but not necessarily helpful discoveries. There were altogether seven riverside bungalows. The first one, reading from the village and upstream, was that which was occupied by Francis and Miss Higgs. The next one, rented by Mrs. Bradley, was ordinarily the property of the naturalist Campbell, who went north during the summer, and was accustomed not to return to Wetwode for at least three months. Bungalow three was taken, apparently regularly, by two wet-fly fishermen named Tavis and Grandall. They were accustomed to come down every Friday during the coarse-fishing season and to return to London by car each Monday morning. Thus, unless the murder had been committed during a week-end, they could not be held to be material witnesses, and, unless they were the murderers, could be wiped off.

The fourth bungalow was owned by a local boat-builder's family. It was used intermittently during the summer by various members of the clan, but was never let to outsiders. Bungalow five was even less interesting. It was derelict and untenanted, and had been so since it had caught fire some six years previously. There was nothing there.

In respect of number six there was a good deal of information forthcoming. It appeared that it was rented all the year round by a man named Darnwell. He was said to come from London, to be moderately well-off, and to entertain ladies of a type known to those of good understanding, but of limited or inhibited vocabulary, as floosies.

Bungalow seven was rented regularly every summer by a pleasant middle-aged couple who were accustomed to invite young people of their acquaintance, particularly their son and their son's friends, to spend week-ends with them during June, July and August.

Mrs. Bradley, who, when she liked, could charm the jewel out of a toad's head, was soon on excellent terms with all her neighbours. The seven bungalows, isolated as they were from the rest of the village whose postal address they bore, had become a self-contained community into which even the promiscuous Mr. Darnwell and his various 'nieces' had been accepted. The little outpost was, in fact, as much interested in Mrs. Bradley as she was in its members, and she experienced not the slightest difficulty in becoming acquainted with all of them.

It seemed to her unlikely that any outsider could have fastened the body to the bottom of the dinghy. Anyone from outside, so to say, would have become too much the focus of attention, for the job, involving, as it did, a certain amount of hammering, could hardly have been done except, in apparent innocence, by daylight.

She soon gathered that boat-repairing was a subject now under *tabu* among the residents. She could scarcely blame them. They were intelligent persons, and they realized (as clearly as she did) that to confess to having repaired a boat during the week when Francis and Miss Higgs had been in Great Yarmouth was as quick a way as any of finding one-self explaining the nature of the repairs to a magistrate.

Apart from this common factor, however, there was no other barrier to a completely free discussion of the murder. Every household had its views, and these were assiduously gleaned by Mrs. Bradley. The only people whose opinions she did not ask for were those of Miss Higgs and Francis. The former, anxious for her charge, sought and obtained permission from the police to take him to his grandfather in Hampshire. She was not at all surprised when Sir Adrian did not answer her letter, but she confided to Mrs. Bradley that she was still determined to go.

Mrs. Bradley, having returned her grand-nephew to his own home, settled down to enjoy herself. She kept careful records of her interviews with the residents of the bungalows, and continued to interview these residents with great method and apparent innocence, beginning with the middle-aged couple, whose name was Coppinger. These people she was strongly inclined (on psychological grounds) to write off at once, particularly after she had verified the information which they gave about themselves.

They were blameless and ordinary people. The man was manager of a factory which made bathing costumes. Some connection existed in his mind between his work and the water in which, sooner or later, that work would be immersed. He could not swim, but he loved to be near a river or the sea. This love had brought him one summer to Wetwode and after that he had never spent a holiday anywhere else. His wife was content to be where he was, and his son was the apple of his eye. The family had no enemies, no debts, no secrets (so far as could be determined) and a considerable number of friends.

Mrs. Bradley, apart from the contacts dictated by good-neighbourliness, soon did not trouble any more about them. Their son, a boy of twenty-two, had his own acquaintances, men and girls, and had always avoided Francis, whom he suspected of not being right in the head. The shy and difficult youth might have apprehended this perfectly well, for he had never made the slightest effort to get to know the family.

About Morris Darnwell, who rented the next bungalow, Mrs. Bradley was far less relenting and certain. To begin with, he was something of an enigma in himself, apart from any question of the murder. Anything less like the paunched and astrakhan-collared Lothario of popular conception could scarcely be imagined; still less the blond beast of Teutonic ideology. Darnwell was a monkey-like little man who had the air of sadness common to nearly all simians, a quiet and cultured voice, exquisitely self-effacing manners and an extensive knowledge of Easter Island art.

He aroused Mrs. Bradley's suspicions by his heartily-declared aversion to the dead man. He had been, she thought, much too frank and outspoken to be considered quite genuine. This did not necessarily imply, however, that he was guilty of complicity in the murder.

'Campbell? An unbearable person,' he declared. 'He was no more a naturalist than I am. Less, in fact. Those binoculars of his have had a good deal to answer for. I knew

a woman who committed suicide because of them. He was a
snooper, a blackmailer and a common informer. Any one of
a hundred people might have killed him. That touch of
fastening the body with those hoops to the bottom of the
dinghy was unique, though. The police ought to be able to
make something out of that. Macabre, don't you think? The
bottom of a dinghy is not at all the kind of hiding-place that
the average mind could have conceived. You're a psychologist.
Can't you make anything out of it?'

Mrs. Bradley grinned politely and said truthfully that her
main interest had been in the reactions of young Mr. Caux.

'Yes, he's an odd lad,' agreed Darnwell. 'A wonderful
swimmer and diver.' He looked speculatively at Mrs.
Bradley, but she refused the gambit, saying carelessly:

'There's always some natural compensation for bodily or
mental infirmity, don't you think?'

Upon the subject of his own whereabouts during the week
of the murder, Darnwell was disconcertingly frank.

'That may have been the week I had Annie here. Macheath
was right about women. Nothing unbends the mind like
them. If I were sleeping with Annie—and she rejects my
favours too often, much too often—a man might play
Drake's drum underneath the windows and I shouldn't
notice it.'

'The inference is that the job was done by daylight,' said
Mrs. Bradley. Darnwell waved thin hands as delicately-
fashioned as the antennae of a butterfly, and shook his head
strongly.

'All the more reason for my having known nothing about
it. Annie and I would stay in bed until twelve and then go
into the village or out in the car for lunch. These people
always tinker with their boats in the early morning. I still
say I shouldn't have noticed. Such are the penalties of love.'

Mrs. Bradley left it at that, but she put a question mark
against Morris Darnwell's name in her notebook. His
observations, however, provided another line of investigation. Presumably he had given the same information to the
police as he had to her, but Mrs. Bradley's detective instinct

(or, as she, probably honestly, preferred to call it, her insatiable curiosity) prompted her to take independent action upon what she had learned.

This independent action soon bore fruit. It was proved that the dead man had indeed been both a public informer and a blackmailer. The list of his victims went into hundreds. Except that she had a personal desire to know the truth about his death, Mrs. Bradley would have lost interest in him. Someone, she concluded, goaded beyond reason, had decided to make an end of unbearable trouble. She now felt not the slightest sympathy for the dead man. Blackmailers, in her opinion, were far worse than murderers, but in the murder itself she took deep interest.

She turned her attention to the occupants of bungalow four, owned by the boat-builder's family. During the week in question it had been used by the boat-builder's cousin, a man named Lafferty, his wife and two daughters. Mrs. Bradley wrinkled her yellow forehead over the name Lafferty and then asked him a direct question, but not of a kind to be resented.

'The international swimmer?'

'Used to be. Too old now. I'm forty-five. Still run my local club, though, and the two girls are coming on nicely. Meet the wife, Jane Court that was. You've probably heard of her, too. Nereid Swimming Club president and star turn in 1930-31. Only missed the Olympic team by a toucher. Personally, I'd have included her, but perhaps I'm prejudiced.'

Mrs. Bradley was prejudiced, too. She found that her mind refused to consider these people as possible murderers. In any case, the bizarre business of attaching the body to the bottom of the dinghy by iron bands and staples would most certainly have been accomplished on land. It could not have been done under water. Therefore the proof of an ability to swim and dive scarcely entered into the matter, except that she felt that in the murderer's place she would have wanted to satisfy herself that the body was still in position, still well and firmly fastened, after the dinghy had been put back into the boathouse.

It seemed to her likely that the job itself had been done in the boathouse. This would afford a certain amount of cover (although not very much) for nefarious and secret activities, and would only have involved raising the dinghy on to the wooden slats which sloped in a gentle ramp from the concrete surround to the water. From this position, too, it would have been fairly easy for a powerful and determined man to have turned the dinghy over again and refloated it, even with the added weight of the dead man and the iron-work, although with the help of a second man, a boy, or even a woman, the task would have been much easier. She did not therefore rule out her original idea that there might have been two persons involved, but she thought there must have been a leading spirit in the affair.

The clue which the police were most inclined to follow up was that the body had been fastened with what were obviously specially prepared pieces of iron. The corpse had been secured by the neck, by each upper arm and by each thigh, and the staples used had points so sharp that a single blow from a hammer would have been sufficient to drive them into the stout wooden frame of the dinghy. The police, after consultation, had decided that if they could discover where all this apparatus had been made or purchased, the identity of the person who had used it would soon be apparent.

Mrs. Bradley was not able (even if she had been interested enough to want to do so) to follow up any such line of investigation. It was the psychology of the murderer which interested her. One thing, she assumed, the murderer had not realized; that the body would be discovered so comparatively soon. He must have hoped and anticipated that by the time it was discovered it would be unrecognizable and unidentifiable. And yet, like Rupert Brooke's poetic non-entity, she knew doubts that would not be denied.

She puzzled for some time upon this oversight on the part of the murderer. It almost looked as though he could not, after all, have been one of the bungalow community, unless he were Francis himself, for the other people surely would have known that Francis was a keen swimmer and was also capable of either rowing or sailing the dinghy, and that the raised centre-board and the behaviour of the boat on its new and terrible keel would immediately attract his attention. There was still the same argument, however, in favour of the murderer's having been someone on the spot, well known to the rest of the inhabitants, for otherwise, she argued, he would scarcely have been able to come and go without being noticed; and that the work had been done under cover of darkness she found herself unable to believe.

She spent some hours in searching the burnt-out, derelict bungalow after the police had abandoned (for the time only, perhaps) their own search for clues in the immediate neighbourhood, but nothing there gave her any help. The evidence of fire and the equally deplorable evidence of the hosed water which had put out the fire, were all that she discovered. The dead man had been coshed and his skull broken. He could well have been killed in the derelict bungalow except that there was no trace of blood there, but he could equally well have been killed elsewhere and his body transported by car.

The only bungalow residents still on Mrs. Bradley's list were the two fishermen, Grandall and Tavis, but it had been clearly proved by the police that neither of them had been in Wetwode at the time of the murder. Their alibis, however, were not, to Mrs. Bradley, satisfactory. Grandall had been in Switzerland, where his mother, an invalid, had had a serious relapse so that he had been sent for at short notice, and Tavis had remained in London because he was not interested in going to Wetwode alone. On the other hand, the police had wiped the two men off their list of possible suspects, and, under these circumstances, Mrs. Bradley was prepared to do no more than note down the fact that it had proved extraordinarily useful to Tavis and Grandall that the latter's mother had contrived her serious illness at such a convenient time.

The police soon ferreted out the blacksmith who had made the iron bands and supplied the staples used by the murderer to fasten the body to the bottom of the dinghy. He lived less than ten miles from Wetwode and he declared that none of the inhabitants of the bungalows, man, woman or adolescent, was the person by whom he had been commissioned. There was no reason to think that he was either lying or mistaken, and he was able to describe in reasonable detail his customer. Unfortunately, in the era of mass-produced, off-the-peg clothes, the description of a middle-aged, strongly-built, high-complexioned man wearing a tweed jacket, a woollen pullover, flannel trousers, a soft hat and a raincoat, did not carry the enquiry further forward. The police confronted him with all the possible suspects, one by one, but the blacksmith, an unimpressionable, sober, non-suggestible Norfolk man, was firm. His customer, he was positively certain, had not been in the least like any of them. He added one further clue, but it did not seem a very helpful one. The customer had spoken, he thought, like a West Country man. He had not been a Norfolk man or a Londoner.

He refused to attempt to imitate the accent, and this Mrs. Bradley thought was perhaps as well, since it might have been even less helpful than his refusal to commit himself on the subject.

It was at this interesting and unhelpful juncture that Miss Higgs, shopping with Francis in the village, slipped on the steps of the Universal Emporium and broke her left leg. She also struck her head, and the resultant concussion made it impossible for her to be allowed visitors at the hospital to which she was taken.

Mrs. Bradley left messages of sympathy, and also a note which stated that she proposed to take Francis to his grandfather, whose address she had previously acquired from Miss Higgs. It seemed unlikely that Miss Higgs would be in a fit state to receive the messages or to read the note for some days.

Although, according to Miss Higgs, Sir Adrian had not even troubled to reply to letters, Mrs. Bradley had no doubt of her own ability to return his grandson to his care now that Miss Higgs was no longer able to assume responsibility for the youth. The idea of personal failure was, and had always been, absent from Mrs. Bradley's consciousness. In any case, she had no intention whatsoever of finding herself in the position of guardian angel. Francis was Sir Adrian's responsibility, and she proposed to plant that responsibility firmly where it belonged. Without attempting to convey her intentions to the boy, she simply packed his bags, sent for her chauffeur, and directed the car to Mede.

CHAPTER SIX

Mede

★

'. . . I say that our race would be happy if we could only fully satisfy our love and return each to his primitive nature and find his beloved.'

Plato: *Symposium*

★

EVEN Sir Adrian, sporting an eye reminiscent of an over-ripe plum, could not contrive to have the cricket match resumed on the Saturday. There had been a *mêlée* of a sumptuous kind, in the immortal words of Private Mulvaney, following the discovery of the visiting captain's body, and into this *fracas* (to Tom Donagh's astonishment) Derek, his pupil, had entered with considerable spirit.

He had come back on to the field at the first sounds, and, shrieking, in a high girlish voice near to tears, 'Don't you dare touch my Grand,' he had sailed in with some pretty right hooks which connected neatly with the ears and ribs of those towards whom they were aimed. In addition, until the police arrived, battle was remorselessly waged between the two elevens and their supporters until the field around the pavilion resembled an *abattoir* and crawled with bright blood and crept with tiny strips torn *berserk*-like from cricket shirts and fancy scarves.

Tom, in self-defence, had put in two or three shrewd punches, and then had dragged his charge from the *maelstrom* and hustled him back into the house. He was absolved from having to make any attempt to rescue his employer, for Sir Adrian had already retired hurt, and was the first person to telephone for the police. These arrived in force from

Lymington, broke up the affray, and, at Sir Adrian's instigation, arrested most of the visiting team.

It then occurred to Sir Adrian to mention the murder, and the local doctor, who had been acting as one of the scorers, made his report. This was subsequently endorsed by the police surgeon, and after the body had been photographed and removed, the police investigation began in earnest, and, owing to the extraordinary nature of the circumstances, those arrested for disturbing the peace were released so that they might testify (to the best of their ability) without there being any reason to have them suppose that they would be subjected to unfair pressure.

Statements were taken from everybody on the ground before either cricketers or onlookers could depart, but, at first sight, there was remarkably little to be learnt. The body had been found in the room devoted to showers and washbowls on the visiting team's side of the pavilion.

The pavilion at Mede was a well-constructed building very simple in plan. Three wooden steps ran the whole length of the verandah (which had no rail) and at the centre back was a door leading to a through passage which ended in another door some forty feet away. It was customary for the home team to use this back door when they came to the pavilion from the house.

On either side of the passage opened the dressing-rooms; the room on the left was for the home team, that on the right for the visitors. Opening off these dressing-rooms, still further to the left and right respectively, were wash-rooms containing bowls and showers, and at the end of the passage were a kitchen used only for the preparation of tea—lunch was taken at the house—and a small, well-stocked bar. The kitchen was on the visitors' side of the pavilion, the bar on the home side.

The dead man was lying sprawled along the line of the showers. There were four of these and his head was on one of the drains. The door had been partly pulled to, probably (the police thought) by the murderer, so that from the outer room, that is, the dressing or changing-room, the body was out of the line of vision.

Alibis were prolific among both spectators and players. The spectators, thanks to Sir Adrian's arrangement whereby they were cut off from the pavilion by the tall fence (which they had surmounted in order to join in the affray but which no one had scaled during the match) could be ruled out at once and were soon allowed to return home. Members of the visiting eleven were more subtly and closely questioned, but it did not appear that any of them could be involved. They had either already batted or else were waiting to bat, and in both cases they claimed that all could be accounted for, since all, except the two players actually at the wickets when the murder must have been committed, had been seated on the verandah of the pavilion intent on the game.

The opposing eleven, (Sir Adrian and his side), were likewise accounted for (except for Derek Caux), since they had been fielding at the time, and the two umpires, of course, had been on duty. It seemed clear at first that person or persons unknown must be guilty unless Derek Caux himself had done the deed. The barman and the two youths who looked after the kitchen could provide one another with alibis similar to those of the visiting team. They also, and in one another's company, had been watching the game from the far end of the pavilion steps, they said. There seemed no reason to disbelieve them.

According to the medical evidence, (which was again reviewed and analysed at the inquest), the unfortunate captain of Bruke must have been struck down with his own cricket bat almost as soon as he had retired to the pavilion after having been given out—or, rather, after having elected to put himself out. The handle of the bat showed no fingerprints. Death had been not instantaneous but to all intents and purposes so, for the victim could not have recovered consciousness. To the relief (if such it could be considered) of his friends, it was made clear by the doctors that even if the attack had been known of immediately it had been delivered, his life could not have been saved.

Sir Adrian, who seemed cheerful, ate a large dinner at a late hour and discussed the murder with gusto. Derek, who seemed tired, ate very little and half-way through the meal asked to be excused, left the dining-room, and did not return. Tom, who naturally was anxious to learn what he could about the dead man, chiefly out of what he himself recognized to be a rather unworthy feeling of Sunday newspaper curiosity, gleaned what he could from Sir Adrian's apparently unguarded remarks, but went to bed not very much the wiser for them.

One point, according to Sir Adrian, did emerge. The dead man was known to have one great enemy. As, however, it seemed impossible that this man could have killed him, the fact (if fact it was) did not much impress Tom.

'Yes, if he hadn't been umpiring at the time, which he most certainly was,' said Sir Adrian, 'it would have been Peter Cornish. Bad blood between him and Witt for years. Began during the war, although nobody ever quite knew the rights and wrongs. Remember when there was that appalling shortage of wines and spirits? Well, it seemed to break out about then. I don't know whether it was black market stuff or something of that sort. Often tried to get the truth out of Cornish, but he used to turn quiet and very nasty. He wouldn't stick at much. I remember his losing his temper during a darts match once. He wasn't playing, but somebody from Bruke was making trouble. Cornish borrowed a couple of darts from one of our fellows and literally pinned back the ears of the chap who was making the fuss. Fellow happened to be standing with his back to a door and leaning against it, don't you know, and Cornish just flipped the darts hard at him, and, before anybody realized what was happening, one of the darts had gone into the lobe of his left ear, and there he was, squealing like a pig, pinned to the planks of the door. Didn't see it myself. Wish I had. Oh, he's a quick-tempered bloke, get him roused.'

'What happened about it?' asked Tom, who did not believe the story and who had an uneasy feeling that Sir Adrian had some ulterior motive in telling it.

'Nothing. Cornish pulled out the dart, gave the fellow a

double whisky and threw him out. Chap left the district soon after. Couldn't live it down, you see. Got the kids calling after him, and all that kind of thing. Oh, people behave themselves in Cornish's pub, I can tell you.'

'What kind of fellow was Witt—apart from anything he had to do with Cornish?'

'A rat,' said Sir Adrian concisely. 'Don't ask me to put my finger on the spot. I can't. Decent family connections, too, but a heel. De-bagged at Oxford, interviewed by the Jockey Club—nothing actually *said* either time, so far as I can find out, and, of course, he wasn't warned *off*—I'm not claiming that!—but there's always been a slightly foul smell about him.'

'Has he lived in Bruke all his life?'

'No. The family property was in East Anglia, I believe, but they sold up when taxes and death duties began to drain the life out of the place. He came to Bruke a year or two ago, well after the end of the war. Bought a smallish house in the village and gradually edged himself in. This is the second year he's captained the eleven. They lost their best bat near the end of the war and were glad to get him.'

When dinner was over Tom decided to take a stroll round the cricket field. His real object, although he would scarcely confess it to himself, was to try to discover some clue to the identity of the murderer. It was too much to believe that somebody had sneaked through the house and so to the pavilion, yet if both teams and all the spectators were exonerated there seemed nothing else to believe, and there was something on Tom's mind and conscience, and he thought that a lonely stroll on the deserted field might help him to clear his thoughts.

His walk was a short one, however. A large form loomed at him and an official voice said kindly:

'Sorry, sir, but you must smoke your cigar in the garden, like, to-night, if you wants a bit of fresh air.'

Tom had not realized that the police would still be in possession of the pavilion and its approaches. He apologized,

C

bade the officer good night, went back into the house and up to his own room. He switched on the light and found Derek, still in his evening clothes, seated upon the bed.

'Hullo,' he said. 'Thought you'd turned in long ago.'

'No,' said Derek, turning his large eyes on Tom. 'I wanted to ask your advice.'

'About this afternoon?'

'Yes. Mr. Donagh, do they know exactly when Mr. Witt was killed?'

'Near enough, I expect. It must have been almost directly he'd finished his innings.'

'Yes, because otherwise his own men would have missed him. They would expect him, when he'd had a wash, or whatever he wanted, to come to the verandah and watch the rest of the play.'

Tom had not thought of this method of assessing the time of Witt's death, but he could see the force of it.

'Yes, that's about right,' he said, 'and somebody—the scorers, probably—will be pretty certain to know when his innings finished.'

'You remember I wasn't fielding all the time? Grand made me go and lie down after lunch because he thought the rain was too heavy. I don't see that I have any alibi, sir.'

'Oh, Lord!' said Tom, in great relief. 'Thank goodness you've mentioned it first! I thought I was going to have to, and I didn't know what to do about it! Still, everybody else on the field would have known, so I had almost decided to say nothing, especially as I'm sure you didn't do it.'

'That's awfully nice of you, sir. To—not to have been going to say anything, I mean. But do you think *I* ought to say something to the police?'

'I shouldn't worry,' said Tom. 'Somebody's sure to blow the gaff on you as soon as the police get down to brass tacks.'

'Do you think so?'

'Well, some of the Bruke fellows will, even if our own blokes keep their traps shut.'

Dreek looked vastly relieved.

'Oh, that's all right, then,' he said. 'Thank you so much

for helping me. And you don't think you yourself are going to say anything about it?'

'I don't see at present why I should.' He was very glad later that he had not made a more definite promise. 'There's only this, though, old man,' he added awkwardly. 'As it's bound to come out sooner or later, you *might* be better advised to mention it yourself. I don't know, really, but what it mightn't be a good idea in the end.'

'Oh, *no?*' cried Derek, looking wildly scared. 'Oh, no! I don't want to, really! It's too much to ask! It's too much!'

'All right, then, don't do it,' said Tom. 'Anyway, sleep on it. Things often look quite different in the morning.'

The morning brought another surprise, and one of a different kind. Derek, looking blithe, came down as Tom was in the middle of breakfast. Sir Adrian had had his meal early and was at the moment passionately disputing with the police the possession of his pavilion and cricket-pitch.

'Hullo,' said Tom. 'Sleep well?'

'Yes, indeed, sir. Oh, dear! Fried eggs again! Isn't there *anything* else?'

'Kippers.'

Derek helped himself and sat down.

'I think I shall go for a good long walk, sir. The police will be about, and they frighten me. I'm sure I shall find myself telling them things, true and untrue, if they begin to question me. I'm better out of the way.'

Tom wondered whether the police would allow him to remove himself from their vicinity so easily. It could only be a matter of time, he thought, before somebody, either in Mede or Bruke, made reference, with or without malice aforethought, to the fact that Derek had not been fielding at the probable time of Witt's death.

To his surprise, the police made no demur at all when Derek decided, at ten o'clock, to leave the house; but, to his considerable annoyance, they did question his own right to go as far as the village in search of tobacco.

'If you will kindly tell me the brand which you prefer, sir,

I will gladly go and get it for you myself,' said the smart young constable.

'Huh! Hendon?' said Tom disagreeably. The smart young constable paid no attention to him whatsoever. Tom, who was well-balanced and honest, apologized. 'But you *did* let young Caux go out,' he explained.

'Yes, sir. We have no reason at present to worry about young Mr. Caux.'

'Meaning you have about me, then?'

'No, sir, of course not.'

Tom was puzzled. If he had been on the job, he considered—meaning that if he had been a policeman—he would have been the very last person to suspect Thomas Donagh of having been concerned in this particular murder. He did not, at that moment, suspect Sir Adrian of having provided some subversive propaganda, but this thought came to him later.

Derek had eaten his breakfast, an unusually large one for him, and then had gone out. Tom had not enquired where he was going; he assumed that it was to the village. At any rate, Derek returned at eleven o'clock in high excitement.

'Mr. Donagh, do you believe in Fate?'

'I suppose so, in a way. Do you?'

'Do you believe in döppelgangers, then?'

'In what?'

'Oh, you know! Your image coming out of a mirror and all that sort of thing. Or your twin. I think I've seen my twin.'

'Your twin?'

'Oh, yes, sir. I told you. Francis. We were parted when Grand took me on, and Francis was sent away.'

'Oh, yes, of course. Do you really mean that you've seen him?'

'They're coming here now. I rushed ahead to tell Grand. It must be Francis. I know it must. Where is Grand? Is he back yet?'

'I don't know where he is,' said Tom. 'Will he—er——'

'No, I'm afraid he won't be very pleased. That's why I thought I ought to tell him. He's never even let me mention Francis, once I've begun on the subject.'

He went off, almost at a trot, and reappeared shortly in resplendent raiment and with his hair newly brushed.

'Hullo,' said Tom. 'Determined to outshine the twin brother?'

'Oh, he has a lady with him,' explained Derek. 'At least, she looks like a witch but I suppose she's human.'

At this moment the bell rang, and after the slightest pause Henry ushered in Francis Caux and his new and involuntary guardian, Mrs. Lestrange Bradley. Derek went forward at once to do the honours, and the deaf and dumb boy began to speak.

'You are Derry. I am glad to see you. I am Francis. We are twins. There was a dead man underneath the boat. I do not like dead men. Do you like dead men?'

'Have you ever seen a tree walking?' Mrs. Bradley enquired. Giving her a look of extreme horror, Derek fainted.

CHAPTER SEVEN

The Questing Fairy

★

'But when to dine she takes her seat,
What shall be our Tita's meat?'

Michael Drayton: *The Fay's Marriage*

★

MRS. BRADLEY cackled.
'Your half of this nutshell appears to be sensitive to superstitious ideas,' she observed conversationally to Donagh. 'Why should that be, I wonder?'

She knelt beside the fallen youth and, to Tom's astonishment, (for she was elderly and looked frail), lifted him on to a chair. She patted him lightly on both cheeks, observed in a deep and musical voice that he was subject to hysteria, and then quickly brought him round.

'It isn't anything to do with hysteria,' Tom explained. 'We've had rather a ghastly experience here. A man was set on and killed in our cricket pavilion the other day, and naturally Derek's upset.'

'Interesting,' said Mrs. Bradley benevolently. She peered at her patient and then looked calmly at his twin brother. 'You see, you are the better man,' she remarked. 'I observe, too, that you have recovered those powers of speech which you lost at the age of . . .'

'Six,' said Derek faintly, sitting up. 'We were six when my father and mother were killed. Or were we seven? Francis was with them. He never really talked again, and the accident had made him deaf as well, so Grand wouldn't have him live with us. I hate Grand. I always have.'

'Nobody would have guessed it,' said Tom drily,

70

recollecting various sickly manifestations of babyish affection on Derek's part and of senile doting on that of his grandsire.

'I had to pretend. I might have killed him.'

Tom mentally dismissed this as adolescent moonshine.

'Well,' he said, 'it remains to be seen what he'll think of Francis now.'

'Who is Grand?' asked Francis. His speech was hoarse but perfectly comprehensible. 'Does he live in this house?'

'Apparently,' Mrs. Bradley replied. 'May I ask whether you, too, are a member of the family?' she added, looking at Tom.

'No. I'm a holiday tutor. I don't know much about things, I'm afraid. I began work less than a week ago. But from what I've gathered, I doubt whether Sir Adrian . . .'

Mrs. Bradley nodded.

'I know. But I'm afraid there was nothing else for it.' Briefly she explained the circumstances which had led to the visit. 'So there seemed nothing else that I could do,' she concluded. 'I can scarcely, on such short acquaintanceship, make myself responsible for the young man, and yet it was not reasonable to leave him alone at Wetwode.'

'Wetwode? In Norfolk? I know it well. Spent several yachting holidays on the rivers and Broads.' The boys had wandered off and were examining the portraits of cricketers on the walls. 'So that unfortunate twin found this body under the dinghy,' Tom continued in a low tone.

'Yes. It seems that the centre-board of the dinghy was up, and this puzzled him. Then possibly he tried to row the boat, but it must have been at once obvious that there was something wrong. He then may have dived in to find out what was the matter, and at first found no way to communicate to anyone else the dreadful thing he had seen. I do not claim that that is exactly what happened, but it may have been.'

'And that didn't loose his tongue, but meeting Derek did. Extraordinary that that should have been the greater shock. Well, look here, I'd better go and find Sir Adrian.' He grinned. 'He's a funny chap, and the news of his grandson's return had better be broken to him gently.'

He sauntered away. In about ten minutes he returned with the baronet. Sir Adrian's face was beaming.

'Well, well, well!' he said. 'Well, well, well, well, well!'

But Francis flinched from him.

'He meant we were seven, not six,' he said wildly, adressing Mrs. Bradley in his guttural tones.

Back in Wetwode Mrs. Bradley reconsidered her plans. There seemed no point in remaining longer at the bungalow unless she wanted to find out more about her neighbours. There seemed little chance of that at the moment, so she wrote to her friend the Chief Constable of Hampshire pointing out that she would be at her Hampshire residence, the Stone House, Wandles Parva, for the following few weeks. She added that she would be interested to know how events shaped at Mede.

He drove over on the following morning and found her cutting roses for the house.

'Ah,' he said, regarding with approval mingled with awe her beehive hat tied under the chin with purple ribbon, her thick tweed costume (unsuited to the warmth of the day) and her motoring gloves and elastic-sided boots. 'Glad to find you at home.'

'Come in and have some shandy,' said Mrs. Bradley. Henri, her cook and butler, who knew better than to produce shandy when there was whisky and soda in the house, demonstrated with the decanter, a siphon and some sandwiches, and brought Mrs. Bradley sherry and biscuits.

'This business at Mede,' said the Chief Constable. 'Not too good, you know. There has been trouble and bad feeling for donkey's years . . . long before my time . . . between Mede and Bruke, and one merely concludes that at last it has come to a head. As it happens, and really most fortunately, Witt wasn't really a local man at all, for otherwise things would be very much worse than they are. He came from Southampton way a year or two ago, and, as

far as we can find out, the only person in Mede who
knew him previously was the inn-keeper there, the man
Cornish.'

'How did you discover that?'

'Cornish came across with it quite openly at the inquest.'

'He was called to the inquest, then?'

'He asked to be. Said that he was the best person to swear
to the dead man's identity just because he *had* known him
longer than anybody else at Mede.'

'Curious; because there was no doubt about Witt's
identity, was there?'

'None at all. I think myself that the fellow just wanted to
be important. He's an inn-keeper, after all, and has to
consider his public.'

'Like any other artist. Yes, I suppose that would be it.'

'On the other hand,' said the Chief Constable slowly,
'there's this to be said. Preliminary enquiries on the part of
Detective-Superintendent Cowley . . . you know Cowley, I
believe? . . . have established that Witt and Cornish did not
get on at all well. Against that there's the cast-iron fact that
of all the people who couldn't possibly have murdered Witt,
Cornish is the man. He didn't even go into the pavilion
when the teams changed over, but remained on the field
inspecting the pitch with the other umpire, the man that
the Bruke eleven brought over.'

'What about the medical evidence? Did anything new
come up?'

'Not a thing. It was fair and clearly stated and amounted
to what we knew already. Witt must have been killed almost
directly he'd finished his innings. He had been cracked over
the head with his own bat and could not have recovered
consciousness.'

'So it must have been one of his own side who did it?'

'It looks like that . . . or, rather, it *would* if they hadn't all
got such fool-proof alibis. Besides, there's another thing, as
Sir Adrian Caux quite fairly pointed out to Detective-
Superintendent Cowley. The feeling between the two villages
ran so high that it was most unlikely . . . *impossible* is Sir

Adrian's word . . . that one of the Bruke team would have done in his skipper before the end of the match.'

'Still, given an opportunity to avenge a real grievance . . .'

'There doesn't seem to have been so much as the shadow of a grievance anywhere, except for this ill-feeling between him and the landlord of the *Frenchman's Inn*. Witt was well-thought-of as a cricketer, was open-handed at the local, no complaints of him as an employer . . .'

'Whom did he employ, and in what capacity?'

'He's a retired military man turned farmer, and he employs most of Bruke. It's only a small place, you know . . . smaller even than Mede. I say, Beatrice, I wish you could go along and look into things. If it weren't that it was a physical impossibility for Cornish to have done it, I'd make him my one and only suspect. It's the only bit of bad blood we know about, so far, and why *should* Cornish, after all, have almost demanded to be the one to offer evidence of identification?'

'We agreed that it was for purposes of personal publicity.'

'Yes, I know. All right. You'll go along there, then, and psycho-analyse the inhabitants?'

'I haven't said so. But I should like to renew my acquaintance with Detective-Superintendent Cowley, and, besides, I am anxious to know what Sir Adrian Caux is going to do about his grandson Francis. I feel responsible for the youth until Miss Higgs comes out of hospital. I am inclined to visit her soon and she is certain to want first-hand tidings of her charge.'

'Francis Caux? Oh, that's the other twin, isn't it? Derek's younger brother.'

'I don't know which was born first. There is no doubt at present which will inherit the property, however. Poor Francis apparently lost the powers of speech and hearing as the result of a severe shock when he was six years old—or rather—it seems more likely—seven.'

'So he ceased to be Sir Adrian's cup of tea, whether he is the older twin or not? Yes, I see. Well, you know where to find me if anything crops up, and I do hope it will. We don't get much of this sort of thing in Hampshire, and I want it cleared up quickly.'

'What are the chances, in your opinion, of a stranger, someone outside either village, having done it?'

'Slight. It would have been possible, of course, if he could have got to the pavilion from the house. But what about the time? How could a stranger have arranged to be on the spot just at the crucial moment?'

'I don't know. I see your point, of course. Obviously he could not have foreseen the minute when Witt would be given out.'

'And there's another thing about that. It appears that Witt almost put himself out. He was anxious to be out. That was clear.'

'Why? Is the reason known?'

'The Bruke eleven, supported (for a change) by the Mede men, say that it was because of the weather. Witt was very anxious to put Mede in on a difficult wicket. I know what you're suggesting, though. You're wondering whether Witt had an appointment with someone at a certain time and put himself out so that he could keep it.'

'It seems possible.'

'Bear it in mind, then; although, if you knew the amount of bad feeling behind this match, you wouldn't be surprised if what we've been told is the literal, absolute truth. Neither team would hesitate to pull a fast one to make the game go their way.'

Mrs. Bradley believed that the literal truth had been told. She doubted, simply, whether it was the whole truth. She went back to Mede, therefore, with an unbiassed mind. It seemed to her that the twin brothers were the crux of the affair, although how and why she did not at the moment understand.

Mede was a lovely little village. Standing, next day, at the crossroads between Mede and Bruke, she saw bramble hedges already hard with small green fruit, tall untrimmed hawthorns pointing straight leaf-rods to the sky, broad fields under pasture and crops, harebells along the roadside, and oak trees bordering lush ditches.

'Not much hedging and ditching been done here yet,' said a voice which came apparently from a tremendous mass of wild clematis on the hedge. Mrs. Bradley turned and saw Tom Donagh step on to the road.

'Good morning,' she said. 'I was under the impression that you had left the neighbourhood.'

'No. Sir Adrian wants me to stay on. Says he can't cope with both those infernal twins—his words, incidentally, not mine—so I'm to continue as bear-leader. You haven't walked all the way from Brockenhurst, have you?'

'No. From Bruke, where I left my car.'

'Ah. Coming to see Francis? I'm sorry I'm not in a position to offer you lunch . . . unless . . . I say! Do have it with me at the pub!'

'But won't Sir Adrian expect you to lunch with the twins?'

'He can't have everything. I'm staying on as a favour, and, I'm glad to say, with better pay. I can ring him up from the *Frenchman* and let him know I shan't be back. He can entertain the policemen who seem to be permanently on and about the estate.'

'Ah, yes. Do they make any progress?'

'Not so's you'd notice. They've got their eye on Derek, of course, but I don't really think they suspect him, although it was very awkward that he should have been off the field when the murder seems to have happened. Oh, Lord! I didn't mean to let *that* out! I shouldn't have told you. Please forget it!'

'I ought to warn you,' said Mrs. Bradley, 'before I accept your hospitality, that I am commissioned (unofficially at present) to have a general look-round on behalf of the Chief Constable of the county; so that anything you may choose to tell me will inevitably figure in my report.' She leered hideously and Tom Donagh grinned and shrugged.

'Fair enough,' he said. 'I don't care all that much about Sir Adrian, but he'll go nuts if the police aren't cleared out pretty soon. Would it be pertinent to enquire why you are a buddy of the Chief Constable?'

'Certainly, child. I live in Wandles Parva.'

'Lovely little place, but . . . er . . .'

'I've worked with him before. We are old friends.'

'Good heavens! You're not Mrs. *Lestrange* Bradley? By Jove, of course, you must be! I say! We *are* going places! I suppose you wouldn't come along next term and give my Detection Fan Club (schoolboys of about thirteen) a talk on some of your cases, would you?'

Mrs. Bradley grimaced and said that she would be delighted. Tom fell into step beside her and soon they passed a farm gate (set on a slant where a farm track joined the road) and came to a couple of cottages. It was not far from these to the village and the *Frenchman's Inn*.

It was not yet noon, so, except for a couple of old men and the landlord, the bar was empty.

'Morning, Cornish,' said Tom. 'What's for lunch?'

'If I'd knowed *you* was coming, sir, it would have been peacock pie,' replied the landlord disagreeably. 'As it is, it'll be the usual roast pork, tetties and greens, followed by apple pie and cheese.'

'Expect two, then, and mind the tablecloth's clean.'

The landlord laughed without mirth and eyed Mrs. Bradley, trying to sum her up.

'Or the lady could have cold 'am and an 'ard-boiled egg, followed by 'ot treacle tart, if she's a mind.'

Mrs. Bradley grinned with a mirthlessness which matched that of the landlord precisely, and opted for roast pork and greens.

'Is it possible to get a room here?' she added. The landlord scratched his head, and then yelled hoarsely for someone called Norah. From the room behind the bar emerged a wispy woman with grey hair and an apologetic smile.

'Yes, Samson?' she said. 'Good morning, I'm sure, Mr. Donagh.'

'Meet Mrs. Bradley,' said Tom. 'Look here, Mrs. Cornish, can you fix her up with a room?'

'A room?' The woman glanced at her husband.

'Well, can you?' he roughly enquired.

'Yes, if you think so, Samson. There's the top front, if that 'ud do. I'll see it's properly aired, Ma'am, and you'd find the 'ouse very clean.'

'Good. And the charge?' said Tom. The woman hesitated, and looked at her husband again.

'What do *you* think, Samson?'

'Three guineas and all found,' replied the landlord. 'Think you could do it on that?'

'If the lady thinks fit.'

'She does,' Mrs. Bradley replied. 'And I shall also need comfortable quarters for my man and a garage for the car. Can you do all that as well?' The woman assured her eagerly that she could. She did not so much as glance at her husband this time.

'What time is lunch?' asked Tom.

'One o'clock, sir. Pork won't roast afore then,' replied Mrs. Cornish timidly, returning to her earlier manner.

'Fine. Let's sit in here and have some sherry, shall we?' said Tom. 'And mind now, Cornish, none of your nasty grocer's stuff. I have a hunch that Mrs. Bradley is a connoisseur, so let's have up a bottle of that Black Market stuff of yours.'

Mrs. Bradley, with a strength which amazed the young man, scooped Tom away from the counter as the landlord's great fist shot forward. Mrs. Cornish cried out, and her husband, recovering himself, turned furiously on her.

'Easy on, Cornish,' said Tom. 'I don't know what I've said to upset you, but it's nothing to do with your wife. Good Lord, man! Can't you take a joke.'

'Not that one he can't, sir,' said Mrs. Cornish pathetically. She laid a hand on her husband's forearm but he shook it away immediately. 'It was cruel hard, during the war, sir, to get decent stuff, as you know.'

'Hold your tongue, you silly bitch!' shouted Cornish.

'And you hold yours,' said Mrs. Bradley pleasantly. Her black eyes held so much menace, however, that the landlord confusedly apologized, and not so very much later he, his wife, Tom and Mrs. Bradley were gathered around a bottle which might have been placed before kings.

The lunch was a great success. Mrs. Cornish was a very sound cook and Tom and Mrs. Bradley had conceived a mutual love for one another. When the meal was over, Tom said tentatively:

'Now what, if anything?'

'I shall walk back to Bruke and bring George and the car here,' Mrs. Bradley replied.

'Oh, that, of course. What then?'

'Then I shall try to discover what the chances were of some stranger's having been able to get through the house and into the pavilion from the rear. It seems clear, from the proceedings at the inquest, that none of the spectators could have got through. To what extent would it distress you if your pupil, Derek Caux, proved to be an accessory before the fact?'

'Meaning that he opened the front door of the house to the murderer?'

'Meaning exactly that, child.'

'But that would involve Sir Adrian. It was *his* idea that Derek should take a short rest.'

'Helpful.'

'I don't see how.'

'Neither do I, at present, child. But, unless some further evidence turns up, it seems likely that whoever murdered Mr. Witt must have come through the house to the pavilion. Were *all* Sir Adrian's servants in the eleven?'

'Yes, they were.'

'So that clears them out of the way unless one was suborned and left the front and back doors open.'

'Widens the field a bit, doesn't it?'

'A fair field and no favour,' said Mrs. Bradley inappositely. 'I shall now walk back to Bruke.'

'May I come with you?'

'Surely, if your duties permit.'

'In for a penny, in for a pound,' said Tom. 'Let's take the short cut across the fields.'

CHAPTER EIGHT

Bruke

★

*'Five justices' hands at it; and witnesses more than
my pack will hold.'*

Shakespeare: *A Winter's Tale*

★

THE TINY village of Bruke was distant some three miles
from the *Frenchman* at Mede, and was distinguished
for its late-Norman church and the remains of a
twelfth-century castle. These were situated half a mile and a
quarter of a mile respectively from the village itself, for the
church, according to custom, had been built on demesne land.

Mrs. Bradley and Tom Donagh reached the church in an
hour after leaving the inn, for the weather was too pleasant
and the signs of summer in woods and fields too delightful
for haste. They walked round the exterior walls of the
church, being careful to observe the superstition of widder-
shins and then entered its dim and chilly silence.

The castle they by-passed, for their inspection of the
church had taken some time. They reached the village at a
quarter to three and found George, the chauffeur, patiently
sitting on the step of Mrs. Bradley's car. He was smoking a
cigarette and reading *Poems of To-day*.

'Please don't throw it away, George,' said his employer,
referring to the cigarette. 'Have you had any lunch?'

'Ample, madam. There is that about the countryside, in
most cases.'

'Splendid.' And Mrs. Bradley, who had made her plans,
ordered a return to the village proper, for they were,
roughly-speaking, on its outskirts.

She had a list of the Bruke eleven with their addresses, together with the name and address of the umpire they had taken with them to the match against Mede, and it was her intention to spend the rest of the afternoon, and, if necessary, the early part of the evening, in interviewing as many of the men as she could find. As feeling between the two villages was so strong, she did not anticipate having much trouble in getting the Bruke players to talk about their captain's sudden and unnatural death, although with what enthusiasm they would greet the questions of a stranger she did not know.

She went first to the local blacksmith because she felt sure of finding him at home. The publican she knew she could visit after the evening opening time, and there was a good chance that several of the team—supposing that she had not been able to interview them during working hours—would be in the hostelry with him.

The blacksmith was putting back the iron rim on a cart-wheel. Mrs. Bradley and Tom got out of the car and watched the sparks fly. The blacksmith lowered his hammer.

'Direct ee somewhere, like?' he kindly enquired.

'No. Don't stop for us. Do you mind us watching?'

'Not a bit. Won't see the likes of any of us much longer, I don't suppose.' He set to again and soon finished his task.

'And now,' said Mrs. Bradley, 'I should be very much obliged if you would answer a few questions.'

The blacksmith altered his benevolent expression.

'I don't know what you be going to ask me,' he said, 'but I've said all I be going to say about poor Mr. Witt.'

'I shouldn't dream of asking you about poor Mr. Witt,' Mrs. Bradley promptly replied. 'A dreadful occurrence, and you are quite right not to want to talk about it. It must have been a most terrible shock to everybody who knew him.'

'Ah, so it were,' the blacksmith agreed. 'Mind you, he were a good batsman and us'll miss him sorely, but he were a stranger hereabouts. Hadn't lived in the village only a couple of year. 'Twas the rector found him for us, like, else us shouldn't have knowed aught about him.'

'Not pubbable or clubbable?' suggested Tom. The black-smith eyed him for a minute or two, and then said slowly:

'Oh, you be one of they Mede chaps. I didn't recognize ee at first in different clo'es and no cap.'

'I did play for Mede, yes,' said Tom.

'Ah!' The blacksmith picked up his hammer, regarded it carefully, took each hand away in turn and spat on each palm. 'Ah, so ee did,' he said in a tone of menace. Then gentler thoughts prevailed. He put the hammer down. 'But ee be a stranger, too. Not a Mede man, eh?' he enquired.

Tom, relaxing, said no, he was not a Mede man.

'I'm a holiday tutor to Derek Caux,' he added. The blacksmith spat—on to a heap of rusty iron ploughshares this time.

'If that lad was mine,' he said sourly, 'I'd dress un in petticoats, *I* 'ud.'

'Oh, no! He's not as bad as all that,' said Tom. 'And he's delicate, you know. It makes a difference.'

The blacksmith wagged his head sombrely.

'If he was mine (which, thank God, un ain't) I'd dress un in petticoats,' he repeated.

'He's not a bad cricketer, anyway,' argued Tom.

'He ain't as bad a cricketer as that un as messed up poor Mr. Witt's 'ead with his own bat,' agreed the blacksmith. 'And if I knowed for sartain who done that, I'd strangle the truth out of un.'

'The police haven't got very far,' said Mrs. Bradley, venturing into the conversation once more.

'Police! Police can't follow the nose in front of their faces. Back you anything you like there's one chap in Mede that know more than he've told the police.'

'Ah, the landlord of the *Frenchman's Inn*,' said Mrs. Bradley. 'Yes, we heard a rumour of that, but there can't be anything in it.'

'And why for not?'

'According to the reports he was out on the field when Mr. Witt was killed.'

'Ah. And now I'll tell ee a funny thing. First time Mr.

Witt played for Bruke, Cornish . . . that's him you're talking about . . . he says, "Oh, so you've found me, 'ave ee?" And then un spits, same like if I was to do here.' He demonstrated, cleverly missing Tom's shoe by an inch and a half. Tom moved away. 'Ah, that's what un done. Since that day they've never spoke to one another. But actually to 'ave killed Mr. Witt, well, no, I don't see 'ow un could a-managed that, like. But they blokes over to Mede, they be a rare bad lot. I wonder somebody didn't warn ee,' he added to Tom, 'before you got yourself mucked up with the likes of they. And now, ma'am, what was it ee wanted to ask me?'

'Whether the church is registered for births, deaths and marriages.'

'Marriages, yes. As to t'other two, I reckon us be all registered for they.' They left him bellowing delightedly at his own wit.

'What does, "So you've found me, have you?" sound like to you, Mr. Donagh?' Mrs. Bradley enquired, when George had let in the clutch and they were on their way to the house wherein lived the Bruke umpire.

'Blackmail,' Tom replied promptly. Mrs. Bradley leered affectionately at him.

'I think so, too,' she said, 'but how are we going to prove it?'

'Even if we could, it wouldn't help us, would it? I mean, this landlord chap is so definitely out of it. I don't even see how he could have been an accomplice. Now if it had been Sir Adrian, and he had persuaded Derek to do the actual killing, all would have been plain sailing. But Sir Adrian was fielding and although Derek . . . and, anyway, I can't see Derek committing a crime.'

'Can't you? And yet I saw his twin brother Francis push Miss Higgs into the river, you know.'

'Really? But twins may not have the same ideas about homicide.'

'True, child. And here we are at Mr. Townshend's gate, if I mistake not.'

Mr. Townshend, the Bruke umpire, was a retired schoolmaster. He had bought two cottages in Bruke before there was a housing shortage—that is to say, a considerable number of years before his retirement—and had had them converted, at inconsiderable cost, into one. From that point he had become his own carpenter, joiner and handyman. It had been his hobby to spend his holidays roaming the countryside in search of good materials from old houses in process of demolition and of acquiring—often for very little money—such items as mantelpieces, panelling, doors and tiles. The result was heterogeneous but, to the owner, satisfying in the extreme.

He opened the door himself.

'Come in, come in,' he said. 'Mrs. Brook and son, no doubt. Come in, come in, come in.'

'Not under false pretences,' said Mrs. Bradley sternly. 'I am not Mrs. Brook, and this is not my son. This is Mr. Tom Donagh, of the Mede cricket eleven, and I am Mrs. Bradley from the village of Wandles Parva.'

'Wandles? Ah, I've often wished we could get a fixture with them. You might examine the chances. Are Wandles very strong this year? We could give them next Saturday fortnight. Do please come in.'

Mrs. Bradley, committed to a description of the Wandles Parva eleven, found herself in an unexpectedly strong position, for the vicar of Wandles had preached a sermon on cricket the Sunday morning before she had left. She had an excellent memory, and, in any case, knew by sight, if not always personally, the men who composed the Wandles team, and she and her host were soon earnestly chatting.

A pleasant-faced woman brought in afternoon tea.

'The wife,' said the umpire. 'Mrs. Bradley from Wandles Parva, dear, and Mr. Tom Donagh, one of our erstwhile opponents from Mede. Sit down, dear. Sit down. Sit down. Sit down.'

'From Mede?' said the woman. 'Oh, dear!'

'Yes, dear. But Mr. Donagh is a stranger, you must remember. He could not have known the Mede reputation when he came.'

'The Bruke reputation isn't too hot, according to Sir Adrian Caux,' said Tom, grinning.

'Oh, I don't know. I don't know. You must allow for a certain amount of local feeling, of course. Personally, I've always felt that the match with Mede was a mistake, but it doesn't do to say so. I did suggest it once at a parish meeting, but even the rector was against me, and as for Wheeler, who is a churchwarden and ought to know better, all *he* had to say was (excuse me, dear, and you, Mrs. Bradley) "What? And let those something Medes think we're something well afraid of them!" So what can one do? I don't even umpire fairly; but that is scarcely my fault. What's sauce for the goose is sauce for the gander, you know, and if that oafish man Cornish would be quite unbiassed, so would I. It would be a treat to play against a decent village like Wandles,' he added wistfully.

Mrs. Bradley promised to do what she could. 'And I'll tell you what,' she added, suddenly inspired. 'If you get the fixture, what about asking Mr. Donagh here to bat for you?'

'In Witt's place, you mean? I don't know, I'm sure. No offence, Mr. Donagh, of course, but to begin with I am not, of course, the captain, and, to go on with, I don't know how the team would feel about co-opting somebody who'd already played for Mede.'

'Pretty rotten, I should think,' said Tom. 'That was a ghastly business. Got any theories about it?'

'Any number. Any number. Yes, yes, of course. I see it in these ways: first, that young Derek Caux did it; second, that one of those fellows in the bar or the kitchen did it; third, that Witt did it himself; fourth, that somebody sneaked from Mede House to the back of the pavilion and did it; fifth, that one of the spectators did it.'

'Yes, but——'

'Objections to these theories and footnotes upon them: first, out of character; too violent a crime. Second, firm alibis for them all: *footnote*, unless they are in collusion. Third, not an easy way to kill oneself, and the bat was too far from the body: *footnote*, suicide, practically speaking,

ruled out. Fourth, by far the most likely hypothesis, and the
one upon which the police should concentrate the greater
part of their attention. *Footnote*, it would involve the con-
nivance of somebody at Mede House; *second footnote*, and
it would have been very difficult to time, unless Witt himself
had made a definite appointment with his murderer and so
got himself out at the required time, which, to me, seems
highly unlikely: still, murder *is* unlikely. Fifth, I know the
ground and I do not see how one of the spectators could
have got into the pavilion.'

'Well!' said Tom. 'I congratulate you, sir! If I may say so,
a beak of the purest water.'

'Yes, yes. The gift of exposition has not been taken away
from me. As to the more flattering part of the description . . .'
He simpered touchingly.

'Anyway, you have the thing in a nutshell,' said Mrs.
Bradley. 'Among your theories there must be the correct
interpretation of what has happened. I myself incline to
your fourth view. I think somebody came through the house
to the pavilion, and I think, with you, that that must
indicate some sort of collusion between somebody in the
Mede (or, of course, the Bruke) eleven and the murderer.'

'The Bruke eleven,' said her host thoughtfully. 'Yes, of
course. There are always wheels within wheels!' He did not
commit himself further except to add, 'And that might
embrace a considerable number of people. Although the
village would be bound to support poor Witt against anybody in Mede—local feeling, you know—there is no doubt
that here he was not what is known as generally popular.'

Mrs. Bradley was more than interested, and Donagh was
positively agog.

'How do you mean, sir?' he asked. But Mr. Townshend
had gone fully as far as he had planned, and possibly a trifle
farther.

'I also am a Bruke man, although only by adoption,' he
replied.

Mrs. Bradley, feeling that she had obtained all the
information she could possibly expect from the Bruke

umpire, rose to go. Tom Donagh had one more shot in his locker.

'Suppose it were a Bruke fellow who did in poor Mr. Witt, who would be your choice?' he demanded. But the ex-schoolmaster declined to commit himself.

'You had better ask others,' he observed.

'A really nice man,' said Mrs. Bradley when they rejoined George and the car. Donagh most cordially agreed. 'In fact, Bruke, so far, easily score over Mede,' he said. 'They seem, somehow, a lot more normal.'

'It depends upon what you mean,' said Mrs. Bradley. 'And I am not particularly quoting our delightful Joad when I say so. Would you call the blacksmith normal, for instance?'

Tom considered this question. He could not answer it, and, by the time they got to their next port of call, the farmhouse of bowler Burt, he had not attempted to do so.

Farmer Burt lived between Bruke and the neighbouring hamlet of Trout, and when they arrived at the farmhouse he was not at home. His wife, a large, flat-faced, placid woman, said that she did not expect him home until seven. He was lending a hand . . . at what she did not add. She asked whether they would leave a message, and she was obviously mesmerized by Mrs. Bradley's sharp black eyes. Mrs. Bradley politely declined to leave any message and Tom asked whether the woman could direct them to where Mr. Burt might be found.

'He be over the ten-acre,' said Mrs. Burt, waving a plump, indefinite hand. 'Unless he be going over to Ricks.'

Tom had seen the name Ricks on a sign-post and said that no doubt they would run into Mr. Burt all right.

'Nuisance,' he remarked, as they got back into the car. 'Think he'll be able to tell us anything, even if we *do* find him?'

Mrs. Bradley said that she doubted it, and spoke sincerely. Tom was not at all sure that he would recognize Burt again if he saw him, particularly if he saw him at a distance; but, as it happened, they were lucky. The car, going slowly, skirted a small wood, and Farmer Burt was in the act of climbing a stile between the edge of the wood and a field of mangold-wurzels. Tom recognized him at once, and George pulled up.

The farmer, a tall man in tweeds and a countryman's round hat, took the pipe from his mouth and stared as Tom came towards him.

'Well,' he said, 'and who'd a-thought of seeing *you* in Bruke, sir!'

'I don't see why not,' said Tom.

'Can we offer you a lift?' asked Mrs. Bradley. The farmer turned his gaze on her and did not answer. He then looked at Tom again.

'Asking for trouble, ain't ee?' he said, putting his pipe in his pocket.

'I don't think so,' Tom replied. 'Why?'

'Why? Well, I reckon Mede men don't come hereabouts, that's all.'

'I'm not a Mede man, in the sense you mean. Why shouldn't I come to Bruke?'

'Un'ealthy,' said the farmer, shaking his head. 'Un'ealthy, sir. That's why. Sir Adrian ud murder ee if he knew.'

'Sir Adrian? I thought you meant the Bruke men might.'

'Us don't 'old with murder and such in Bruke. Us 'appens to be civilized here.'

'You're talking about Mr. Witt, I know. But that was nothing on earth to do with me. I only played in the match because I'm tutoring Sir Adrian's grandson, as you and all the others jolly well know. It was the most frightful thing to happen, but I wasn't at all mixed up in it.'

'There's no smoke without fire.'

'I don't know what you're talking about. Hop in, if you're going to, and we'll take you over to Ricks.'

'Ah, all right, then, I will. No, I won't. Wouldn't do me no good to be seen hobbin' and nobbin' wi' thee, would it, now?'

'Just as you like.' Tom, who had stepped out on to the road, got into the car again. Mrs. Bradley leaned across him.

'If you won't let us give you a lift into Ricks, perhaps you would permit me to accompany you on foot,' she said to Burt. 'I represent the police, and there are some questions I want to ask you.'

She opened the door of the car on her own side and got out. The farmer looked puzzled and extremely ill-at-ease.

'Why, thank you kindly, ma'am,' he said awkwardly. 'No reason why you shouldn't walk along o' me, I suppose, if you've a mind. You wouldn't be one of these 'ere police-women, would you?'

'I am a consulting psychiatrist to the Home Office.'

'Psychiatrist, eh?' They began to move away from the car. 'So that young Caux boy *was* mixed up in it! Didn't see what else could be the answer.'

'There is no reason to suspect Mr. Derek Caux so far. Why should you hit upon *him?*'

'Barmy,' said the farmer, touching his own head furtively. 'Barmy as a coot. Stands to reason. More of a gal than a boy. Had a young cockerel once . . .'

'Hermaphrodite fowls are not a rarity. I once had a bantam pullet . . .' The conversation became technically physiological, and by the time they reached the hamlet of Ricks, which they gained by taking a short cut across one of Farmer Burt's own fields, Mrs. Bradley was able to return to the subject she really wished to discuss. There was now a fair chance that the farmer would be prepared to answer all her questions.

'I be only going to pick up a pup,' he said, pausing at a wooden door in the wall of a long garden. 'I won't be more than half a minute.'

He was as good as his word. In a very short time indeed he came out again with the puppy snuggled in the breast of his coat.

''Tis for Mother,' he announced. 'Her gets pretty lonesome now and again with me out nearly all day.' The puppy whined and shivered and then relaxed. Mrs. Bradley gently stroked his wide head. 'Nice little dogs, these be. I got his two brothers in my yard, but they're trained for outside, and

Mother, her wanted a house-dog. If you're staying in Bruke you better drop in and have a cup of tea with her one day. Be company, like. Her don't have much people to talk to.'

'What does *she* think about Mr. Witt's death?' asked Mrs. Bradley.

'Mother? Her don't say much. Her don't *know* much. All her's ever said to me was that Mr. Witt shouldn't never have come to the village. One of our gals went over to work for him once . . . married now, her is, and gone to live Winchester way . . . but her soon run home again. Nothing *wrong*, you know, but she didn't seem to care about the place. Said people used to come away cryin' after they'd visited Mr. Witt, and it kind of got on her nerves. Gals is fanciful creeters. Not as she ever 'eard or see any 'arm . . . just that they used to leave *cryin*'.'

'Blackmail,' said Mrs. Bradley, as though to herself. The farmer nodded.

'That's what I reckon,' he said simply. 'He was supposed to be retired Regular Army, but he didn't seem much like an Army man to me, and nobody ever *did* know quite 'ow 'e come by his money.'

'Did any local people visit him and come away distressed, do you know?'

'I couldn't say, ma'am, I'm sure. I doubt it. Margy would have mentioned it, I should think.'

'Were you surprised when Mr. Witt got himself out so determinedly in the cricket match? Mr. Donagh told me that he almost ran from the wicket.'

'Surprised? No, I weren't surprised. Us wanted to get out quick and put Mede in on a sticky wicket.'

'It didn't occur to you that Mr. Witt might have an appointment with someone at the back of the pavilion?'

'Why, no. I never thought nought about it. Why should it be anythin' o' that?'

Mrs. Bradley felt that there was no further information to be obtained from the farmer, and she did not pursue the subject. In the lane leading to the farmhouse George had parked the car. Tom Donagh was no longer in it.

George got out when he saw his employer coming, and opened the back-seat door. Mr. Burt vouchsafed one more remark.

'You'd best ask Cornish what happened between him and Mr. Witt when Cornish kept the *Old Rum Puncheon* at Gardling,' he observed. 'That's where *that* all begun. You know, when the G.I. troops was stationed over there in the war. Mr. Witt had a room at the place for a bit. Never paid a penny for it, neither, or so I did hear tell. But mind how you sets about asking un. He be a proper old madman when he's roused.'

This fact did not interest Mrs. Bradley, but the octopus-arm of blackmail, which writhed and twined around every aspect of the case, most certainly did.

CHAPTER NINE

Pons Asinorum

★

*'Suddenly. amid these elements, I became aware that
on the other side of the Sea of Azof we had an interested
spectator.'*

Henry James: *The Turn of the Screw*

★

THERE was plenty to go on, Mrs. Bradley decided. She listed the points in her mind and then in her notebook. First and foremost there was the strange weight of coincidence. Unless she had sadly underestimated the brain-power of at least one of the twins, it was sheer bad luck that Derek should have been absent from the field at the time of Witt's murder.

Secondly, there was the obvious nigger in the wood-pile, Witt himself. He must have had more victims than one. The field of his activities could well be a very large one, and as it was not humanly or physically possible for the brutal land-lord of the *Frenchman* to have murdered him, search would have to be made among his victims for somebody who had had means and opportunity, as well as motive, for the murder. The means and the motive seemed clear enough. As for opportunity, Mrs. Bradley could not do other than believe that it had been provided by young Derek Caux, who must have opened the house to the murderer, unless he were the murderer himself.

There was nothing she could do in all this that the police could not do far better. She was not in the least degree sorry that a blackmailer had met his end. It was another poisonous pest out of the way, and was therefore a distinct gain to society. Of the other dead man, so far, she knew very little. What she badly wanted to know was the connection, if any, between the two murders, and whether it was likely that Francis Caux had had any hand in either. She was willing to believe him innocent; nevertheless, he had been deeply wronged by his grandfather and might have stored up sufficient venom in his mind to have become completely anti-social.

Mrs. Bradley could not forget how she had seen him push Miss Higgs into the river. It had seemed, later, that he was exasperated at being unable to communicate to her the news of the dead man in the boathouse, but against this theory there now had to be set two facts which appeared to conflict with it.

First, if he had really wanted Miss Higgs to know of his dreadful discovery he could at least have led her to the boathouse and pointed to the dinghy, or (as he was undoubtedly a considerable artist) he could have sketched the horrid corpse. Secondly, of the two events, surely the discovery of the dinghy's grisly keel should have occasioned Francis a greater shock than the meeting with his twin brother; yet the latter event had caused him to prove that he had recovered his powers of speech, and not the former.

There was not much doubt, either, that both boys were to some degree abnormal and degenerate. Whether they were sufficiently lacking in conscience to have been accessories to an act of murder she did not know, but she was inclined to think that a boy as spoilt and indulged as Derek and one as unfairly treated as Francis might be capable of criminal activities.

Then there was young Tom Donagh. She pondered at length upon Tom. She could understand that he might have decided to take a tutoring post to see him through part of the long summer vacation, but she could not see why he should have agreed to continue it in circumstances as peculiar and as murky as those which had come about. She wondered what held him, and decided that it might be youthful curiosity. And yet it surprised her that a schoolmaster, of all people, should not object to being one of the central figures in a case of murder. His name had been in the papers already, a fact of which he was aware.

Whatever Tom's reasons for continuing in his job, one thing seemed certain. He had had no hand in either of the murders. This fact brought Mrs. Bradley's mind back again to the beautiful and extraordinary twins. There was one small point which nagged at her. She felt that, after Derek's fainting fit, she possessed some information which, sooner or later, would have to be made public. She wondered when, and how, to publish it.

In a sense it was pure theory, and there seemed no chance of proving it to be fact, but it would fit other facts, although even this did not sway her. She knew. She knew that she knew.

Her thoughts turned to Sir Adrian, that self-opinionated and unethical tyrant. She might have supposed him to be at the bottom of all the trouble but for the fact that she did not believe he would have used his over-loved Derek as an accessory to the murder of Witt. She could not think that he would have exposed the lad to such a risk. Therefore possibly Sir Adrian knew what *she* knew.

At any rate, Sir Adrian himself could not have killed Witt. His alibi was unshakable. It was useless to speculate upon the identity of Witt's murderer, in fact, until far more was known of Witt's activities as a blackmailer; but, again, his death might have had nothing at all to do with these activities. It might have been the result of a sudden, unpremeditated quarrel or something done in a moment of panic. The smash-your-skull type of murder was far more likely to be carried out under sudden emotional stress rather than as the result of long-term hatred or a planned revenge.

That brought her back to Derek Caux again. The boy was emotionally unstable; she was prepared, out of her long experience as a psychologist, to swear to that. He had all the symptoms . . . restlessness, a pathological desire to please and to be admired, a girlish face and physique, a petulant, high-pitched voice, nervous hands, a fear (disguised as love) of his grandfather. He was a prototype, in fact, of the panic-murderer, and might be completely upset . . . driven berserk, in fact . . . by something which would have on a normal boy no effect whatsoever.

She weighed the *pro* and *con* of all her theories, and came, as was her wont, to a definite decision.

'That's it,' she thought. 'The trouble is how to prove it.'

'What do you think?' asked Tom Donagh, presenting himself at the *Frenchman's Inn* on the following morning. 'Sir Adrian's decided it's bad for Derek to stay in the house after the murder. Thinks he's brooding about it. He isn't. He's brooding about his brother. Sir Adrian ain't nice to your Francis, and it worries Derek.'

'I suppose you mean that Francis is to be sent back to the riverside bungalow, and Derek, too. And that gives food for thought—thought being as much in need of sustenance as are the vile bodies to which it is harnessed.'

'How did you guess about Francis and Derek?'

'It is the obvious thing.'

'But the riverside bungalow might be worse for Francis than Mede House is for Derek.'

'Exactly. And you are to go with them.'

'Yes. That's Sir Adrian's idea. We're to boat and fish and swim, and goodness knows what-all.'

'It will be interesting to see whether Francis has overcome his repugnance to the river.'

'Why, are you coming down, too?'

'A little later. Farmer Burt introduced an interesting and possibly a valuable sidelight on the relationship between the landlord here and Mr. Witt.'

'But I thought we were quite certain that Cornish is definitely out of the affair. He's the one person who couldn't *possibly* have killed Witt.'

'Yes, I know, child.'

'Oh, well, I'd better pop back. Pity it isn't opening time. I might have had a pint while I was here.'

'As a resident visitor,' said Mrs. Bradley primly, 'and if

you will risk your, I trust, unsullied reputation by coming up to the bed-sitting-room with which I have been provided, I shall be happy to call for the refreshment to which you allude.'

Cornish brought the beer himself and set it down on the table in the window.

'Nice day,' he said without enthusiasm. 'Rain later, I shouldn't wonder.'

'Mr. Cornish,' said Mrs. Bradley, 'I wonder whether you would do me a favour?'

'Willingly, ma'am.' But it was clear that he did not mean this.

'Would you be kind enough to tell me why you left the *Old Rum Puncheon?*'

The landlord stared at her.

'Why I left the *Old Rum Puncheon?*' he repeated. I't was on account of marrying Norah.'

'You took great exception to a remark made in all innocence by Mr. Donagh here. I wondered whether there was any connection between the two things.'

The landlord's fleshy face darkened. Tom put down his tankard.

'There was no connection, 'course not,' said Cornish sullenly. 'What connection *could* there be?'

'People have been blackmailed before now for trafficking in stolen liquor, Mr. Cornish.'

Cornish breathed heavily and lifted a clenched fist. Then he dropped his arm and contrived to laugh.

'No doubt. But that wouldn't interest *me*,' he said. He turned away, and a moment later they could hear him shouting threateningly for his wife.

'*Not* a man I should ever have wanted to marry,' remarked Mrs. Bradley drily. 'I think we are entitled to assume that he *did* traffic in stolen liquor, probably at Black Market prices, of course, and *knowing* it to have been stolen.'

'But . . . a country pub-keeper? It wouldn't have paid him to do it.'

'Oh, yes, it would, if his customers were American airmen.'

'Oh, I *see!* So that's what old Burt let out of the bag, was it? And if Witt had found out, and had been blackmailing Cornish, there would be a cast-iron motive for murder. But as Cornish can't *be* the murderer, I don't see how it helps us.'

'Neither do I, at present, child.'

'Besides, why wait so long? The war's been over for years.'

'Yes, but you remember the remark made by Cornish when Mr. Witt turned up at the Mede and Bruke cricket match on that first occasion? It sounded then as though Cornish had managed to get away from Witt and keep his whereabouts a secret, and then Witt turned up again . . . whether accidentally or on purpose we may never know.'

'Still, Cornish didn't kill Witt, so that's that.'

'True, child.' But she did not seem downcast about it.

'When shall we see you at Wetwode, I wonder?' asked Tom.

'In a day or two. Possibly the day after you three go down there.'

'Good. I shall look forward to it. You know . . .' he eyed her with friendly suspicion . . . 'you've got something up your sleeve about Witt's death. Do you know more about it than you've said?'

'I have nothing up my sleeve except twins,' Mrs. Bradley replied. Tom laughed. He liked her immensely.

'Yes, come to think of it,' he said, 'and, as a matter of fact, I've thought of it a good many times during the past day or so, it *is* a bit odd that the twins should be mixed up in two quite different murders. Still, perhaps things happen like that.'

'It takes a considerable amount of explaining,' said Mrs. Bradley gravely.

'You don't think . . . no, I don't, either. I mean, I know nothing much about either of the lads, but I still say I can't imagine young Derek killing anybody. It isn't that he's all that good a chap . . . in fact, most of the time 1 can't stick

D

the cissy little oddity . . . but murder just isn't up his street, if you know what I mean.'

'Ah, well, we must wait upon events. And now, do have another pint of beer.'

'No, thanks. Cornish might poison it after what you've just said to him.'

'So you feel like that about Cornish. Curiously enough, so do I. Well, perhaps we should take the road. When does your new term begin?'

'Not until Thursday fortnight, but 1 shall get back a bit earlier than that. I'm being given the Remove, and I'll have to get something ready for the devils, I suppose. It's a peculiar form, isn't it? Rather a compliment to get it, really. I was given the tiny boys last term, and felt a combination of Nanny and Old Father Time. Most devitalizing!'

'Life is a see-saw of disappointments and compensations.'

'One compensation,' said Tom Donagh, grinning, 'is that I received a very fat cheque from Sir Adrian this morning for consenting to stay on longer than we had originally agreed that I should.'

'All the same, the money was more than you had expected?'

'Yes, a good deal more. I gather I'm to keep my mouth shut about something, but what that something is I haven't the foggiest idea, and I'm certainly not going to enquire.'

'And Derek?' Mrs. Bradley enquired. 'He is glad that you're going to stay on?'

'I can't make out Derek,' Tom Donagh replied. 'There's something on that lad's mind. He's on the verge of confiding in me, I think, and I'm not at all certain I want his confidences. You see, the devil of it is that, after all, he was the only member of our eleven who was in a position to slam Witt on the head with that bat. I keep coming back to that fact, in spite of what I feel about the unlikelihood of his being a possible murderer. But, look here, what about you? Shall you stay on here any longer?'

'For a time, child, yes. And if I were a person interested in wagers, I would propose one here and now. You bet, (in moderation), I suppose?'

'Say on. You interest me. I'm an Irishman, don't forget, so your question is really unnecessary.'

'I do not forget it, but I would not like you to waste your money, so I ought in fairness to tell you that I feel I am betting on a psychological certainty.'

'That's trailing your coat with a vengeance! But do let's know what you mean!'

'I was about to remark that it would not surprise me in the least if Sir Adrian joined the party at Wetwode.'

'Oh, I don't think he will. There isn't any cricket there, for one thing, and he doesn't like Francis for another.'

'You will see that I am right,' said Mrs. Bradley. Her prophecy proved to be true. Two days after Tom had taken Derek and Francis to the bungalow, Sir Adrian arrived, and, in his own way, (which was that of interfering belligerently with all that was being done by the police to establish the identity of the Wetwode murderer), took charge of all that was going on, both in and about the bungalow and all along the riverside as well.

'What I want to know,' said Sir Adrian to Tom, at the end of a couple of days, 'is to whom this dinghy originally belonged.'

This approach to the question puzzled and interested Tom. It worried him, too, for he had learned the answer already from Mrs. Bradley.

'To whom it originally belonged?' he echoed, sounding stupid. Sir Adrian made a contemptuous noise in his throat.

'That's what I said,' he retorted. 'On the money I paid Miss Higgs, I don't see that she could have afforded to hire or purchase a sailing dinghy. And if it *wasn't* her dinghy, that seems to let my grandson out.'

'But, surely, sir . . .'

Sir Adrian shook his head.

'No use blinking facts, my boy, and the facts look fishy . . . damned fishy. There's Derry was in a position to have knocked off that rotten feller Witt, and there's his twin brother has to go and find the body of this other blasted feller fastened under the dinghy. I'd go bail for Derry with

my life—*you* know that by this time—but what does the
whole affair—both the affairs, in fact—what does the whole
thing look like?'

This plain speaking, although much to Tom's liking in
some respects, since it crystallized his own doubts, nevertheless was strong meat, coming from Sir Adrian. Nothing was
more probable, as Tom well knew, than that, considering
the peculiar circumstances, both twins might have something
to answer for. Whether the something was murder he did
not know. There were, however, such kittle cattle as
accessories either before or after the fact.

Mrs. Bradley, urgently sent for by Tom, and, upon her
arrival at the village inn, confronted by these doubts and
fears, was more than interested to learn that Sir Adrian was
seriously worried. She and Tom reasoned the matter closely
whilst the launch which Mrs. Bradley had hired chugged
gently along the river reaches.

Between intervals of falling in love with wet woods more
nostalgic than those of Kipling, and of listening entranced,
in the intervals when they shut off the launch's engine, to
the green and soil-laden waters of the river washing amorously
up to the roots of the foremost trees, they discussed the two
murders until both were bored with these, and the slight tide
up from Thurne Mouth, slapping into the reeds and
running up into and washing back from the black-avised
and super-natural banks, seemed the only thing worthy of
philosophy.

They returned from this excursion to find Sir Adrian
almost demented.

'What *is* this?' he shouted. 'Who's been talking against
my grandson?'

'Derek? *I* don't know,' replied Tom, who felt that the
question was really an adverse comment upon his absence
from the bungalow, although he had stipulated for two
hours' leave each day.

'Derry? No. Derry's all right, except that he's an ass.
Frankie is the one I'm talking about!'

Mrs. Bradley was entranced; Tom was astonished, knowing Sir Adrian's antipathy to the supposedly deaf and dumb youth.

'Francis?' he said feebly. 'Why should anybody talk about Francis?'

'If I knew, I'd wring their necks! How dare they say my grandson's a murderer? Eh? How dare they? That's what *I* want to know.'

'Who are the They?' asked Mrs. Bradley.

'How should *I* know? It's all over the village.'

'Where did you hear it, then?'

'Madam, that's no business of yours.'

'Of course it is,' said Mrs. Bradley calmly. 'Who has been calling him a murderer?'

'If I knew that,' said Sir Adrian with intensity, 'I would throttle him. As for you,' he added, addressing Tom, 'you thick-skinned, money-grubbing satellite, I don't want you anywhere near my boys. Understand?'

'Good-bye, sir,' said Tom.

'You be damned!' said Sir Adrian. 'I might be murdered myself for all you'd care!'

Tom was suddenly sorry for the self-willed, frightened, dotingly-foolish old man.

'I'll stay as long as you want me, sir,' he said. 'Until term begins, that is.'

'Tchah! You'll stay as long as you think you will,' said Sir Adrian. 'I know your type. But you can go to the devil! Get out of here! I don't want you any more! Understand?'

'Then I'll call it a day, sir,' said Tom.

CHAPTER TEN

Caliban *v.* Sycorax *v.* a Faun

★

*'. . . wish to express their gratitude to all who have so
generously contributed . . .'*

The Book of the Norwich Festival, 1951

★

'And what do you propose to do now?' Mrs. Bradley and Tom Donagh were again in the launch, which was making its idle and attractive way up the river towards the nearest Broad.

'I don't know,' replied Tom. 'Sir Adrian paid me again,' he added, 'up to date, and, of course, I'm completely curious to know what has made him change his attitude towards Francis.'

'So you're not going to stay and see this thing to an end?'

'I'd like to . . . but is it going to have an end? Of course, the police may get something, but it seems to me that there isn't much chance of our finding out anything that they can't.'

'True, child. And yet I cannot believe that there is very much reason why we should not satisfy our own curiosity. Of one thing I think we may rest assured.'

'Those bloody twins. I agree. They had something to do with it. That sticks out a mile. I can see what Derek did, of course. He must have opened the house to Witt's murderer.'

'There *could* be another explanation. He could have been providing that murderer with an alibi.'

'By having people think he did it? Oh, come, now! He wouldn't stick his neck out that far! Besides, we've nothing to go on. There's nothing we actually know. We've got a

suspect in old Cornish at the pub, but beyond that . . . and
we know he couldn't have done it . . .'

'We also know, from the medical evidence . . . in which,
by the way, I concur, and I was the first person, except for
the boy who dived down to find it, to see the body, remember . . . more or less when the Wetwode corpse was put into
the water. That occurred when Francis and Miss Higgs
were in Great Yarmouth.'

'I get you. You mean we've got to find out whether
Francis could have sneaked back here to help in the murder,
and, if he could, when he did. But I'm afraid I don't see how
we begin.'

'We begin by going back to Mede.'

'To the pub, you mean? Right. But won't Sir Adrian
soon know that we're there?'

' "What's Hecuba to him or he to Hecuba?" ' asked Mrs.
Bradley facetiously. Tom Donagh grinned.

'Right,' he said again. 'To Mede. "Boot, saddle, to horse
and away!" And in case you were thinking of tackling
Landlord Cornish again . . .'

'Oh, but I am. He is our chief point of contact. He was
blackmailed by Mr. Witt for obtaining Black Market
wines and spirits. So much we know. What we do not
know is . . .'

'Whether he had sufficient motive for murdering Witt,
and, if he had, who actually committed the murder for him,
what that mysterious bloke's reward was, and what connection there was, if any, between Witt's murder and the death
of this fellow Campbell at Wetwode.'

Mrs. Bradley beamed upon the intelligent young man.

' "Quite right, Humphrey, quite right." And you'd better
leave Landlord Cornish entirely to me.'

'Not on your life! I don't trust his temper. I'm certain he
knocks that wife of his about, the dirty brute.'

'You think he might attempt to knock *me* about?'

'I wouldn't like to bet on it either way. You'd do better
to have me at hand. Chivalry in defence of the tougher and
wilier sex is my middle name. Didn't you know?'

'You keep out of it, dear child. Not chivalry but sinuous and guileful argument is what is wanted here.'

She had her way, and Donagh was left in the bar whilst Mrs. Bradley addressed the landlord in the airless and slightly smelly sanctity of his private sitting-room. Eschewing guile, she came straight to the point.

'Now, look here, Mr. Cornish, I have no doubt that you can help me, and I hope you will.'

'No credit. That's the motto of this house. If you can't pay, ma'am, out you go, same as everybody else.'

'You misunderstand me. May I ask how well you are acquainted with the mentality and outlook of young Mr. Derek Caux?'

'Eh?' He glowered at her suspiciously.

'It's like this, Mr. Cornish. As matters stand at present, it seems more than likely that in the course of the next few days Mr. Derek Caux may be arrested as an accessory to the fact of murder, if not for the murder itself.'

'Him? Couldn't do no 'arm to a bluebottle! Him do a murder? 'Tis onnatural.'

He spoke with restraint. His piggish, bloodshot little eyes had flickered uncertainly. He was wary and on his guard. She had frightened him. So much was clear. She continued soberly:

'It seems likely that during his temporary absence from the field . . .'

'His grandad ordered him off. There wasn't nothing murderous in that! Treats him more like a gal than a lad, he do. A half a dozen good 'idings wouldn't do the young . . . no 'arm. That's what he'd get if he was my boy. What that one needs is toughening up a bit. Don't do to act sorft wi' boys.'

'No doubt. But I'm glad to have your opinion that he is incapable of murder. What I was about to put to you, however, is this: whilst he was off the field, is it likely, in your opinion, that he would have opened the house to the murderer?'

'I dunno.' He seemed more at ease now. 'What do ee want to know for?'

'I am a psychologist, and, as such, I am interested in Mr. Caux. You see . . . and let's not beat about the bush, if you please, Mr. Cornish . . . so far as is known at present, except for Derek Caux, everybody on the spot at the time of the murder can be accounted for and has an alibi. You yourself, for example . . .'

'I was out on field. Everybody knows that!'

'Exactly. You, the only person in Mede who seems to have had the smallest reason for wanting Mr. Witt out of the way, are the very last person who can possibly be suspected.'

She had not expected to be able to get the whole of that statement out without provoking an explosion, but the landlord merely sat biting his lips and concentrating his attention on the ink-stained, beer-splashed table-cover.

'Well?' he said at last. 'What of it?'

'This. Do you know of anybody else who had got into difficulties because of Mr. Witt's activities?'

'Witt was a——!'

'I'm quite sure he was, and no doubt his death will act as a soporific in more cases than your own.'

'Eh?'

'A number of people will sleep better for the knowledge that Mr. Witt is dead.'

'Ah, that's a fact, that is, I reckon. He can't do no more 'arm, the —— ——.'

'I know. I know. Blackmail is the most dastardly of crimes. You yourself, now . . .'

'Look 'ere, you keep me out of it, or else I'll slit your scrawny little gizzard, you old——'

'Be reasonable, Mr. Cornish. That is exactly the kind of threat which is open to misinterpretation by the police.'

'Don't you threaten *me* with the police!'

'Why not? You seem to have gone in considerable awe of them for some years.'

Cornish gaped at her. Her philosophical response to his bullying put him out of countenance.

'I 'ad my reasons,' he growled. 'Bloody poke-nosed

perishers! What business is it of theirs if a pore chap tries
to turn an honest penny?'

'It wasn't a particularly honest one, was it? But I'm not
moralizing now.'

'Better not, neither! I ain't 'ere to be proach at!'

'Preached. So you think I may reassure his grandfather
that Mr. Derek Caux can have had nothing to do with the
death of Mr. Witt?'

'The old buzzard! Makes the lad a laughin' stock, so he
do. That boy wouldn't have nothing to do with anybody's
death asseptin' of his own, killing hisself with his own
book-larnin'.'

Mrs. Bradley nodded, thanked him for his co-operation,
(at which he blinked), and joined Tom in the bar. She
accepted a glass of sherry, and when they were outside
again she informed Tom, who asked her how she had got
on, that she thought she would find somewhere else to
stay if she decided to come back to Mede. Tom whistled.

'Like that, is it?'

'I've frightened him, and badly. He knows something, I
think, and that something may involve Derek Caux.'

'As you suspected.'

'Well, the coincidences in this business trouble me.'

'It was the old man who sent Derek in to have a rest, you
know.'

'I do not lose sight of that fact, child, nor of the other
important fact that Derek dislikes his grandfather to the
point of loathing him.'

'Meaning?'

'That the opposite may be equally true. Sir Adrian may
detest the boy as much as the boy detests him.'

'Oh, come, now! You'd scarcely say that if you saw them
together as *I* have!'

'Then I had better see them together. Let us return to
Wetwode. Or are you inclined to visit Brittany? The molluscs
there are well regarded.'

Tom looked at her sharply, but her expression was bland.
He said lamely:

'I rather want to stay here. This business has got me. It's enormously interesting. The only thing is . . .'

'Yes, I know. You are not prepared (and who shall blame you?) to behave like a snake in the grass.'

'The trouble is, you see, that you've made me definitely suspicious of young Derek, and it seems more than a shade over the odds to win the bloke's confidence, and all that, and take his grandfather's money, if I'm more or less a spy in the camp. Do you know what I think I'll do? I'll go back, get Derek on his own, and bust him wide open. I'll make him tell me exactly what he did while he was off the field of play.'

'Risky, child, don't you think? And, remember, he has successfully resisted every attempt of the police to do the same thing. He doesn't lack brains. He has parried their every attack.'

'Yes, but the police have to handle him with gloves on.'

'And you think you would not be thus inhibited?'

'Perhaps you're right. I would be.'

'You wouldn't fool Sir Adrian, you know. He would at once jump to the conclusion that you suspect Derek if you attempted to contact the boy again.'

'What *shall* I do, then? I'd much rather have it out with Derek.'

'There is someone else whom *I'd* rather talk to,' said Mrs. Bradley thoughtfully.

'Walters, the butler fellow? I wouldn't mind betting he's got the tabs on most things that have happened in that house.'

'I wasn't thinking of Walters. If he has any sense he'll mind his own and his master's business.'

'I can't think whom you mean, then.'

'Miss Higgs. There are one or two leading questions which suggest themselves to me, and which I feel that she can and will answer.'

Miss Higgs, unfortunately, was still in hospital and it seemed unfair to trouble her although she was going on well. In the interval, therefore, Mrs. Bradley returned to her riverside bungalow and Tom went to visit some cousins who lived in London.

Sir Adrian greeted Mrs. Bradley coolly when he met her, and she, in her turn, showed no sign of having any further interest in him or in his affairs.

The fishermen, Tavis and Grandall, meanwhile came under Mrs. Bradley's scrutiny. They seemed harmless enough, and, apart from anything to do with the murder of Campbell, she was glad to make their further acquaintance.

She had stalked her prey warily. She had informed herself of their habits by careful observation over the space of two week-ends. On the third Saturday she ventured to speak to them in the saloon bar of the hotel.

'I note that the roach are particularly amiable at present.'

Tavis, a Welshman much like a favourite actor of her acquaintance, looked at her cheekily and appraisingly over the top of his tankard.

'Indeed, yes,' he agreed cautiously. 'You will be a fisherman yourself, no doubt?'

'By no means,' Mrs. Bradley blandly informed him. 'I have an over-mastering distaste for taking the life of any creature. Besides, what so delightful to watch as the cold ecstasies of fish?'

'A crank, eh?' said Grandall, a dark and keen-eyed man of about forty-eight. 'No time for cranks.'

'How right you are.' She regarded him with benign and irritating interest. 'I think I had better restore myself immediately to your good graces. I am (as people say) "in with" the police. I want all the information which you can give me about the death of your near neighbour, Mr. Campbell.'

'Police, eh?' said Grandall, whose conversation seemed to follow a pattern and not an involved one. 'No time for the police. Nosey parkers. Besides, you once talked to us before. We've nothing to say.'

Tavis had different ideas.

'I would not say that, man. No, I would think twice before I said that. What did you want us to tell you, girl *bach?*'

Mrs. Bradley blinked her sharp black eyes at him. His handsome, cheeky, cunning face smiled winningly at her.

'Come away, where the Prime Minister can't hear us,' she said, indicating Grandall. She led the way to a small table. Grandall stayed only long enough to order a round of drinks (one of which, to her surprise, was for Mrs. Bradley) before he joined them.

'Prime Minister, eh?' he remarked. 'Well, if I am, it's his own fault. He talks too much, and you've got a pal in the village. Silly kind of woman. Blabs her head off.'

It was a sufficiently apt description of the old school friend, and Mrs. Bradley did not contest it.

'I want to know all about Miss Higgs and Mr. Francis Caux,' she said.

'Miss Higgs, eh?'

'Yes, but I would rather hear it from Mr. Tavis, you know.'

'Tavis, eh? And what should he know that I don't know?'

'Time will provide the answer. What say you, Mr. Tavis?'

Tavis winked at his companion, less with the intent and suggestion of deceiving her, Mrs. Bradley decided, than of implying that the two of them had better be prepared to support and help one another.

'Well, now,' he said, 'Miss Higgs, is it?'

'I don't agree with women bringing up boys,' said Grandall belligerently. Mrs. Bradley waved him away, inclined her head towards the Loki-like Welshman, and raised her eyebrows.

'Miss Higgs it is,' she said; and, while Grandall relapsed into sulky silence, Tavis told her what he knew, or what he saw fit to have it presumed that he knew.

'She came here when we did. We have fished here eleven years.'

'Eleven from seventeen leaves six, or, in the case of years, which have twelve months, seven. Good enough, Mr. Tavis. Go on.'

'Don't be a bloody fool, Gareth,' said Grandall suddenly and urgently. Tavis turned on him.

'And why not, man? Why not? Do you want your neck in a noose, then? Do as she asks you, and be quiet.'

Grandall muttered, put his head on the table and appeared to fall asleep.

'War wounds?' Mrs. Bradley suggested. Tavis nodded.

'Right through the head. Very lucky to be alive to-day, or, maybe, not so lucky,' he admitted. 'I will tell you what you want to know. It was this way, then: a long time ago I said to Thomas . . . that is, to Grandall, you know . . . Thomas, I said, what do you make of Miss Higgs and this boy *bach* she have with her? Why, nothing, says he, but that she cannot be his mother. And why cannot she be his mother? Oh, that, he says, she is not related to him at all. She is just by way of being his guardian, isn't it? Well, I did not know what to make of that, but when she gets to know us . . . you know the way it is . . . she tells me about it. The poor boy is deaf and dumb, and his friends don't want him, see? So she gets a small salary to take him off their hands, and there it is, and that is all I know.'

'Thank you, Mr. Tavis. May I ask one more question? It may be irrelevant or it may not . . . I cannot tell until I receive your answer.'

'What is it, then?'

'How many times has Mr. Grandall been down here without you . . . and how many times have you been here without him?'

Tavis laughed, and with genuine amusement.

'You want to fix the murder on one of us, then?'

'Not at all, but a truthful answer to my question might help me.'

'Well, then, there is this. Two years ago, it might be, I was here without Grandall, but I don't know that he was ever here without me.'

'And on that occasion, when you were here without Mr. Grandall, I think that Miss Higgs confided something to you.'

'Why should you be thinking that, I wonder?'

'Let us say that I don't think it. I know it.'

A certain wariness in his eyes and the form of his answer, told her that the shot had gone home.

'Ah, well,' he said, 'if you know it I will not deny it. Yes, then, I had a few words with Miss Higgs. Interesting words, too. She was wondering whether the boy was still as deaf and dumb as he seemed.'

'How long ago was this?'

'Oh, let me see, now. I said two years, didn't I? Maybe it would have been last June two years. It was the beginning of the season, see?'

'And the boy would have been fifteen. Do you know, Mr. Tavis, that some people think that at fifteen years old human beings reach the summit of their mental powers?'

'Who am I to deny it, then, girl *bach?*' Back came the impudent and warily confiding smile. He was a singularly attractive person.

'Splendid. What else did she tell you?'

'Oh, that she was afraid.'

'Afraid of what?'

'The boy. He was growing up, she said.'

'What details did she supply?'

'She said he was getting to be too much for her.'

'Did she ever refer to that again?'

'Not to my knowledge, no.'

'What did you think she meant?'

'I thought she meant the girls in the village, like. See?'

'Ah, yes, of course. Thank you very much, Mr. Tavis.'

'And what will you do now, I wonder?' asked Tavis innocently.

'Go back to Mede, perhaps . . . or perhaps have a look round the village.'

'Oh, there! They won't tell you what you want to know, you know.'

'Perhaps I can draw my own conclusions.'

'Oh, I have not lied to you, indeed,' he said very quickly. 'It's the truth I've been telling you, now.'

'Yes, I believe you have,' said Mrs. Bradley. 'And, even if you haven't, I'm grateful to you. Remember me to Mr. Grandall.' She looked compassionately upon the sleeping man.

CHAPTER ELEVEN

Dorcas

★

'Torch-bearer, if thou canst not fire two hearts with equal flame, either quench or shift the fire that burns in one.'

Rufinus—translated by Shane Leslie

★

'YOU LOOK rather pleased,' said Tom Donagh, meeting Mrs. Bradley for lunch at her expense.

'I *am* pleased,' Mrs. Bradley replied. 'A great light has been shed upon this case.'

'Which case?—We have two, you know.'

'I have not overlooked that point, child. I refer to the case at Wetwode.'

'Well, if *you've* got any further, the police haven't. I've scanned the papers until I'm pie-eyed.'

'They may not enjoy the full confidence of the police, child.'

'Who gave you the new dope, anyway?'

'Mr. Gareth Tavis, the coarse fisherman.'

'Is he? I thought Welsh public opinion was dead against all crudeness! Sorry! No, what did he say?'

Mrs. Bradley told him. Tom whistled.

'I don't know why we didn't think of girls,' he said.

'I did,' Mrs. Bradley placidly responded, 'but I wanted someone else to mention them.'

'I've never questioned Derek, either, about girls.'

'One can't. It is a subject that crops up if it is going to be mentioned at all.'

'And yet,' said Tom, pursuing his own line of thought,

'one had girls oneself. Why should one not assume that one's pupils, so to speak, have them?'

'These suppositions so often complicate life. No school-master worthy the name associates such matters with his charges.'

'No, I suppose you're right. It *would* make things rather awkward. *Mens sana in corpore sano* doesn't include the obvious. What did friend Tavis have to say?'

'Merely that Miss Higgs told him two years ago that Francis was becoming too much for her and that he supposed she was referring to the village girls.'

'Aha! Francis would be much more likely than Derek to toddle along that way. Sir Adrian keeps a wary eye on his grandson. Derek doesn't get much freedom when one comes to think of it.'

'One so seldom comes to think of anything.'

'One thinks,' said Tom shrewdly, 'that this entrancing conversation has now come to a full stop. Am I right? Road closed until preliminary survey has been made?'

'Quite right. I must tackle the village gossips as I cannot yet come at poor Miss Higgs.'

'How do you propose to begin?'

'By engaging a housekeeper, child.'

'One of the village girls' mums?'

'You show an intelligence far beyond your years.' Tom grinned. She leered affectionately at him. 'And to obtain the services to which I refer, I shall go first to my old school-friend Cissie Cra . . . Mabel Parkinson.'

'I didn't know you'd got an old school-friend living in those parts. I thought you said you hung out in Hampshire, same like Sir Adrian at Mede.'

'To achieve even the most modest degree of success, child, it is essential to have old school-friends everywhere.'

'Yours must be different from mine, then. All mine seem good for is to touch me for a drink, or even, in extreme cases, for cash.'

They parted amicably, and Mrs. Bradley drove to her friend's house. Mabel Parkinson was at home. She was engaged in the pastime of studying palmistry. A couple of books were open on the table, and she was concentrating upon pressing her right hand (covered with some powdery black substance) upon a virgin sheet of paper. Mrs. Bradley, fearful of interrupting a rite, waited patiently at the open French windows until, with a sigh of satisfaction, the practitioner surveyed the result of her handiwork.

'Good-day, dear Mabel,' said Mrs. Bradley in a voice which would scarcely have startled a fawn. Mabel Parkinson looked up.

'Oh, it's you, Beatrice. Do come in. Don't most people call you Adela these days?'

'Yes. Helen Simpson began it, since when I have decidedly preferred it. Now, Mabel, I want some domestic help in my bungalow, and I thought you might know of somebody suitable.'

'Oh, dear! It isn't very easy in these days, you know. Besides, they all want such an enormous amount of money, besides cups of tea at all hours, in which they put at least half one's sugar ration as well.'

'These are difficulties which must be faced. I am no longer at leisure to do my own tidying-up. I am sure you know of somebody who would come.'

'The only person I know of wouldn't suit you.'

'Indeed? Why not?'

'She and her daughter were caught red-handed.'

'Shop-lifting?'

'Yes. In Norwich. It was *not* their first offence. They let the girl off, as she was only fourteen and was judged to be under the mother's influence, but the woman was given a prison sentence.'

'What did the girl do while the mother was away?'

Mabel Parkinson (not at all a bad sort, Mrs. Bradley had long ago decided) looked down at the black fingerprints and palm-print which had come out with remarkable detail upon the specially-prepared paper. When she looked up her eyes were troubled.

'The girl looked after the younger children. There isn't a

father. She got into mischief, I'm afraid. The usual trouble
. . . boys. No supervision, you see, except what the vicar
could manage, and, being a man and a bachelor, *he* was at
a sad disadvantage. I tried my hand once, but met with
nothing but abuse and impudence. You know what these
people are like nowadays.'

'I do indeed. Well, Mabel, your Mrs. . . .'

'Sludger.'

'Sludger appears to be just the person I want. What is her
temperament? Shop-lifters are seldom taciturn. Can she be
trusted to gossip freely while she sits down to her elevenses
and so forth? Is she the type to muck-rake the village whilst
she drops the household china at the sink? Will she pause
during the shaking of rugs to vilify her neighbours and
friends?'

Mabel Parkinson's face had cleared.

'You're looking for some information to help you in this
dreadful murder case,' she said with relief. 'You don't really
want a charwoman. Well, Norfolk people don't gossip
much, as a rule, but the Sludgers don't come from Norfolk.
I don't know where they *do* come from, but Mrs. Sludger
isn't popular in the village, so, if it's scandal you're asking
for, you won't go very far wrong if you engage her. But for
goodness sake don't say I didn't warn you of what she is
like. And now, do let me read your hand. I'm just learning
how to do it, and I want to see as many different hands as I
can. You don't mind if I black it all over? The black comes
off quite well afterwards.'

Mrs. Sludger lived in a small, dirty cottage, in the bare-
earth garden of which she kept hens. She opened a door
which might have led into a sewer, judging by the odour
which assaulted Mrs. Bradley's aristocratic nose, and looked
at her visitor suspiciously.

'I don't want no tracks and I don't want no districk
visitors,' she said.

'I possess no tracts except one which puts forward some
powerful arguments in favour of the sterilization of the

mentally unsound and which I do not happen to have with me, and I am not a district visitor but a prospective employer.'

'Employer?'

'Yes. I want somebody to keep my bungalow clean and tidy.'

'Clean?'

'Yes.'

'And tidy?'

'Yes.'

' 'Ow much you offering?'

'What are the local rates?'

'Rates?'

'Yes.'

'You mean, what do ladies pay around 'ere?'

'Exactly. What do ladies pay around here?'

'Well . . .' She broke off and put her head back inside the malodourous door. ' 'Ere, Efful! Come 'ere! I warnt yer!'

A clean, well-dressed, pretty girl of about sixteen appeared.

'Well, mum?'

' 'Ere's a lady wants me to go out and oblige. What did you say Mrs. Up the Road pays that Mrs. Reepham?'

'Two and threepence, mum.'

' 'Ow many hours?' the woman demanded, turning again to Mrs. Bradley.

'Two hours every morning from ten o'clock until twelve, no Saturdays.'

'What you fink, Efful?'

'Please yourself, mum.'

'All right,' said the woman, smiling genially. 'If it don't suit me I can always turn it in. When shall I start? Termorrer?'

'Certainly. I shall expect you at ten, then.'

'Righty-oh. Ta-ta, and ta for the orfer. Oh, you won't warnt no cookin' done, I don't suppose?'

'No cooking.'

'O.K. then. See you termorrer. Efful, you better put my overall froo the wash.'

To Mrs. Bradley's surprise she turned up to time the next morning. This fact was not destined for repetition, but Mrs.

Bradley found that the experiment of engaging her was successful. True, she complained, at half-hourly intervals, of her palpitations, which, apparently, only a nice cup of tea and a snack could reduce to law and order, but she was a well-informed and unmalicious gossip, and Mrs. Bradley soon learned all that there was to know about the village.

Curiously enough, Mrs. Sludger was sufficiently detached and fair-minded not to resent the attitude of the village towards herself.

'Mind you, I don't reely fink they need 'ave put me inside for nickin' a couple o' blouses,' she observed, 'but the magistrate, 'e said as 'ow an example got to be made because too much of it seemed to be goin' on. Mind you, there's Mrs. I-Could-Tell-You-Oo but no names no pack-drill, goes to every jumble sale for ten mile or more around 'ere, and what she don't know about knockin' the stuff orf the tables accidental-like and 'elping to pick it up, ain't nobody's business. Still, I'm not complainin'! It made a bit of a change, like, and I got shut of the kids, although what Efful got up to, I shouldn't wonder if she did.'

Mrs. Bradley pricked up her ears, but continued her task of sorting out and throwing away correspondence with undiminished zeal.

'A very nice girl, Ethel,' she observed. 'She appears to be both pretty and intelligent, a combination of qualities sufficiently rare to be remarkable.'

'You know,' said Mrs. Sludger, peering under the book-case to find out whether, perhaps, that part of the floor could be left untouched that day, 'I must say, if you'll excuse me, I does like the way you talks. All them long words, and I suppose you knows what you means. I orfen says to Efful, when I goes 'ome of a morning, that it's as good as learnin' a forring langwidge to 'ear what you got to say when you got the Micky in yer.'

Mrs. Bradley, unaware until this moment of harbouring the Micky, steered the conversation deftly back upon the rails.

'Ethel, I suppose, learnt French at school.'

'French? Efful learn French? I should soon 'ave gorn up and give them teachers a bit of my mind if she 'ad. Waste enough time at school as it was, so she did. Fair 'ated it. Keepin' 'em on till fifteen! Did you ever 'ear of anythink so daft? When they might be out earnin' good money!'

'And is she earning good money now?'

'Well, it's me palpitations, you see. I 'ave to 'ave 'elp; I can't 'elp it.'

'But I suppose she gets plenty of fun. Young girls need fun, I always think.'

'Fun? Well, I dunno about that. She's kind of broody, Efful is. "If you was an 'en, I'd know what to do wiv yer," I says, "but being as 'ow you ain't an 'en, Gawd 'elp yer, 'e probally won't," I says. It's all on account of young Mr. Caux, you know, dear.'

She abandoned her devices and sat back on her heels.

'Young Mr. Caux? Oh, really?' said Mrs. Bradley, feeling sure that the desired information was now about to emerge. 'Rather a handsome young man. A pity he has such an affliction.'

'Oh, well, if 'e 'adn't, I doubt if 'e'd ever 'ave looked at Efful,' said Mrs. Sludger with her usual staggering matter-of-factness. 'But it's after 'im Efful goes broody, though I've told 'er of it orfen enough. "It isn't no good you a-frettin' yourself about 'im, Efful," I says. "After all, 'e's a gent, 'owever peculiar 'e may be, pore boy. And 'e *is* deaf and dumb!" But she ain't 'avin' nothink o' that. "Sometimes 'e is, and sometimes 'e ain't," she says. I didn't like the sound o' that, and so I can tell you, dear. "You just be'ave your-self," I says. "I know *that* sort o' talk. Goin's-on never did no gal no good yet, and I'm the livin' example." You see, dear, Efful might 'ave 'ad a farver but for me, so I 'aves to keep me eye on 'er, and 'ave done, ever since twelve. But when I was in for that there free munce, well, you never can tell, but I don't think no 'arm, as nothing 'appened.'

More than ever did Mrs. Bradley look forward to the time when Miss Higgs could be asked some leading questions. There was one thing in particular that she badly

wanted to know. It was the result of a wild surmise on her
part. Her mind had pounced on it during Mrs. Sludger's
oration. It seemed in the last degree unlikely that it would
be answered in the affirmative, and yet it was such an
attractive question that she sincerely hoped for an encouraging reply.

'I wonder,' she said, 'whether you would have any
objection to my asking Ethel one question about young
Mr. Caux?'

'She won't answer yer, I daresay, and I don't know 'ow
to make 'er. I never '*ave* lifted my 'and to any of 'em except
it might be to give young Bert a clip be'ind the ear'ole,
and . . .'

'I don't think Ethel will object to this particular question,
Mrs. Sludger. I have no intention of hurting her feelings or
of raising any moral or sociological issues.'

'I could listen to yer all day, dear,' said Mrs. Sludger
admiringly. 'Only,' she added virtuously, 'I got me work
to do.'

She peered inside the teapot, picked up the kettle and
shook it, received no encouragement from either receptacle,
so, sighing, picked up a pail and stood it, with a resigned
little clanking, in the sink.

Mrs. Bradley managed a word with Ethel in her own
home while her mother was semi-occupied at the bungalow.
She liked Ethel, and came to the point at once.

'Ethel,' she said, 'take me out to look at your chickens.
There is something I want to talk to you about.'

'If mum's half-inched anything I'm sorry, but you did
know about her before you took her on,' said Ethel
defensively.

'It's nothing to do with your mother at all. It's just something I want to know. I'm going to ask three people the
same question. You are the first. If you answer me truthfully
it will help me very much. If you tell me a lie it will hinder
me, but, of course, only for a comparatively short time. If
you refuse to answer, well, it is your business and I shan't
press you. Fair enough?'

'Fair enough,' said Ethel. She rinsed her hands under the scullery tap, dried them on her handkerchief—the roller towel hanging behind the back door had seen better days in more respects than one—and led the way into the yard.

'You used to be friendly with Mr. Francis Caux.'

'Mum told you?'

'Yes.'

'Nobody else?'

'Nobody else, so far.'

'No harm in it. We never done anything wrong.'

'Of course not. Why should you? But, Ethel, while you were friendly with him, did you ever suspect that he might be two people?'

'Frankie Caux? Two people?'

'Yes. Was he always . . . Frankie Caux?'

Ethel's lovely eyes widened. She looked distressed.

'Oh, but . . . Oh, but . . .'

'Never mind,' said Mrs. Bradley. 'I won't worry you about it.' To her intense interest and gratification, the girl's answer could scarcely be construed as a negative one. She left Ethel to think things over. She did not underrate the girl's intelligence. She expected a voluntary statement from Ethel, and that at a very early date.

She tried the question next on Sir Adrian, whom she encountered exercising his charges on the road to Salhouse. The boys, who were dressed more or less alike in tweed jackets and flannel trousers, strolled on ahead. Mrs. Bradley walked very slowly indeed to make certain that Derek was out of earshot, and then said:

'How are the twins getting on?'

'Famously. Francis doesn't utter a lot, of course, but he makes do, and his lip-reading seems very much improved,' said Sir Adrian impressively.

'Extraordinary, isn't it?'

'How do you mean?'

'Well, here is this unfortunate youth rendered pathologically deaf and dumb as the result of a shock received in early childhood. He receives another shock when he discovers a dead body pinned to the bottom of a dinghy, but this, apparently, affects him comparatively slightly. I mean, I know he endangered Miss Higgs' life by calling her attention to the fact that the river held horrors, but he himself seemed physically unchanged. Then comes this third shock, the shock of meeting the twin brother from whom he has been parted for ten years. He recovers to some extent the lost powers of speech. Lip-reading, which, for some reason, he has never mastered, comes to him just as easily.'

'Yes? Could be like that, couldn't it?'

'I am not saying that it could not. We know very little indeed, even now, about the workings of the subconscious mind. I will, however, go as far as to say that I have never *known* it to happen quite like that.'

'He only talks little-kid talk, if you know what I mean. It's as though he's picked up again where he left off at seven,' said Sir Adrian, defensively.

'Yes?'

'What's on your mind?' asked the baronet, glancing at her beaky little mouth. 'You're doubtful about something. "Bubbled and troubled" as the poet Gay has it. Unburden yourself. What bites you?'

'A question I want to put to you. How well would you say you know Derek?'

'Oh, not well, of course. He's a strange boy. Why?'

'Have you ever thought he was Francis?'

'Francis?' Sir Adrian looked astounded. 'Oh, no, I never confuse them. Besides, Francis has a much healthier appetite than Derek! He's quite a good trencherman, whereas Derek is finicky and, as often as not, eats almost nothing.'

'No, a healthy appetite *is* a difficult thing to disguise,' Mrs. Bradley agreed. 'Even more difficult, though, is the task of eating food which one does not want. To force children to eat when they are not in the mood for eating, or to make them eat things for which they have no taste, has always seemed to me very cruel.'

She walked on and caught up with the boys. Sir Adrian lingered behind.

'And how is Sir Adrian?' Mrs. Bradley enquired. Derek turned, his beautiful face filled with pleasure.

'Oh, how *very* kind of you to ask after Grand!' he said. 'Isn't it kind of Mrs. Bradley, Francis?' Francis, who was looking over a gate, made no response until Derek took him gently by the arm and caused him to turn round. Then he repeated the question. His brother smiled. His luminous eyes widened.

'Very kind,' he said throatily. 'Very kind to ask about Grand.' Then he turned and looked over the gate again.

'And you won't get much more,' said Sir Adrian, joining them. Derek laughed.

'He makes wonderful progress,' he said, 'but there's a long way to go yet, a very long way, isn't there, Grand, dear? *You* ought to know, if anyone does.'

And Derek, with his talent for an irritating by-play of public demonstrations of affection, put his arm round his brother's waist and rested his head on his brother's shoulder. Sir Adrian gazed sentimentally at them. Mrs. Bradley did not know the word *Punk*. If she had, she would probably have used it.

CHAPTER TWELVE

Castor and Pollux

★

*'Of all the delusions with which he deceives mortality,
there is not any that puzzleth me more than the Legerde-
main of Changelings.'*

Sir Thomas Browne: *Religio Medici*

★

SIR ADRIAN, who, after their last meeting seemed inclined
to ignore the fact that Mrs. Bradley was his nearest
neighbour, suddenly confided to her one morning that
Scotland Yard had been called in on both the Mede and the
Wetwode murders.

He was seated in a deck-chair on his riverside lawn. She
was correcting the proofs of an article for the journal
Psychopathology, and had a small table placed almost in
line with his chair but on the opposite side of the little
staithe which ran between the two small properties.

'Really?' she said. 'I wondered how long it would be.'

'Wrote to the Assistant Commissioner myself,' said Sir
Adrian proudly. 'Told him it was time to do away with all
the damned nonsense and get down to brass tacks.'

'I don't blame you. Are Scotland Yard sending a detective-
inspector down here, then? I haven't seen one yet.'

'Ah, that's where the Yard excel, you know. He'll make
his way down here and put up at the pub and pretend to be
a fisherman. Then, when he's got us all weighed up, he'll
take off his sheep's clothing and begin putting us all through
our paces, but not before he's pretty sure of himself. *You'll
see.*'

Mrs. Bradley, who had worked with several detective-inspectors from Scotland Yard, and who was consulting psychiatrist to the Home Office, grinned like an alligator and said that she supposed so. She then asked after Miss Higgs.

'Oh, Francis wants to go and see her in hospital. Morbid. Boy always *was* morbid. Can't be helped, of course, although Derry's company does him a world of good. I've been rather remiss there, I'm afraid.'

'Do you find any difficulty in distinguishing him from his brother, now that they are together again and are so much alike to look at?'

'Of course not! I couldn't mistake Derry for poor Frankie. Mind you, I shall be very glad when Higgs can take her job on again. Want to have Derry to myself. Want to get back to Mede. Want to get back to cricket and a quiet life. Still, shall arrange for them to meet, and all that. Been rather remiss. Yes, yes. Been rather remiss. Still, done what I can to make amends. Can't have Frankie tagging on until Doomsday. Too much to expect, what?'

'And Derek? Will he agree to having Francis go back to Miss Higgs?'

Sir Adrian moodily ground a daisy root into the lawn with the heel of a heavy shoe.

'I can't make the lad out,' he said, in something between a groan and a growl. 'Dashed if I can. All he seems to want is to be arm-round-neck with his brother, and they're out together all day long.'

'Natural, at their age, surely?'

'Yes, if they'd been brought up together, perhaps, but they haven't set eyes on one another for ten years, and now it's "Derry" and "Frankie" and cheek by jowl and David and Jonathan all the blessed day. I don't get a look in anywhere, and Derry and I were such pals. Besides, I don't like it. It isn't good for Derry. It isn't healthy. What's that thing Shakespeare wrote? You know the one I mean. Well, it's more like that than anything else I can think of.'

Mrs. Bradley could think of quite a number of things written by Shakespeare which might conceivably be appropriate to the situation described by Sir Adrian, but she fancied that he would be unlikely to know any of them. She murmured, in her beautiful voice, 'Ah, well . . . "youth's a stuff will not endure," you know.'

'That's it. Had it on the tip of my tongue but can never spit these things out until somebody gives me the cue. That's it, exactly. "Journeys end in lovers' meeting." That's the line I wanted. It's like that, you know . . . or like two silly girls together. Giggling and laughing and plotting in corners . . . it's giving me the fidgets.'

He humped himself round in his chair, picked up the book he had been reading, and ignored Mrs. Bradley for the rest of the time she was there. She studied him covertly and thoughtfully. There was an incongruity here, she decided. Even when allowance had been made for an old man's jealousy, his remarks about Francis did not ring true, particularly those in which he affected to feel sorry for the boy. He was not sorry for him; he hated him; and behind the sycophantic expressions of remorse, there was fear.

She finished correcting her proofs and then untied the canoe and paddled upstream and under the bridge to the hotel. Here she tied up, walked ashore up the boathouse steps and went into the hotel for a mid-morning glass of sherry. Her immediate interest was not so much her elevenses . . . although the hotel sherry was good . . . as that, having paid for a drink, she felt at liberty to use the hotel telephone which was situated in the small alcove at the foot of the stairs and had the great advantage of being absolutely private so long as nobody else was in the hall. She rang up the Assistant Commissioner at New Scotland Yard, and after the minimum of delay was connected. She asked whom he was sending to Norfolk to investigate the murders at Mede and Wetwode.

'I suppose you'd like Gavin,' said the Assistant Commissioner, 'and you can have him. He's been looking into that Goodwood affair, but it's about to break very nicely, so you can have him, because it's all over bar the shouting down there. You might get Mede and Wetwode settled as soon as ever you can, Beatrice, because of the State Visit next month. Gavin is our handsomest young man at present, and so I think we shall put him in charge of the security arrangements, as the visitor is a lady. I know your *beaux yeux* can do most things, but they're not to keep Gavin tied up.'

Well pleased with the result of her call, Mrs. Bradley returned to her canoe and paddled upstream again past the moored houseboats, the riverside lawns and the tea-gardens. Once she was beyond the ugly railway bridge which carried the branch line to the sea, she was in another world. From the thick black ooze on the right bank writhed the greyish roots of the trees in wet woods that stretched in haunted fantasy as far inland as she could see. On the left bank it was sunny and green, and even the slight disturbance of the water from her flashing and dripping paddle sent tiny waves to suck in and out among the hollow-stalked valerian and the arrow-heads, among tussock-sedge, fen-sedge, and reeds, among sweet-grass, saw-sedge, and the thin-stemmed ragged robin.

She kept out in mid-stream to pass over the eel-fishers' nets, and round the next bend she saw a boat ahead of her. Unwilling for company, she paddled in to the side and lay up in a sluggish spot between two beds of great sedge, whose broad-bladed leaves hid her and her slender craft from view. The canoe stuck its nose amid the stiff and sword-like plants and Mrs. Bradley sat still and watched a Montagu's harrier as it floated, buoyant and watchful, in the clear, rapt, Norfolk sky.

Suddenly she heard a voice which she recognized.

'*Carex Paniculata.*'

'Tussock sedge,' replied a voice which sounded almost exactly like the first one.

'Right. Now you.'

'*Glyceria Maxima.*'

'Reed sweet-grass.'

'Yes. *Carex* . . .'

'It's my turn. All right, then, although I see you know it. *Carex Acutiformis.*'

'Fen sedge. We won't count that one, then. What about
Phragmites Communis?'

'Despite its Soviet-type nomenclature, dear, I think it is
merely the common reed. Let us see what you can do with
Calamagrostis Canescens.'

'Reminiscent of magic dogs, darling. But I think I will say
it is the purple small-reed.'

'Well, that ought to be enough to settle Grand's hash. He
suspicions us, as the saying goes. How's the dim Miss Higgs?'

'Pretty well, I think. Look, let's get back to the boat. I
want to swim, and the best place is half-a-mile further on. It
will be shallow enough for you and deep enough for me.
And there's a bit of grass there where we can practise that
new quick-step variation, or, contrariwise, lie and ponder on
the beauty of fair women and brave men.'

The voices faded. Mrs. Bradley's keen ear could detect
the sound of them for some little time, but she could not
distinguish any words. Soberly pleased that one of her most
fantastic theories was now proved, she pushed off from the
bank and paddled rapidly and efficiently upstream, passing
the Caux twins whose dinghy was in process of running up
a mainsail.

She waved to the boys, and one of them called back a
cheerful greeting. Soon she had lost sight of them round the
bend. When she reached the huge white mill which spanned
the river she paddled in to the side, pulled the canoe on to
the shelving bank, and sat on the short grass to rest.

While she rested she meditated, but her thoughts returned
always to one focal point. The case was closed until she or
Gavin . . . preferably she *and* Gavin . . . could interview Miss
Higgs. There was no reasonable doubt now that the twin
boys were in the habit of changing places. There was no
doubt at all but that Francis was no more deaf and dumb
than Derek . . . but, then, there never, to her, had been very
much doubt about that.

She wondered how long the game of changing places and
so hoodwinking their grandfather had been going on, and
what had led the boys to begin it. Miss Higgs, of course,

might have been in collusion with them, but, if so, the drastic action of Francis in pushing her into the river seemed unaccountable. Besides, she had begun to give the game away during her first long conversation with Mrs. Bradley.

Mrs. Bradley went over that conversation in her mind. One point had been clear, two others had still to be cleared up. Only one of the boys could play cricket, or, at any rate, only one had any real aptitude for the game. It was possible that only one could swim. It was possible that only one was seriously attracted by girls.

She had another idea, too, and she thought that an interview with Miss Higgs might help to prove it true or false. A tactful approach would be needed, as it was a matter which concerned Miss Higgs herself. It was probable, Mrs. Bradley thought, that one of the twins liked Miss Higgs and the other resented her guardianship. Carrying this thought a stage further, she also had an idea that the twin who liked girls might very well resent the guardianship of a middle-aged woman. From this, the true Derek and not the true Francis had pushed Miss Higgs into the river on the day of Mrs. Bradley's arrival in Wetwode. On the other hand, a badly-frightened Francis might still have done such a thing. The incident, which should have shed light, enveloped the situation in blacker darkness, unless. . . . And the more she thought over a new and startling theory the better she liked it.

There remained an enigma. She could not, at that stage, decide with certainty whether the brothers had exchanged rôles during the cricket match against Bruke. It seemed more than likely that Derek had not taken the risk of allowing Francis to impersonate him in an important match, but, on the other hand, the bad weather could have been held accountable for faults and mistakes which a perfect wicket would render inexcusable.

If Derek had had some overwhelming motive for wanting Witt out of the way, he could have got his brother to take his place in the team and (granted that Francis could contrive to free himself from Miss Higgs for the day without

E

exciting her suspicions) he could have had a perfect alibi
for the murder of the Bruke captain.

But something had gone wrong with the time scheme.
Witt had been killed when neither twin was on the field.
Mrs. Bradley had heard about the match from Tom
Donagh, and she felt that the weather had been the *deus ex
machina* in the affair. The point was not at the time capable
of proof, but it seemed to her more than likely that the
Bruke innings had ended too soon. The match had been
scheduled to last two days, Thursday and Saturday, but the
treacherous wicket had determined Witt's policy. Witt's
policy had been to get his men out as soon as he could, so
as to extricate them from a defensive position in which few
runs could be scored, put Mede in while the wicket was at
its worst, skittle them out, and trust that the weather would
so much improve on the Saturday that his side would have
a second innings and keep Mede in the field until the end of
play. Owing to the peculiar and unethical nature of the
contest . . . that is to say, that a draw was an impossibility
. . . Bruke could thus count upon a resounding victory, for
the match could be won outright whether Mede played a
second innings or not.

Obviously Francis, not much of a cricketer, might still, in
the emergency which faced the brothers, have been trusted
to field, but, on such a sticky wicket . . . or, probably, on
any wicket at all . . . he could not be permitted to bat. A
great risk had been taken . . . that seemed a reasonable
supposition . . . and it might easily have come off but for
the uncertainties of the game (although even these might
have been allowed for to some extent). Undoubtedly it was
the extraordinary conduct of the twin in leaving the field of
play, and so destroying both his own and his brother's
alibi, which had played into the hands of the investigators.

However much she turned the matter over in her mind,
Mrs. Bradley could find only one explanation of this
suicidal and fratricidal omission. Otherwise it had neither
rhyme nor reason; it had blown a careful and daring plan
sky-high. It was something which, whatever their opinion of

Derek-Francis or Francis-Derek as a potential murderer might be, the police could not possibly overlook.

When she discussed her ideas with Gavin, however, that mild-mannered and handsome young police officer looked gloomy, profound and wise.

'Motive,' he said. 'It sticks out a mile that one of the young devils was involved, but until we find a motive we can't pin either of 'em down. You see, whoever Witt was blackmailing, we don't know it was either of *them*.'

'You mean you don't think them capable of murder?'

'I'm dashed if I know. I keep thinking of that Loeb and Leopold business in the States. These two young decadents might easily be the same type. Of course, I've only talked to the one who claims to be Derek. The other one was foxy enough to hand me baby-talk, or something not far removed from it. My instinct . . . you know your J. A. Ferguson's *Campbell of Kilmhor* . . . was to put my sword to the carcase of a muckle ass and see would it louse his tongue, but unfortunately I'm not even permitted to box his ears.'

Gavin had had just the one interview with the boys, and had come to Mrs. Bradley to obtain her latest views and to report his own lack of progress.

'There's another thing,' she said. 'I've been thinking that perhaps we shall not need Miss Higgs' evidence after all. Something happened, the significance of which at first escaped me.'

'How do you mean?'

'I am speaking now of this game or plot of the two boys.'

'The murder or murders?'

'Not altogether. I was thinking only of this change-over of identity.'

'Yes?'

'When I brought Francis (as I thought) to visit his grandfather, one of the twins most spectacularly fainted. It was genuine loss of consciousness. I am too experienced a doctor to have been deceived about that. I thought at first that it was shock through fear of his grandfather, but . . .'

'You mean, so it was,' said Gavin, 'but not for the reason you thought.'

'Right, child. He *was* afraid of his grandfather, who exclaimed, (to my surprise, I admit, for I had heard from Miss Higgs how much he disliked her embarrassing charge), "Well, well, well, well, well," and that in a comparatively genial tone.'

'I see your point. In other words . . . although I should never have been able to work this out for myself . . . the *real* Derek was again masquerading as Francis, and one of the twins, probably Derek, thought that, confronted by the pair of them, his grandfather had recognized the favourite grandson.'

'Exactly. And that being so, all reason for believing that the real Francis was deaf and dumb would be amply and demonstrably disproved.'

'We still need to hear Miss Higgs on the point, though, I feel.'

'She must be approached with considerable tact, then.'

'Yes, I quite realize that. Shall I have first bash at it, or will you?'

'You, I think. Your beauty and charm will overwhelm a middle-aged virgin.'

'I shouldn't be surprised,' said Gavin, moving out of reach of a prodding yellow forefinger. ' "Now lies the earth all Danäe to the stars" . . . a fact of which we policemen, in spite of our modesty, cannot help but sometimes be aware.'

BOOK TWO

The Echoes

'But if you talked to yourself, you did not answer yourself. I am certain I heard two voices.'

Oliver Goldsmith: *She Stoops to Conquer*

CHAPTER THIRTEEN

The Echo Under the Bridge

★

'. . . *answer, echoes, dying, dying, dying.*'
Alfred, Lord Tennyson

★

MRS. BRADLEY retired to the Stone House at Wandles
Parva in slightly saddened mood. In spite of her
conviction that in one way or another the twin
brothers were at least in part responsible for the double
murders . . . the one at Wetwode and the other at Mede . . .
she felt certain that some great wrong had been dealt them
and that wrong had provoked one or both of them to take
vengeance.

The most obvious and likely motive which they might
have had for murder was that one or other of them had been
blackmailed, and, to her, blackmail was one of the more
inexcusable crimes. She tried to work out the possible
reasons for this blackmail, beginning with the first known
fact, that the boys' parents had both been killed at the same
time. She wondered whether there was any possibility that
the deaths of the parents could be brought home to any
negligence, cowardice or need on the part of the boys, but
the fact that the twins could not, at the most, have been
more than seven years old at the time of the crash seemed to
rule out . . . in practical terms, *did* rule out . . . any question
of their responsibility.

That brought the thing nearer home. What could either
Francis or Derek have done since they were seven . . . she
could put it higher . . . since they were sixteen at least . . .
which would give even the most unscrupulous person

sufficient hold over them for his murder to have appeared to be a solution of their difficulties?

This brought another question. Why *two* murders? Granted that the twins would have backed each other up through thick and thin, what two persons in districts as far apart as East Anglia and Hampshire could have been so completely in collusion as to have made life unbearable for both brothers? There was some mysterious factor in all this, and she thought that somewhere in the picture was Sir Adrian Caux. Sir Adrian had accepted the custody of the boys only to separate them at a very early age. They had been old enough to understand and to resent this separation. It had been a heartless business undoubtedly. She decided to see Sir Adrian again.

She found the squire of Mede preoccupied with boats. He was organizing his own regatta, to be rowed and sailed on the River Burwater starting from the very bungalow at which the murder of Campbell had taken place.

This particular point did not, of itself, influence Mrs. Bradley. Her spirit was anything but morbid and she saw no reason why the environs of Wetwode should be sacrosanct because a violent death had taken place there. She greeted Sir Adrian with neighbourly civility and enquired concerning the reason for, and the scope of, his activities.

He replied with what seemed to her to be rather suspicious politeness . . . even warmth . . . that he thought it only right to spend some of his money on the villagers and requested her to help him judge the races.

'I would prefer to compete,' said Mrs. Bradley. 'Is there possibly a class for Canadian canoes?'

'No,' Sir Adrian replied. 'They are not much in evidence on this part of the river, so I didn't make a class for them. Perhaps, though, you could give us an exhibition.'

'In the vulgar sense, that is what it would probably amount to. I think I will enter in the fourteen-foot International class . . . sailing dinghies, you know.'

'We haven't got one.' Sir Adrian looked at her as though he could kill her. 'Why don't you suggest something sensible?'

'I have never heard of a sailing regatta which did not have a fourteen-foot International class,' protested Mrs. Bradley, noting the return to his natural manner.

'Well, you have now. What about the single or double sculls? Quite enough excitement for a woman of your age.'

'Too much effort. I must conserve my energies. Sail or nothing.'

'There's a class for outboard-motor boats. Dinghies, you know.' Sir Adrian's tone had altered again. It was quiet and conciliatory.

'Then there ought not to be. I shall report you to the river conservancy people,' said Mrs. Bradley firmly. 'Who are you to ruin their soft banks?'

'Pish! And that being settled, are you going to help me judge the races or not?'

'Very well. I will help with the judging. I assume that there will be three of us.'

'Three judges? Why three, dear lady?'

He was disingenuous enough to look surprised and slightly perturbed.

'We must have a majority verdict, I feel. It will save time and tempers.'

'Look here,' said Sir Adrian, 'what's your game?'

'To give a fair verdict.'

'Fair to whom?'

'To the victims. I mean, the competitors.'

'Do you doubt my sense of fairness?'

'And my own. One is always biassed.'

Sir Adrian opened his mouth to speak, closed it again, smiled without opening his lips, and then said with false geniality:

'Champagne, oysters, peanuts and Gorgonzola cheese. Am I biassed or not?'

'What could be nicer,' said Mrs. Bradley cordially, 'unless you had said Asti, cornflakes, green gravel and Spanish onions?'

'Why Spanish onions?' Sir Adrian enquired.

'The larger lunacy, I presume,' said Gavin, when, the regatta over and the procession of boats dispersed, he and Mrs. Bradley were walking towards the hotel where her car was parked. 'What was behind it? Do you know?' He was referring to the conversation, or, rather, the tilting match, which Mrs. Bradley had had with Sir Adrian, and of which she had told him, speaking more seriously than she usually did.

'Oh, yes, of course I know. I was warning him, and he didn't like it much.'

'I don't see why he shouldn't. He couldn't have known whether you were accusing Francis or Derek. By the way, do you think he yet knows them apart?'

'He knows better than to give that secret away, child.'

'What are you going to do now?'

'In the classic phrase, I am going to wait . . . and (I hope) see.'

' "Don't seem to know what 'e's waiting for," ' said Gavin, who had picked up the reprehensible habit of quotation from his fiancée, Mrs. Bradley's secretary.

'Sir Adrian is a foeman worthy of my steel,' said Mrs. Bradley complacently, 'and one of the things I am waiting for is to find out exactly why he decided to organize his own small private regatta in a place which holds a big regatta every year.'

'Have you any ideas on the subject? I mean, he's given to mad projects, isn't he? Look at his private cricket ground, and his manservants all paid for their batting and bowling and so on.'

'I know. But I don't think the regatta comes under the heading of a mad project. If it does, then I fancy there was method in the madness.'

'The boathouse?'

'Exactly . . . unless the rather obvious use of the boat-house was to make us think so.'

'Expound.'

'You mean elucidate, I think. The regatta was staged for a purpose. Sir Adrian staged it, therefore the purpose was his.'

'Unless young Derek persuaded him into it.'

'Yes, I agree that that must be taken into consideration and that Derek must be kept in the picture. Well, now, let us take the boathouse first.'

'There couldn't be any clues left there that we poor bobbies overlooked, could there?'

'I don't know. I should scarcely think so, except that even our skilful and gentlemanly Force often do not know what they are looking for, and if one doesn't know what the clues are . . .'

'What the heart doesn't grieve for, the eye doesn't see, in fact.'

'I could not have put that so well, but that is what I meant.'

'Therefore there could have been something about the boathouse which a guilty mind would consider suspicious. Could Sir Adrian's have been the guilty mind?'

'The guilty *mind*, yes. He could have performed of the guilty deeds only one, though, this one here.'

'I say, this begins to stink a bit! You think he worked upon Derek to carry out the other murder?'

'I refuse to commit myself absolutely on that point, but I have it well in the front of my mind.'

'But that would be devil's work!'

'Aptly argued. It is certain that Sir Adrian could not have committed the Mede murder. It is certain that Derek-Francis or Francis-Derek could. It is possible that Sir Adrian could have murdered Campbell, and if what I think about the regatta is true, it seems likely that he did. His choosing to come to Wetwode at all was extremely suspicious. It would have been much easier, as well as far more comfortable, to have had both boys at his own big house in Mede.'

'You begin to convince me that Sir Adrian is the villain of the piece. Tell me all about the regatta, for I feel that thereby hangs a tale.'

'Maybe there does, and maybe there does not. I wish *you* would tell *me* something first. What were the details of the deaths of Sir Adrian's son and his wife?'

'Funny you should ask that. We decided to check up on the Caux family, and it seems that there was nothing in the least suspicious about that crash. Caux had a bad reputation, as I expect you've heard, but he died, and his wife with him, in a very nasty accident on the Great North Road when he was driving his father's car. They swerved into a lorry, and simply didn't stand a chance. It wasn't the lorry driver's fault. A theory was that a wasp had stung Caux just over the eye and he lost control of his vehicle for just a split second, that's all. The wife was sitting in front, beside Caux, and Francis, then a boy of seven, was in the back seat and escaped serious injury. We've combed all the reports, and that's every single thing we can find. It was just one of those things. The Caux car was completely smashed, and afforded no evidence.'

'Who was the lorry driver?'

'A fellow named Spitov . . . a Pole. Repatriated later, and killed in the war. Completely exonerated from blame by the coroner and had had a clean record as a driver.'

'Where was Derek Caux at the time?'

'In bed with measles. That's why he wasn't with them. We've managed to rout out his old nurse, quite a decent, respectable body now living up North. There's nothing more to be got there, I'm afraid.'

'I bow in honour of the hard work of the police. I didn't think there *was* anything to be got from the facts of that accident, but they needed airing if only to show us where not to look for a motive for these two murders. We are where we began, and that is always one kind of progress.'

'Your turn now: the regatta. How come, and what did it learn you?'

'Sir Adrian said that he wanted to spend some money on the villagers. I must say that he gave good prizes . . . five pounds for a win, three for second place and a pound for third. There were five races, two of which, the double sculls and the coxwainless fours, had to be timed instead of rowed off as races. There were too many entrants to make a massed start sufficiently safe.'

'And were there too many? What did you yourself think?
. . . You said you helped with the judging.'

'I agreed that there were too many. But an interesting
point occurred. According to George, my man, on the
previous evening a man came into the hotel public bar . . .
you know, the one round at the side of the house through
the big gates . . . and offered ten shillings to everybody who
proposed to enter for the double sculls and the coxwainless
fours. He said he was doing it for a bet, as people in his
village had been saying that Wetwode men were effete,
effeminate, (those were not the words he used but they give
the general sense of his adjectives and substantives), and
were lacking in local pride, civic sense and even the most
rudimentary kind of courage.'

'Lord! I hope he didn't wait until they were all boozed up
before he began!'

'He did. George, of course, was not present. He was at
my Hampshire house as I had returned there. But I got him
to drive me to Wetwode when I decided to see Sir Adrian
again, and he went in on the morning of the regatta for his
eleven o'clock glass of beer, which he likes very much when
we are staying in villages, although he drinks nothing at all
in London, and found the public bar humming with the
news of the previous night. It transpired, George told me,
that Sir Adrian had deposited money with the barman so
that the villagers could drink the health of himself and his
grandsons, and so, by the time the stranger arrived, the
party was already somewhat livelier than is usual in that
very respectable house.

'The stranger's remarks, therefore, provoked a response
which must have delighted him. Men signed his list who
might well have thought better of it next morning, received
their ten shillings each on the spot, and, of course, could
scarcely withdraw for fear of what would be thought of
them by these (I fancy fictitious) villagers pictured by Sir
Adrian's *agent-provocateur.*'

'Oh, you go as far as that, do you? Well, on the strength of
George's report, yes, I think *I* do, too. This is extraordinarily

interesting. Proceed, moon. Tell me what you deduce from all this subversive ratiocination.'

'Something nasty in the woodshed. I wish we could have obtained a description of the man who offered the ten shilling notes.'

'Probably one of Sir Adrian's servants, you think. Well, I can dimly perceive a way round that, but, of course, if Sir Adrian really was at the bottom of it, his motive might merely be that he wanted a record entry for his races.'

'True. But there is more. Sir Adrian acted as starter, left me at the boathouse with a stop-watch, and he and a twin, in a small launch, accompanied every race to see fair play.'

'I can't see very much in that. I suppose the course was unmarked?'

'Yes. It was from the boathouse entrance . . . the river-end of the staithe, in fact . . . to the Broad and back. The boats had to enter the Broad at its first opening, cross one corner of the Broad, come out at its second opening, and so home.'

'Sounds quite a good arrangement.'

'Yes, it was.'

'What's the matter, then?'

'At one point there was an avoidable, totally unnecessary accident.'

'Oh, Lord! You don't mean . . . ?'

'Engineered? I'm afraid so. What happened was this. The double sculls all went off first, and then the coxwainless fours. When it came to the first heat of the fours Sir Adrian became fussy. We had to wait for twenty minutes, for no apparent reason, whilst he inspected the starters, altered the position of the stake boat and argued with Derek (Francis is keeping up the fiction of being deaf and dumb) about the nice conduct of a blank-shot gun. When he at last allowed matters to proceed, one of the older men pointed out that the proposed course would soon be closed to them because the pleasure launches . . . enormous things which can carry a hundred people . . . would be returning up-river and there would not be room for the crews to pass without getting far too much wash to make the timing fair. He argued that as the course would not be of the same difficulty for all, it would be advisable to put off the fours and run off some of the land sports which were being held for the children. Yachts and motor-cruisers he held to be reasonable hazards and merely a matter of luck. River steamers, which ran to time, could and should be avoided.

'Sir Adrian refused to accept this view, which he apostrophized as being nonsense.

'He sent off the first of the boats. This was manned by four young fellows, one of whom was my diver.'

'Your what?'

'My diver. When it seemed likely that Francis Caux with his clay-modelling had given us details of the disposal of Campbell's body at the bottom of that dinghy . . .'

'Oh, yes, of course. I remember.'

'Yes, well, Sir Adrian's questionable means of obtaining entrants for his regatta, together with his unreasonable waste of time and equally unreasonable refusal to listen to reason, convinced me that, in the vulgar and grammatically meaningless phrase, he could bear watching. To this end I handed the stop-watch to George, who was beside me, and slipped into what had been the back garden of my bungalow. There I had my canoe lying in a little stream too narrow to be called a dyke, and yet fulfilling the function of one.'

'You mean it leads into the Broad?'

'And by a very short cut, for the river winds and bends, whilst my stream, man-made to drain the ground at the backs of the bungalows which otherwise would be an impassable swamp, runs as straight as a ruler to a reed-bank behind which I expected to be able to shelter whilst I watched the march of events.

'The big public launches go out by way of the Broad, but return all the way by river. My plan was to wait until the rowers and Sir Adrian's small launch had passed my hiding-place, and then to follow them up and find out what happened when they met one of the public launches, which, at that time, they were almost bound to do. I did not think that the twin who was steering would turn his head and see me, still less that Sir Adrian, who had a megaphone in order to assist him to keep the course clear, would look round either.

'Fortune favoured me in this. On to the Broad up the first short dyke came the rowing boat, a clumsy tub of a thing let out usually to fishermen holiday-makers. The four young men were sweating and straining, Sir Adrian, a couple of lengths behind them, was exhorting them through the megaphone, and I, paddling vigorously out from behind my reed-bed on to the open Broad, was at once in pursuit, and, of course, in my light craft and on that calm water, had no need to worry lest I should be left behind.

'At the exit from the Broad it happened. A yacht was close in to the bank, and Sir Adrian gave tongue through the megaphone. There was room for the rowers to pull by, but only just. Sir Adrian's launch got round easily and so did I. I could hear nothing but the chug-chugging of Sir Adrian's engine. It blotted out, even to my ears, which, as you probably know, are sharp, the easier, quieter throbbing of the engines of the public launch.

'The rowers did not hear the public launch either, and as they took the broad bend from the end of the second dyke to get back on to the river, round came the pleasure boat. The man in charge saw the rowers and put his helm right over towards the opposite bank. Sir Adrian let fall his megaphone, gave a hoarse scream, clutched the wheel of his launch, thrusting his grandson aside, and *deliberately* (it seemed to me, and I was in an excellent position for seeing the whole incident) deliberately ran down the rowing boat.

'The big launch was round the bend by this time. I doubt very much whether any of her passengers saw what happened. The yacht was also hidden, for she lay at the further end of the dyke and, as I told you, well into the bank, and that dyke is on an almost semi-circular curve. The four men fell into the water and my diver went into the depths. The river (I find upon enquiry) is ten feet deep at that point.

The small launch, Sir Adrian's, has no great draught, most fortunately.'

Gavin looked at her. Her beaky little mouth was pursed up in a tight, triumphant smile.

'Now please don't be aggravating,' he said. 'I gather that Sir Adrian's little plan failed, and that no one was hurt. How was that?'

Mrs. Bradley nearly lifted him out of his chair with a screech which rent the room.

'I saw what was going to happen,' she said, 'and so, of course, did stroke, who happened to be my diver. In any case, he was fore-warned. I warned him myself whilst Sir Adrian was fussing and wasting time. I felt that if the warning was unnecessary, so much the better. It proved to be very necessary. However, to make sure, I called out, just like that . . .'

'Don't do it again, as you love me!'

. . . 'and it gave them all time to jump for it. The diver went down like a stone. Then the yacht people, quanting by the bank, came up to the rescue. We all searched diligently for the diver, but he was not to be found.'

'What?'

'Until late that evening, when I ran him to earth in the eel-catcher's hut that belongs to his uncle Dan.'

'Good heavens! But how on earth did he escape? Under-water swimming?'

'Yes, back into the dyke and so to the Broad, where he surfaced beyond Sir Adrian's ken. Sir Adrian has confessed to the other three men that he lost his head and did the wrong thing. He has compensated them.'

'And what about you? Do you think he knows you've tumbled to what he was up to?'

'It doesn't matter whether he knows or not. He also knows that nothing can be proved except that ostensibly he didn't keep his head in an emergency.'

'Does he think this diving fellow is drowned?'

'I'm sorry you've been away, for the local police,' said Mrs. Bradley with a diabolical leer, 'have been dragging the

river for two days, although the inspector knows perfectly
well that the body isn't there. You have a most co-operative
colleague.'

'1 wouldn't like to tell you what *you've* got!' said Gavin,
laughing. 'Where's the diving chap now?'

'At Wandles Parva. Henri has orders to guard him with
his own life if necessary, and the Chief Constable has an
eye on things too. And now tell me all about Mede.'

'You had better come along down there, I think, and get
out of the way here.'

'You fear that Sir Adrian may attempt to get me out of
the way in a different sense if I stay upon the order of my
going? Perhaps you are right. But we'll go to Wandles first.
I want to be present when you question my diving boy. I
think we are getting very near to the edge of the wood.'

'Well, I wish we could see through the trees, then. Motive,
motive, motive! That's what's holding everything up. I
believe Sir Adrian and his precious grandsons to be the
biggest villains unhung, but until we know what reason
they had for murdering these two men . . .'

'I am hoping great things from my diver. Aren't you ever
going to tell me anything about Mede?'

'That's the devil of it. I've been down there for almost a
week. There isn't a clue to be had.'

'You've questioned the servants?'

'*Ad non compos mentis.* And the only thing I got was that
some tinned food was missing from the pavilion kitchen
after the cricket match played by Sir Adrian's team against
the inmates of a mental hospital. The inference is that one
of the loonies took it. The kitchen is on the visitors' side,
as you probably know.'

'And my friend Mr. Cornish?'

'You had better tackle him yourself. He's a cross-grained
devil, but I don't believe he knows a thing about Witt's
murder.'

CHAPTER FOURTEEN

The Echo Over the Wall

★

*'For I would not spend another winter in this place, if I
thought I should live, which I verily believe I should not,
for ten times the value of the estate . . .'*
The Verney Letters, edited by

Margaret Maria, Lady Verney, LL.D.

★

IT SEEMED better to tackle Miss Higgs first. Upon her
evidence hung the reply to one question which had to be
answered.

Miss Higgs, her leg still in the sling which hung from the
ceiling, seemed glad to see them.

'I thought you'd come,' she said to Mrs. Bradley. 'I
wondered whether perhaps you had come before.'

'No.'

'You knew I'd had a shock. Yes, I can see why you didn't
disturb me. But, bless you, one gets over these things at my
age. Of course, ever since Francis pushed me into the river
I've had my doubts of him, but I didn't really think he'd
push me down the post-office steps, any more than I
thought he'd ever stay out all night. It's funny how you
never think of these things. You think you get to know people.
Of course, nobody ever does get to know anybody else.'

Mrs. Bradley, whose experience did not bear out any of
these statements, deliberately avoided the point which they
premised.

'What we really wondered,' she said, 'was whether you
felt perfectly certain that it was Francis who pushed you
into the river and threw you down the post-office steps.'

That this was the first she had heard of the latter operation she gave no sign. Miss Higgs tried to hoist herself up, was brought to mind of her leg in its cradle, and fell back into her former position.

'Funny you should say that,' she said. Gavin unostentatiously took out his notebook. 'You know, it didn't seem like Francis, either time.'

'Whom did it seem like, then?'

'I don't know. It just wasn't *like* Francis, that's all. He couldn't hear or speak, but somehow I would call him a *loving* boy. At any rate, I am perfectly certain he was very fond of me.'

'Quite,' said Gavin, breaking in. 'But, look, Miss Higgs, are you certain that it was always Francis you had with you? I know that's a leading question, and, therefore, to some extent, inadmissible. But I'm going to press it because your answer may be important . . . very important indeed.'

Miss Higgs looked thoroughly unhappy.

'Of course, I know what you mean,' she said, 'and I suppose I did wrong under the circumstances. You mean when I sneaked little Derek over to see his brother, don't you . . . and kept him with us whilst Sir Adrian was away?'

'But I don't quite know when that was,' said Gavin, earning Mrs. Bradley's later stricture that his attitude was not Calvinistic but Jesuitical. 'If we could get dates, even approximate dates, don't you see . . .'

He pointed out to Mrs. Bradley afterwards that perhaps the Jesuits were wise in their generation.

'Dates? Well, let me see,' said Miss Higgs. 'The boys were turned seven when I first had Francis. Then Sir Adrian wanted to go over to Switzerland . . . Vevey, I think it was, just like *Little Women* . . . but he couldn't, because of the war . . . Derek's education, you know, and that's why I have a feeling I remember the name. Instead, he travelled about to look at various tutorial establishments in safety areas. So I sneaked Derek over to stay with us . . . there was only one servant at Mede that I had to square. I kept Derek a fortnight. But the two boys didn't get on. Little Derek was so bright and intelligent, and poor Francis, with being deaf and dumb . . .'

'Ah, yes, of course,' said Gavin. 'They would hardly have had time to become acquainted.'

'Well, you never know, with twins,' said Miss Higgs, with considerable vigour. 'There are things between twins which the rest of us will never understand.'

'All the same, you formed the opinion that the boys had no points of contact?'

'I *wanted* to form that opinion, perhaps. I dreaded losing Francis. I don't want you to misunderstand me. And if you think that my poor Francis had anything to do with that awful business of pinning that poor man's body under the boat, I can only assure you you're wrong, and that's all I can say.'

'It's no good asking her again whether she ever thought the twins changed places,' said Gavin, when the interview was over. 'Even if she did, she wouldn't say so.'

'We've gained our point, though,' Mrs. Bradley observed. 'We know now that the twins did meet, and how they met, and for how long. And, as she says, nobody knows, even now, how twins react to one another.'

'I still don't see how it helps us.'

'Everything helps us which clears up even one point. We shall now go and see my diver.'

The youth Malachi, graceful and comely, greeted them with reserve. His stay at the Stone House had been enjoyable. There was no doubt about that. He seemed loth, however, to commit himself to giving any definite answers to Gavin's questions.

'Don't worry about your poaching escapades,' said Mrs. Bradley suddenly. 'They do not appear to be germane to the present enquiry.'

'It was only a few brown trout,' said the sinuous youth. Gavin became reassuring.

'That's nothing to do with us. It's a magistrate's job. Now, look here, Malachi, what we want is your story of what happened at the regatta, and, of course, *why* it happened. Begin at the beginning, and don't forget to fill in the gaps. The brown trout are a matter of a fine or a fortnight in quod. What we enquire about now is a hanging matter, so jolly well be careful what you say. Now, then, say on. Let's have it.'

'Mister,' said Malachi, gravely, 'that begin when I dive in and find that poor chap that was pinned on under that boat.'

'Who knew of it besides yourself, myself, my man George and my friend Miss Parkinson, Malachi?' Mrs. Bradley demanded.

Malachi looked doubtful.

'Can't speak to that,' he replied. 'My father, I told him. Didn't think any harm to tell him anything I do.'

'Quite right. It's not your father I am talking about.'

Malachi hesitated, wavered, and then came out with it.

'They know me in these parts. There isn't one doesn't know I can dive to bring up the mermaids if I know they oold dears are there. So Mr. Tavis, that come to me and make to enquire whether I know anything about the man they hold the inquest on. Of course I say no to that, but he persist.'

'Mr. Tavis? That's very interesting,' said Gavin. He made a note. 'Go on, my lad. And don't worry. I don't think there's anything in this to get you into any trouble. What did you say to Mr. Tavis?'

'I don't know what to tell him, five pound note or not. So I say what I think.'

'And that was?'

'I say I think it was Mr. Campbell.'

'Well, we know it was. But when did you get that idea?'

At this the boy came across with it.

'When I dive down to search out the bottom of that boat, I know it was Mr. Campbell. No one else about here know it would have to be him, but I know because I know Mr. Campbell wasn't leaving Wetwode, like he say.'

Gavin exchanged a glance . . . or hoped to . . . with Mrs. Bradley. Her eyes were on Malachi's boots. Not that the boots held any interest for her, but she did not propose to meet the boy's eye. She was on the verge of finding out something which might conclude the case, she imagined.

'Oh, yes,' said Gavin carelessly. 'And how did you come to know that?'

'That told me. "And you hold your tongue," he say. "That isn't for you to know nawthen. But somebody I won't name, he's after me," he say, "because of something I know it doesn't suit him to have somebody know. So I make to go away, but I'll be round and about," he say, "to watch his game and put a few spokes in his wheel." '

'Did you gather who the somebody was?'

'No, I don't know that.' He looked puzzled. 'Except it might be Mr. Grandall that came down here with Mr. Tavis for the fishing.'

'Confusion worse confounded,' said Gavin when this interview was over. 'What did you make of all that?'

'Lies, prevarication and fear,' Mrs. Bradley replied. 'It was nothing to do with Mr. Tavis and nothing to do with Mr. Grandall. I think that, quite by accident, Malachi saw Campbell return when he had pretended to go away. And I think Campbell knew that Francis Caux could speak and hear and understand.'

There Gavin left it. There was no proof, unless something more could be got out of Tavis and Grandall, but this seemed very unlikely, although he persuaded Mrs. Bradley to try the two fishermen again. She paddled down-river to a spot where, on one side, the wet woods, among whose corpse-like roots the river eddied and gurgled, came down to give cover to coots and water-voles, and on the other the water-meadows with their frequent, bordering willows, gave fishermen a stance and some cover.

There she found Tavis and Grandall, as she had hoped. They had moored their punt under the bank, and, with hats tilted over their eyes and a tin of coarse-fishing bait between them, were somnolently holding their rods over eight feet of water.

She knew very much better than to hail them. Dry-fly

fishermen are observers of holy rites, but heaven knows no
fury like the coarse-fish adept who thinks you have scared
his roach or perch.

She paddled, therefore, dreamily downstream, keeping to
the opposite bank and scarcely dipping her paddle until
she had passed them. There was a sweet little dyke further
on, a stream choked with meadowsweet and the umbels of
water-dropwort. Keeping a careful look-out for passing
yachts, she swept across-stream and nosed the canoe expertly
into a bosom of flowers.

She landed and pulled her convenient craft into safety.
Then she strolled along the grassy bank and noiselessly
approached the two fishermen. She arrived at the time that
Grandall had hooked a fish. She waited politely whilst he
gaffed it, and then stepped forward with sycophantic
adulation.

Grandall was pleased.

'Betted Tavis that I'd get one before he did,' he observed
with self-satisfaction. Tavis smiled . . . a secret, Welsh
indication that the bet had gone a little further than that
which of them should catch the first fish.

'Will you wish me luck, now?' he said. Mrs. Bradley sat
down on the bank at a point where her shadow should not
need to cause fish to rely upon their intelligence, and silently
waited. Sure enough, within twenty minutes Tavis had
pulled up a fish of fully a pound and a quarter.

'Good going it is,' said Tavis, 'and very good to see
you, Mrs. Bradley, isn't it? Look you, some luck I was
needing.'

Mrs. Bradley discounted these Celtic circumlocutions.

'I wanted to talk to both of you,' she said. Grandall
sullenly, Tavis triumphantly, put their rods away.

'No more fishing to-day; the light's all wrong,' said
Grandall, huffed at his friend's success.

'I know,' Mrs. Bradley replied. 'Quite unlike the light
that dawned on you when Mr. Campbell was killed.'

Both men looked smug; then Grandall was openly
amused.

'I say, that's a good one,' he said.

'Maybe,' Mrs. Bradley replied. 'Mr. Tavis, at what point did Mr. Campbell realize that Francis Caux could see and hear and understand?'

'Well, look you,' said Tavis earnestly, 'that isn't for me to answer. It is not my way to make trouble.'

'Making all allowance for your point of view, Mr. Tavis, I feel I must press the question. When did he know? And when did he tell you?'

'Oh, last year it would have been, but it did not trouble me. All boys are foxy, indeed, and this one no different from the others. But make me wild, he did, when the young blackguard fouled the fishing. He put down bread . . . ground bait, you see . . . and brought the fish into that little staithe they had. I spoke to him.'

'We threatened to tear his hair off,' put in Grandall conversationally. 'Young Malachi Thetford gave us the tip. He's pretty spry, that lad. So we tackled Francis Caux and frightened him, for all that he pretended not to understand a word we were saying. I know he did, though. I'd have put my boot behind him except for upsetting Miss Higgs. Neighbours, you know, and all that. It doesn't do to fall out with neighbours.'

Mrs. Bradley returned to Hampshire, whither Gavin had preceded her, and had to report no progress.

'If anything turned on the fact that people had begun to realize that Francis Caux was neither deaf nor dumb,' she said, 'then Mr. Grandall and Mr. Tavis should have been the first victims. The fact that neither has suffered so much as a threatening letter leads me to suppose that we can eliminate one item from our calculations.'

'That the deaf and dumb business has had no immediate connection with the murders.'

'Yes.'

'But, all the same, its remote connection is still possible.'

'Yes.'

'Look here, what are you getting at?'

'We have Miss Higgs' express pronouncement that she

was responsible for bringing the boys together again after Sir Adrian had separated them.'

'Granted.'

'Does Miss Higgs, from what we previously knew of her, strike you as the kind of woman who would have done that sort of thing?'

'Well, no. And, of course, she talked of squaring the one servant who was left in charge of Derek whilst Sir Adrian was pottering about to arrange about Derek's education.'

'Quite. Now, to begin with, I do not believe that Sir Adrian left Derek in charge of only one servant. Secondly, to square a person indicates, in the idiom of the moment, to bribe him. Miss Higgs is always pleading poverty.'

'Oh . . . I see.'

'I wish I did,' said Mrs. Bradley sincerely.

'How do you mean?'

'I wish I knew how Miss Higgs comes into the whole thing. She appears to be fond of Francis; she appears not to be quite willing to agree that the twin boys ever changed places; she needs to work for her living, and therefore would be very foolish to risk Sir Adrian's displeasure, and yet she took that risk by bringing the boys together at the first opportunity she had.'

'So far we have only her word for that.'

'Exactly. Yet I think it must be true. Otherwise how would the boys, separated at so tender an age, have got in touch with one another again?'

'Certainly that is a point. As I see it, we've got to question her again, and take a different line of approach.'

'And that would be?'

'Ask her what she knows about landlord Cornish.'

'Staggering,' said Mrs. Bradley admiringly. Gavin regarded her dubiously.

'You think it might work?' he enquired.

'Negatively only. I speak merely from instinct, but instinct warns me that there is no connection whatsoever between Miss Higgs and the landlord of the *Frenchman*.'

Not at all to Mrs. Bradley's surprise, but greatly to the

surprise of Gavin, Miss Higgs herself volunteered the next piece of information. Mrs. Bradley had gone back to stay at the *Frenchman's Arms* in Mede, and had left her address at Wetwode post-office.

'Not to impede you in any way,' wrote Miss Higgs, 'I ought perhaps to say that I knew it couldn't be Francis that pushed me into the river. He would never have done such a thing. You will wish to know (from your enquiries) when the twins might have changed their places. Well, it could have been while Francis and I were spending that week at Great Yarmouth. You see, he used to go swimming every day in the Pool, and, as I never worried about him while he was in the water, I used to sit on the beach, from which you can't possibly see who is in the Pool unless they go up on the high diving boards, which Francis never did, as his ears were funny . . .'

'We never thought of that,' said Gavin, when Mrs. Bradley showed him the letter. 'I mean, about a bloke with bad ears not being able to dive from heights.'

'Quite. But I don't think his ears were bad.'

'Oh, no. This camouflage business. Yet there doesn't seem any reason to suspect that at the age of seven he wasn't suffering from shock.'

'I think he was. At the age of nine it seems that to some extent he may have got over it.'

'You say "to some extent." What do you mean by that, exactly?'

'Exactly, it is difficult to say. I would submit that the physical effects had worn off. The mental trauma probably remained.'

'Then Francis, not Derek, is our man!'

'Maybe.'

'Well, on the strength of this letter I am going to have another bash at Miss Higgs, and that without loss of time.'

Miss Higgs, who could get about a bit, had been discharged from hospital, and was now (at Mrs. Bradley's expressed wish, although Miss Higgs had no knowledge of this) recuperating at the house of the old school friend,

Mabel Parkinson, as there was no one to look after her at the bungalow.

'Yes, she is here,' said Mabel, answering the door to Gavin, 'but I don't know whether she'll see you. She's sick to death of the whole business about these awful murders, and really one can't wonder at it. And why Beatrice had to get *me* involved I can't think. At least, I *can* . . .'

'Quite. An *alma mater* shared is an important problem halved, and I know, Miss Parkinson, that you'd never let an old school-fellow down. Mrs. Bradley has the utmost confidence in you. At a time when she had no one else to whom she could turn, no one else to whom she could entrust this delicate matter, she said to me that she knew she could rely upon Mabel Parkinson.'

Mabel simpered.

'Oh, if the old school tie is involved, you know,' she said, 'of course one does what one can. The only thing is, with Miss Higgs so closely connected with that place where we found the body. . . . Still, I should like to see the murderer that could get the better of *me!*'

'Well, the murderer might try if he thought you knew anything. Do you know anything, Miss Parkinson? If so, I wish you would tell me.'

'Any amount,' said Mabel Parkinson. 'To begin with, I don't trust young Francis Caux.'

'No, we don't much, either.'

'It was quite, quite too odd that he should have found out by accident about that body . . . where it had been hidden and all the rest of it. He *knew* it was there because he'd had previous information. Then, as I see it, the knowledge was on his conscience and upset him . . . or else . . .' Gavin suddenly realized that Miss Parkinson's eyes were shrewd, and her thin mouth intelligent . . . '*or else*,' she repeated emphatically, 'he knew who Beatrice was and thought he'd better come clean and try to disarm her of suspicion.'

'It's most interesting that you should say that,' said Gavin, 'because I personally have a very firm idea . . . amounting, I might say, to a certainty . . . that it wasn't

Francis at all who "discovered" the body, but his brother Derek. But you mustn't let that go any further.'

Miss Parkinson went pink with excitement.

'So *that's* it!' she said. 'Not a word shall escape me, of course. Does Miss Higgs know this?'

'I expect so, but I don't think I should let even her know that you know, if you don't mind. The fewer people to discuss the point the better, at this stage in our enquiry.'

Mabel Parkinson took him upstairs to see Miss Higgs. Miss Higgs had been given the largest bedroom as a bed-sitting-room. It saved her the stairs, as Miss Parkinson pointed out, and was handy for the bathroom and lavatory. Gavin found himself rather in love with Mrs. Bradley's old school chum. She might be a tedious old duck, but of her good-nature and loyalty there could not be any doubt at all. He was glad he had told her about the twin brothers. She deserved a break, he thought.

Miss Higgs, to his consternation, began by being tearful.

'I can't *tell* you how good Miss Parkinson is to me,' she said. 'I've never known kindness like it. Her best bedroom, and everything done for my comfort. Waited on hand and foot . . .' she indicated the two sticks which helped her to get about . . . 'really, one is almost grateful for a broken leg if it shows one that disinterested goodness still exists in this world.'

'Quite so,' said Gavin. Miss Parkinson, patting Miss Higgs kindly on the shoulder, said that she must be getting ready some tea, and that they would all have it together in Miss Higgs' room. 'Look,' went on Gavin to Miss Higgs, 'I don't want to bother you, but there are just one or two things which might help to make my job much easier if I could learn them from a reliable witness like yourself.'

Miss Higgs wiped her eyes.

'I'm a fool,' she said, 'but kindness does break you down when you're not used to it. What do you want to know?'

'First, if it isn't an impertinent question, what do you propose to do when you've fully recovered? Shall you go back to the bungalow to look after Francis Caux?'

'I couldn't. For one thing, I couldn't bear to live there again, especially when I think how terribly Francis has deceived me, and, for another thing, it seems from what dear Miss Parkinson tells me . . . she heard it down in the village . . . that Sir Adrian has adopted both the boys, so I shan't be needed any more. I thought perhaps I would try to get a post as governess to a delicate girl.'

'Right. Well, now, for my next question: you said at our last interview that you knew it couldn't have been Francis who pushed you into the river, and, if he did not, that would account for the fact that he didn't jump in and fish you out. But had you ever suspected, *before that*, that the boys changed places?'

'Not really. Of course, it did shock me very much when I found that the boy had been misbehaving in the village with that girl.'

'But, all the same, you still thought it was Francis?'

'What else could I think? I never *dreamed* it was Derek. How could I?'

'Right. Now, another point . . . and I do hope you'll answer me quite frankly. You see, it's murder I'm investigating and it begins to look very fishy for one or both of those two boys. You told us that you sneaked Derek away from Mede at a time when Sir Adrian was absent, and had both children with you for a fortnight here at Wetwode. Now, they are very striking-looking boys and the village has always been interested, I take it, in your poor little deaf-and-dumb charge. Didn't it cause a considerable sensation when his twin, indistinguishable from him in appearance, turned up at the bungalow?'

'No. You see, nobody ever saw them together. I had explained very carefully to Derek, who was always strikingly intelligent, that if it ever came to his grandfather's knowledge that he had gone to stay with his brother, I should be dismissed and he would never see Francis again.'

'I see. One more question, Miss Higgs, and I think I'm through. You say you didn't know that the boys had ever changed places, but, from the answer you've just given me,

I may take it, I presume, that you *did* know they often met?'

'They met every year at the summer holiday time,' replied Miss Higgs.

'How on earth did you manage that?'

'I didn't manage it. Derek managed it, and I don't know how he did, and he has never told me. But for a week every year he has been with us at whatever seaside place I chose for Francis.'

'You wrote to him, then?'

'No, never. And I never found out how he knew, but, of course, the dates were always roughly the same. Sometimes he would get there on the same day as we did, and sometimes a day or so later. I chose a different place every year for five years, so that the fact of their being twins and so handsome and so much the image of each other should not be talked about too much, but that was my whole share in the matter. And I told you a lie last time. It wasn't I who squared the Mede servants. It was Derek, even at that tender age.'

'Thank you very much indeed, Miss Higgs. You've been more than helpful.'

'All the same, I don't believe . . . I never *will* believe . . . that Francis was mixed up in those dreadful murders!'

'Quite,' said Gavin; and was much too kind-hearted to point out the foolishness of this statement. 'After all, she obviously never really knew one from t'other,' he said to Mrs. Bradley later on. 'How could Derek always fix the date, though?'

'He didn't this year, at any rate. This year Miss Higgs took Francis away in June. It has always been at the beginning of the grouse season before.'

'Of course! Lord Averdon's grouse moor! Yes, you told me. As simple as that!'

CHAPTER FIFTEEN

The Echo Heard at the Inn

★

'Thou hast shaved many a poor soul close enough . . .
thou art only meeting thy reward.'
The Brothers Grimm: *The Jew in the Bush*

★

'WELL, there is no doubt about one thing,' said Mrs. Bradley. They were in Mede, in her private sitting-room at the *Frenchman's Inn*. 'Campbell was killed because he knew too much.'

'Knew that there were two boys and that they changed places, you mean. Could the same apply to Witt?'

'I don't know.'

'But how should Campbell? . . . Oh, yes, of course! He was a naturalist, wasn't he? Watched birds and crept about in woods and things . . .'

'And had a very efficient pair of binoculars, yes.'

'Um, that adds up all right. I wonder how Derek managed to sneak away so many times, though, without Sir Adrian being the wiser? You'd think that, sooner or later, someone would blow the gaff.'

'That is where you tell me something more about the household at Mede.'

'But I can't, you know. I can't shake them. They're like the wise old owl, I think, the more they know the less they speak. It's very disheartening. You don't think that the two deaths are entirely disconnected, and that the landlord here killed Witt because of the blackmail over that stolen Black Market liquor?'

'I might think so if it had been physically possible, child,

160

but, you see, it wasn't. No, no. It was one of the twins, or, at any rate, one of the twins was an accessory before the fact. We've realized that all the time. The only thing which still puzzles me is why on earth the one who was supposed to be playing cricket chose the time of the murder to absent himself from the field.'

'Yes, that *is* a licker! Unless, of course, it was deliberate, and he *meant* to do the other twin down.'

' "Now, husband, you have nick'd the matter. To have him impeached and . . ." '

'Yes. *Beggar's Opera* or no *Beggar's Opera*, it means hanging all right,' said Gavin soberly. 'We make a dead set, then, at Derek Caux.'

'I think we must, otherwise he might murder Sir Adrian!'

'I say, you don't really think that, do you?'

'I wish I didn't, child, but there it is.'

'We ought to tip the old boy off.'

'I have thought of that. Can you imagine the result?'

'Well, yes, I can, unless . . . you don't think he may have rumbled Derek by this time?'

'If he has he would never admit it.'

'No, I suppose not. Look here, how do we get this dissolute kid?'

'Your finger-print experts might help.'

'Jove, yes. You mean that, as even identical twins don't have identical finger-prints, we may be able to prove that Francis visited the house at Mede when the boys changed places. Apart from Donagh's evidence that one of the Mede servants let out that Sir Adrian is invited every year to shoot over the coverts of Lord Averdon, whose team has an annual fixture with the village eleven at Mede, we're pretty sure they had a game at swopping places. But if what we've gathered is true, the precious Derek would have had servants galore round his neck whilst his grandfather was away. Do you mean to say that *none* of them gave him away?'

'So far as we know they did not. Of course, Sir Adrian may be unpopular.'

'Or young Derek may be feared.'

F

'Few things would surprise me less. Evil *is* fearful, and people are really rather superstitious about it. There seems to be a human, or sub-human, instinct which regards evil as being far more powerful than good.'

'It's queer, that. Look here, why don't *you* tackle those Mede servants again? You'd get far more out of them than I've been able to do.'

'Very well. I will try. After all, we've a fair amount to go on.'

But the Mede servants were either staunch or fearful, or . . . as Mrs. Bradley, against her will, assumed . . . more mercenary than either.

'Yes, I expect he did bribe them,' said Gavin, referring to Derek. 'And, after all, if Donagh is to be believed, they all sold their souls long ago in consenting to be played as amateurs when, hang it all, their very pay depended upon their cricket. If that isn't blatant professionalism I don't know what is. Let's tackle old Cornish again.'

Landlord Cornish, approached again, was not particularly pleased.

'Look here,' he said, 'what's the game? I ain't here to be stooged by the police.'

'Certainly not,' said Mrs. Bradley smoothly. '*Ne pleurez pas,*' she added genially. '*Nous avons besoin de vous, monsieur. Attendez bien. Je vous ouvre mon coeur.*'

These execrable sentences produced a marked effect.

'Oh, if *that's* your lay,' said Cornish, 'why couldn't you say so before? I'll come clean all right. Only, you see, that there Witt, he stuck in my gizzard, as you might say. What might you want for to know?'

'We want to know who, besides yourself, had a motive for wanting Mr. Witt out of the way,' said Mrs. Bradley before Gavin could speak. Gavin drew his stomach in and mentally flexed his arm, for the landlord's attitude was menacing. Mrs. Bradley cackled.

'We know you didn't kill Witt,' she said. 'Who did?'

'I reckon it was young Caux,' the landlord answered sullenly. 'But ask me why . . . I don't know. It's just as it seemed to work out.'

'You mean his absence from the field at what turned out to be a crucial time?'

'Nay, I don't mean nothing. Let sleeping dogs lie, that's my motto.'

'You surprise me,' said Gavin sincerely. 'I should have thought you were the kind of bloke to stir them up with a pole.'

'Hey, Liza!' bellowed Cornish suddenly. His unhappy wife appeared. 'Speak up, now, girl! Did I, or did I not, have anything to do with Mr. Witt's murder?'

'Oh, no, of course you didn't,' said Mrs. Cornish, distressed. 'Only, I always thought you'd have liked to have had,' she added plaintively. She glanced in a terrified way from one face to another. 'I do hope I haven't said the wrong thing,' she added, cringing before her husband.

'Not you, lass, not you!' he responded. 'You don't often say the right thing, devil knows, but this time you've hit the nail on the head, my girl. Here, have a drink.'

He poured out a glass of port and handed it over the counter. Mrs. Cornish was so amazed that she nearly dropped it.

'And what can you make of that?' asked Gavin anxiously, when he and Mrs. Bradley were back in her private sitting-room upstairs. Mrs. Bradley shook her head.

'Nothing, except that we know he did not kill Witt and that there seems nothing whatever to connect him with Campbell.'

'So we're just as we were.'

'Not quite. That was an astonishing remark that Mrs. Cornish made. I think we should follow it up.'

'Cornish will probably have her life if we do.'

'I can prevent his being rough with her, I think. We know now why he hated and feared Witt, and the case, after all, has never come to court.'

'Good Lord! You're not proposing to blackmail Cornish on the strength of that stolen liquor?'

'Certainly not. But there is no harm in making use of information in our possession to protect that miserable little woman.'

'But that *would* be blackmail!'

'Very well, child. I now become a blackmailer, then. Kindly press that bell.'

The maidservant answered it.

'I wish to see the manager,' said Mrs. Bradley grandly. The child fled, consternation in her eyes. Mrs. Bradley cackled. 'That ought to bring Cornish post-haste. He will conclude that I am going to complain,' she remarked in satisfied tones.

Up came the landlord, almost bursting.

'If this house ain't good enough . . .' he began. Mrs. Bradley motioned him to a chair and Gavin gave him a cigarette. These tactics were sufficiently mystifying to calm him. He did not sit down, but he stood there, hulking and sulky, twirling the cigarette between a banana-like thumb and finger.

'Our business is confidential,' said Mrs. Bradley, 'and we should like Mrs. Cornish to help us.'

'Her? Got no more sense than she was born with! . . . Ah, and if you think you can squeeze anything out of her as'll get me into trouble with the police, you got another think coming. She never saw nothing, and she don't know nothing, see?'

'Quite,' said Gavin, 'but unfortunately for you, *I* am in a position to know a good deal, and, from what I know, I could soon learn a great deal more. That little Black Market manipulation of yours in stolen spirits hasn't disappeared into the place where good dogs go, or anywhere else, you know.'

'We are going to question your wife. I am perfectly willing for you to be present at the interview, but you are not to prompt her,' said Mrs. Bradley. 'And if you behave yourself, your *crime* . . .' she underlined the word boldly, keeping her black eyes fixed on his face . . . 'will remain resting in a decent obscurity which is undeserved by you, and which will last for just as long as your wife remains unterrorized and is not browbeaten by you. You're a marked man, Mr. Cornish, and don't you forget it.'

Cornish turned a curious greenish colour. Then he flung the cigarette on the floor, stamped on it, and lurched at Mrs. Bradley like a drunken man. Gavin leapt up, but the little old woman kept him back. She stepped aside, and Cornish crashed heavily, one arm flung over the seat of an armchair, the other trailing on the floor. His head fell forward. His gross body slumped.

Mrs. Bradley knelt down to find his pulse. She could not. She got up.

'Please help me to turn him over,' she said, 'although I don't think there's any doubt that he's dead.'

Gavin helped her, but his police experience made it inevitable that he should agree with her verdict.

'Heart, I suppose,' he said. 'Well, the world won't be any the worse for *his* going out of it. Will you tell Mrs. Cornish while I send for the fellow's own doctor? He'd better see the body. There'll have to be an inquest, I suppose.'

This proved unnecessary. The dead man had been under treatment for the past two years for heart attacks.

'Told him he'd go off like this if he couldn't take things easier,' said the local doctor, a cheerful man of forty. 'One thing, it's saved that wife of his a good many hidings of late. I told him he'd kill himself if he went on knocking her about in the way he did. He was a real brute, you know.'

Mrs. Cornish took the news of her husband's death with indifference.

'I hoped he'd go sudden,' she said. Neither Gavin nor Mrs. Bradley felt inclined to ask her what she meant.

'What will you do now, Mrs. Cornish?' Gavin asked sympathetically, when the funeral, well-attended by the village, was over and he and Mrs. Bradley were again at the inn. The widow was in black, and looked remarkably well.

'Oh, this place belongs of me, you know,' she said. 'I put Cornish in as landlord when we married, thinking folks like a man about the place, but I never made nothing over to him in his name. My poor father worked the 'ouse up and give it a good name and that, and whatever Cornish done to me, I wasn't going to sign nothing away. My dad would have turned in his grave. He never wanted me to marry 'im in the first place, but Cornish was a fine-looking chap in them days, and I thought I knew best, as gals do.' She sighed, and then looked round the bar parlour with evident pride. 'I kep' it all nice,' she said wistfully, 'and it's all mine now. I wouldn't wish 'im back.'

Gavin thought he had never heard so unanswerable an epitaph. They gave her a couple of days, and then decided to ask her for the interview at which they had promised Cornish should be present.

'Look here, Mrs. Cornish,' said Gavin, 'you can give us some help, I think.' She regarded him woodenly. 'We know all about Mr. Witt and the hold he had over Mr. Cornish, but that's all washed up now. What we'd like you to tell us, if you will, is of anything you recollect concerning a man called Campbell. No doubt you've seen his name in the papers.'

She shook her head.

'I never knew but one man called Campbell,' she said. 'Used to come fishing when old Mr. Cornish had the *Fisher's Inn*, not so very far from 'ere. Me and Cornish was courting at the time. Mr. Campbell, he was mad on birds and such, and could say the Latting names of every plant you could show 'im. But very 'ard up 'e was, Mr. Campbell was. Used to give 'em 'is fish to 'elp pay 'is bill. Then 'e seemed to be better off. A whole sight better off. Bought 'imself a nice pair of field-glasses, and a microscope thing, and a couple of guns and a new trout-rod . . . everything.'

'And had you ever any idea of what might have happened to provide him with all this extra money?'

'No. He once mentioned his aunt, but Cornish, when he was in his cups . . . he used to drink deep as a young man although the doctor often warned him not . . . he says one day as how if Mr. Campbell had any old aunt it was . . . well, I won't repeat what he said, it being unfit for Christian ears . . . but, anyway, that's what he said.'

'So you formed your own conclusions as to where the money came from, Mrs. Cornish?'

'I didn't dream. 'Tweren't no business o' mine. But

Cornish, 'e did say as 'ow 'e believed Mr. Campbell and Mr. Witt was two of a kind. I've learned what 'e meant by that since. At the time I didn't enquire. I knowed it meant nothing very good.'

'Tell us some more about Campbell.'

'I can't. Him and Mr. Witt was pretty thick, and that's all I know.'

'I say,' said Gavin at a venture, 'you don't remember a man called Tavis, I suppose?' She shook her head. The name obviously meant nothing to her. 'Or Grandall? A Mr. Grandall? Did *he* ever come to the *Fisher's Inn*, do you know?'

'Not as I ever heard tell on. Of course, as soon as we was married, old Mr. Cornish died and Cornish took on the 'ouse. But he didn't make no sort of job of it, and when my old dad died and I found I'd been left this 'ouse we moved in 'ere. But . . . what did you say the names was?'

'Tavis and Grandall.'

'No, I don't think they could 'ave come. That's like Davis and Randall, ain't it?'

'Like enough, but not quite right. Why, did you know a Davis and a Randall?'

'Oh, no. It just struck me, that's all.'

'Sometimes I can dimly see why Cornish struck her,' said Gavin, very sourly, when he and Mrs. Bradley were alone. 'She's not exactly helpful to us, is she?'

'She has established a very definite connection between Campbell and Witt.'

'And as they were both murdered it might have been Cornish who did in Campbell. I don't believe that, you know.'

'Who does? The point is that Witt initiated (or could have initiated) Campbell into the mysteries of the blackmailer's art, and that is very important. If we could prove that Campbell blackmailed Francis Caux on the subject of the exchange of identities between the twins, we might be well on the way to finding the motive for both the murders.'

'We've got to this point before, but there doesn't seem to be any proof.'

'This is where I tackle Mr. Darnwell again,' said Mrs.

Bradley serenely. 'I am now in a much better position to ask him questions than I was when I saw him before.'

'Darnwell?'

'The entertainer of nieces. The joy and the scandal of Wetwode. The expert on Easter Island art. The most interesting man I've met since I first met *you!*'

Gavin grinned.

'Tell me more,' he said.

'No,' Mrs. Bradley replied. 'The statements I should be compelled to make are not fit for a young man's ears. Get you to London and learn what you can of his reputation in the City; of his bank-balance; his acquaintances; his war record (if any); his expectations under wills; his true nationality; the hotels and restaurants he frequents; his flat, his servants, his travels abroad, his ox, his ass, and anything else that is his.'

'In other words . . . scram,' said Gavin. 'All right, then. I'll leave you to all your devilment unassisted. Let me know how you get on and whom I shall ask to bail you out when you get into serious trouble. I suppose it had better be my Laura. She seems to respect your brains, although heaven knows why.'

'I will wave to you across the court of the Old Bailey, if not before,' said Mrs. Bradley. Gavin looked at her mistrustfully.

'I still can't see the wood for the trees,' he said, 'but I suppose you've got the fox in the bag all right.'

'I wish I supposed so, too,' said Mrs. Bradley, 'but I do think Mr. Darnwell can help us, and I do think that I'm the better person to tackle him. I shall go to-morrow. Meanwhile, I mean what I say. You look up his antecedents, and if you can get on the track of one of his nieces, that might possibly help us.'

'You underrate my powers of imagination,' said Gavin with a great deal of dignity. 'You mean that Derek-Francis may have tried to snaffle one of Mr. Darnwell's young ladies.'

Mrs. Bradley hooted with laughter and made him a fencer's salute with the poker she picked out of the grate.

'Good luck to your hunting,' she said.

CHAPTER SIXTEEN

The Echo Out of the Wood

★

'. . . the primroses and crocuses were hidden under
wintry drifts; the larks were silent, the young leaves of
the early trees smitten and blackened.'

Emily Bronte: *Wuthering Heights*

★

'NICE to see you,' said Darnwell. 'Meet Sadie. Sadie, a
drink for Mrs. Bradley.'

'Thank you,' Mrs. Bradley responded. 'Your very
good health, Mr. Darnwell. So this is niece Sadie. She does
the family credit, if I may say so.'

'Oh, gosh, Sam!' said Sadie, displaying a lovely set of
teeth in a good-humoured, slightly embarrassed smile. 'The
lady's rumbled you.'

'As who would not?' agreed Mr. Darnwell lightly. 'Hop
it, darling, and give Mrs. Bradley the floor. I think she has
come here on business.'

'Trust you!' said Sadie, treating Mrs. Bradley to an
admiring and eloquent glance. 'If she knows of a shop for a
poor girl out of a job . . .'

'You're not out of a job,' said Darnwell. 'Go away, dear.
Little pigs have big ears.'

'And big swine have long snouts . . . especially if it's anything to their own advantage,' retorted the young lady,
laughing happily. She went out of the room and Mrs.
Bradley saw her go past the window.

'She's a nice kid,' said Mr. Darnwell indulgently. 'One of
the very best. I wish I *could* find her a shop. But you know
what it is these days. Farces with five characters and a

169

walking-on part. Musicals at a premium. What did you need to unload? I'm entirely at your service, I need not say.'

'I've come for information about the late Mr. Campbell.'

'What, again?' He registered horror. 'I thought you were my pal.'

'I'm not sure that I am not,' Mrs. Bradley sedately observed, 'but I fancy that you could give me some information which would help me to find Campbell's murderer.'

'Not sure that I want to find him,' said Darnwell thoughtfully. 'Bit of a mess, our Mr. Campbell. You might think I ought not to be calling the saucepan black, so to speak, but I can assure you that my little love-nest here don't *begin* to add up to the harm that Campbell did. I don't have any morals, in the accepted sense of the term, but the gals don't come to much harm, and they do get three square meals a day and a dollop in the kitty to be going on with until they can find a shop. You'll not find one of 'em ever to say I gave her a dirty deal.'

'I am convinced that your only concern is to make certain that the indigent are fed, clothed and indulged, and, in any case, your morals are nothing to do with me. I should never dream of concerning myself with them. No, Mr. Darnwell; I am merely going to ask you a direct and simple question: did Campbell ever try to blackmail you?'

Mr. Darnwell looked amused.

'Sure he did,' he responded.

'On the subject of your nieces?'

'Sure. I was no taker. I crowned him with Maimie's tap-dance shoe . . . it was Maimie I had staying here at the time . . . and told him to run and tell the police. No bum of that calibre,' said Mr. Darnwell righteously, 'tells a gentleman of little leisure but very good taste where he gets off.'

'Admirable,' said Mrs. Bradley; and meant it. 'Were there any repercussions?'

'No. He steered clear after that, although he did waylay Sonia one day . . . it was Sonia was staying with me then . . . and asked her a couple of questions about me and my ways.'

'And the result?'

'Sonia couldn't believe her ears. "What?" she said. "You something I won't repeat! Do you take me for *that* sort of girl?" '

'And wasn't she?' asked Mrs. Bradley, interested.

'She wasn't interested in etchings, if that's what you mean,' said Mr. Darnwell, grinning, 'but she was useful at darning and mending. You'd be surprised how domesticated some of these girls are. You see, it's a bit difficult, having servants here. Now, when I was living on Easter Island while a spot of financial difficulty blew itself out . . .'

Mrs. Bradley begged him to keep Easter Island, in which, she said, she was interested to the point of fascination, until there was time for him to do the subject justice. Darnwell begged her pardon, and the conversation reverted to Sonia.

'No, she couldn't believe her ears,' said Darnwell emphatically, 'and when he went on to the next question . . . holding out a ten-pound note, mark you, the kind of present I never let these girls see as it puts ideas in their heads . . . she just kicked his shins for all she was worth and fled back here and collapsed. She can act, that girl. I got her a job in films. She's doing well. I never hear from her now. You know,' he added solemnly, 'I'm not *all* bad. You'd really be surprised.'

'I don't know that I should,' Mrs. Bradley politely rejoined. 'But Campbell?'

'I don't know any more. He left me alone after that. He was limping for days.'

'You don't know any more that has to do with you personally, but you know a good deal more than you have said.'

'Maybe. But, look, he was a nasty fellow. Why not leave well alone? You can take it one of his victims got fed up with him. Does it really matter which one?'

'Yes, because I want to prevent another murder.'

'Oh? An innocent victim this time?'

'Do you know, I have given the matter some thought, and I'm not at all sure I believe that there are very many *innocent* victims of murder. After all, silliness . . . and some of them have been extremely silly . . . is hardly innocence, is it?'

'So the proposed victim is very far from innocent, I take it.'

'Very far indeed.'

'Yet you want to save his life? . . . or is it hers?'

'It is his. It is the life of Sir Adrian Caux.'

'That madman? I've seen quite a bit of him since he's been living so close. Who's trying to do him in? His precious grandson?'

'Yes, I think so.'

'Are you serious? I caught young Francis with Doreen last year . . . it was Doreen I had staying here then . . . and he was quite frightening the poor girl. I kicked him well and I kicked him truly. Then I held him by the collar and told him what I thought of him. I didn't mince my words. He wasn't deaf and dumb then. He let out a yell you could have heard at Dover, and then, while I talked, he went red to the roots of his hair. If ever a boy's ears burnt, his did. He understood what I was saying all right.'

'That is more than interesting.'

'Mind you, I kept my weather eye open for the little beauty after that, but he didn't give any more trouble.'

'No, I imagine not. But could we get back to Campbell? What else do you know about him?'

'Not much, and that's the truth. It isn't that I'm holding out on you.'

'Perhaps I could help your memory. I should not think you are a highly suggestible man, so you won't turn my promptings into leading questions. First, I take it that Campbell was a genuine naturalist.'

'He was until he used his nature study to cover his other little occupation, the one I mentioned.'

'Blackmail. Yes. And yet once a naturalist . . . it's a fascinating business, you know.'

'Oh, quite. But, of course, hide-outs built in the woods or in reed-beds can be handy for lots of things, can't they? Look here, I'll tell you what. I found one of 'em once. I'll take you to it if you like.'

'I would like it immensely. Now, at once, please.'

'All right. I'll just let Sadie know.' He raised his voice.

'You back, Sadie?' There was no answer. Darnwell excused himself to Mrs. Bradley, but she, who had had no previous experience of love-nests, followed him out. They went round the bungalow past the windows of the room which they had just left and to the kitchen step at the back. There sat Sadie, surrounded by a dozen pairs of shoes, her own and Darnwell's. She was singing quietly from the music of *Rose-Marie* and cleaning the shoes with vigour and great success.

'Oh, honey-girl,' said Darnwell, genuinely concerned, 'you shouldn't do that when we've got visitors! Just look at those mucky little paws! And, anyway, I don't have girls clean my shoes.'

'To-day you do,' said Sadie sunnily. She got up—a little creature with the natural balance of a dancer—yawned and added, 'What about a nice cup of tea?'

'Get yourself one,' said Darnwell. 'Mrs. Bradley and I are going to take a little walk. You don't want to come, I suppose?'

'Not if I'd be in the way.'

'You would a bit, darling. Shan't be more than about an hour. Got to go to the other side of the village.'

'O.K. big boy. Try and not get your feet wet.' She stooped and picked up a stout pair of shoes. 'Put these on. It rained this morning.'

'See what I mean?' said Darnwell, promptly kicking off his slippers and pulling on the newly-cleaned shoes. 'Treat 'em rough is my motto.' He kissed the nape of Sadie's pretty neck.

He backed out a small motor-launch and he and Mrs. Bradley chugged upstream to the public moorings just below the bridge. Here they tied up and stepped ashore. Darnwell led the way across the road and round the corner past the hotel. From the hotel to the railway station the pavement still bordered the roadway, but at the station it ended, and, once they were under the railway bridge, they were in a country lane.

To the left the pasture and the cornfields dipped to the

river. A church-tower came in view. Hedges divided the
meadows. There were hayricks and oak trees, poppies
among the corn and occasionally the lively blue of the
flax. The road, as though to confound those ignorant persons who believe that all Norfolk is flat, was gently switch-
back, and walking was pleasant and interesting.

After about three-quarters of a mile, a very narrow, rough
lane branched off from the country road.

'Up here,' said Darnwell. High ragged hedges, broken
only occasionally by gates, hid most of the landscape from
view. The church had disappeared among trees, but sudden
flights of swifts indicated that it was at no great distance
from the travellers.

At the end of half a mile the lane divided. Darnwell,
without even a half-glance at what appeared to be the
obvious route, branched off suddenly to the right. Deep
trees shaded the way, and the lane, not more than a track
now, led steadily downhill towards the river.

'And here we are,' said Darnwell. 'Over this gate, and we
can find it.'

The hide-out was a cunning affair made of branches over
a natural hole in the ground. A short distance off was a
clearing, small, but close-turfed and very private.

Mrs. Bradley crawled towards the hide-out. Flies buzzed
around its entrance and there were imprints of birds' feet,
although what the species of bird which had made them she
neither knew nor cared. She lay flat, a thin, inconspicuous
figure, and inveigled from a deep pocket in her skirt a
powerful magnifying glass, and studied the ground. Then
she lay beside the hide-out and unslung field-glasses. With
these she scanned the immediately-surrounding *terrain* and
pronounced judgment.

'A well-chosen spot. I congratulate Mr. Campbell.'

'Looks nice and comfy,' said Darnwell sardonically. Mrs.
Bradley stood up.

'You should know,' she responded serenely. 'I presume
that you fought in the trenches in the 1914 war, and in-
habitated a dug-out?'

'Hell! I thought I looked younger than that. I was only twenty, you know.' He laughed. 'Seen all you want to see here?'

'Not quite.' She walked into the neat little clearing. 'Very few people would come here, I imagine.'

'Very few indeed. It's off the main road . . . if you can call it a main road . . . and the village has about a dozen houses and one well which serves the lot of them. Come and see the well. I don't want to get back sooner than I said. Gives girls wrong impressions.'

'You're a chivalrous man, Mr. Darnwell.'

'Oh, I wouldn't say that. Experience teaches, you know.'

'It teaches very few people. One needs more than average intelligence to learn anything by experience.'

'Have *you* learnt anything by it?'

'One thing which coincides with what you have learnt, I think. It doesn't do to upset other people's dignity. One should never catch one's fellow-sufferers out.'

Darnwell grinned.

'You're telling *me*. So I shan't get home under an hour. Who knows who Sadie might be entertaining!'

'You have the virtuous vice of tolerance, Mr. Darnwell.'

'It makes life easier,' said Darnwell. 'Tell me where I mustn't tread.'

'Stay just where you are, then. That will do very nicely.' She quartered the ground, treading carefully. 'No more clues which mean anything to me,' she announced. 'Come, Mr. Darnwell. Let us take a look at the village and waylay the first small boy we meet.'

'What for?'

'To determine whether he also knows of the hide-out. How did *you* come to find it, by the way?'

'That's telling. But, since you ask, I will tell you. I trailed Campbell to it. It was after he tried his games on with me and failed. I thought two could play, maybe, and so I simply followed him.'

'But didn't he know?'

'Not he. I've been deer-stalking before now. Never got a

glimpse or a smell of me. I was inside the hedge all the time and he was on the road. Next day, when I'd seen him catch a train, I penetrated further and saw the hidey-hole, but I didn't go close up. I didn't want to leave footprints near the entrance.'

'Simple. Yes. I don't suppose it's the only one he had.'

'No. There would have been one, at least, among reeds.'

'I agree with you entirely.'

'That's right. And another one out on the marshes.'

'The marshes?'

'Sure. Go straight on after the bridge instead of turning up by the station, and keep right on past the signpost. Then take the first on the right and still keep on.'

'I will do so, Mr. Darnwell, and I thank you very much. No, I won't come back to your bungalow. I'm going to have tea with a friend of mine in the village.'

They met no village children at all.

When Gavin turned up again Mrs. Bradley had much to tell him, including an interesting fact she had not disclosed to Darnwell. There were traces of blood in the mud at the entrance to the hide-out. She had been back and had possessed herself of a sample. There had been no blood in the derelict bungalow.

'Right,' said Gavin. 'Now what about some little boy in that village? You and Darnwell didn't encounter one, I gather.'

They found one trailing a stick and whistling dolefully, a grimy, chubby child of about eleven. Mrs. Bradley stopped him.

'Do you live here?'

'Yes, I do.'

'Is there a policeman in the village?'

'No.'

'So you boys never worry?'

'Eh?'

'You know that, whatever you get up to, nobody bothers you.'

'My dad do.'

'No doubt. Do you boys play in the woods here?'

'Some do.' He began to edge past her.

'And you?'

'Maybe.'

'Have you ever seen a man with field-glasses watching the birds?'

'No.' He tried to escape but Mrs. Bradley gripped him by the jersey.

'Are you sure?' asked Gavin, joining in at what he thought was the crucial point. 'I am a police officer, and I want to know all about this man. To begin with, can you describe him?'

'If you mean Mr. Campbell, I was with Ben Thetford, but we didn't upset Mr. Campbell.'

'When were you with Ben Thetford?'

'Last year, in our summer holiday.'

'Oh, yes. What was Mr. Campbell doing?'

'Watching through the glasses.'

'Watching what?'

'Courting couples, I reckon to think.'

'Why should you think that?'

'Ben Thetford told me that's what Mr. Campbell do.'

'I see. Is Ben Thetford any relation to Malachi Thetford?'

'Yes. They're uncles.'

'How much?'

'They're uncles.'

'You mean Malachi is Ben's uncle, don't you?'

'Yes. Bertha Coltshall, that marry Malachi Thetford's brother Billy, and Ben, she's his mother.'

'Ah, yes,' said Gavin, disentangling this. 'I suppose it would have been Malachi who told Ben that Mr. Campbell watched courting couples through his field-glasses?'

'I don't know.'

'Did you often go to the hide-out when Mr. Campbell wasn't there?'

'Sometimes.'

'Did you,' said Mrs. Bradley, 'ever go there after Mr. Campbell was dead?'

The boy tried to wrench himself away. When he found he could not escape he began to cry.

'I don't know. I don't know nawthen! Lemme goo! I h'an't done nawthen wrong!'

'All right,' said Gavin. He hesitated, looked at Mrs. Bradley. 'Look here,' he said, 'if you're a sensible chap you'll keep this conversation under your hat. Understand me? Mr. Campbell was murdered. You know that, don't you? Now, you needn't worry about it so long as you don't talk. Are you scared?'

'No, sir.' But he was.

'Good lad. And you won't report that you've seen me and this lady?'

'No. I better tell me dad.'

'All right. There's no harm in that. Where do you live?'

'Number Six, the village.'

'Right. I'll speak to your father myself. I'll tell him you've been helpful. If anyone asks you where you got this half-crown, you tell them you got it showing some people the way to Wroxham Broad.'

'I don't know the way to Wroxham Broad.'

'Oh, well, you think of somewhere, then. Good-bye. I'll be round at your house later on, when your father's at home. It's just confirmatory evidence,' he added to Mrs. Bradley. 'But you were right. It was well worth while. Bit of luck we happened upon the very boy who knew about Campbell's hidey-hole, though.'

'All the village boys knew. If they had not, Campbell might still be alive.'

'How do you make that out, I wonder?'

'He was killed because the twin brothers discovered that he was watching them. Village boys are a good deal more observant, as a rule, than youths of the type of the Caux brothers when it comes to fish, feathers and fur. If the twins discovered the hide-out, the village boys are more than bound to have done so.'

'Ably argued. Where do we go from here?'

'To Sir Adrian Caux, I fancy, unless you desire to find Campbell's little sanctuary on the marshes.'

'I don't think so. We've got what we want. What shall you say to Sir Adrian?'

'I shall advise him to re-make his will.'

'Oh?'

'Of course, child.'

'Ah, yes, I get it. There can be only one reason for the murders of Campbell and Witt. Either or both of them must have been in a position to give away to the grandfather the fact that the boys changed places. They most probably changed places for one chief reason. They are determined to inherit Sir Adrian's worldly goods at an earlier date than his normal earthly span will dictate. It will appear that Derek, his named heir (so I suppose) has killed his grandfather, since no one else will have any obvious motive for encompassing the relative's death. Derek (quite a clever young devil) makes his brother an offer. "You help me," he says, "by mixing up our two identities so that no one can tell t'other from which, and we'll probably both be arrested and have to appear in court. *One* of us has a fool-proof alibi, the other then must be the murderer, *but*, since no one is able to prove which one of us is which, and as one of us is palpably innocent, it turns out that they can't hang either of us. Try us separately, or try us together, it makes no earthly scrap of difference. One of us *is* a murderer and the other is an innocent man. They'll *have* to let us both off, and there we are, with all grandfather's money to spend between us, for, of course, I shall see you get half. We'd better go abroad, I should think. There'll be too much criticism here. But we shall be made for life. It's as easy as falling off a log." And, of course, it probably will be,' Gavin gloomily concluded.

'Nonsense, child. To get the money, one of them will have to be Derek, and whichever one claims to be Derek automatically fixes a rope round his neck. Don't you see?'

'Lord, yes! I suppose that point would have come to my mind in time. Tell me your version, then.'

'It is the same as your own. Like you, the boys haven't quite finished thinking things out.'

'What are you going to tell Sir Adrian about his will, then?'

'The obvious thing. He'll have to make the boys joint heirs and let them both know it if he wants to preserve his life.'

'Or, preferably, cut *both* the young devils out of it.'

'They might kill him then for revenge, and they *might* get away with that, you know. You see, if nothing was coming to either of them, a very big motive for murder would have gone by the board. Revenge, as a motive for murder in England, makes a very poor show compared with financial gain and sexual opportunity.'

'I agree, of course. May I give one word of warning?'

'You may, of course,' said Mrs. Bradley, grinning. 'I think that you mean to tell me to look after myself. But I bear a charmed life, child. The Wandering Jew is not more unlucky than I.'

Gavin courteously snorted. He had not the faintest idea of what she meant.

CHAPTER SEVENTEEN

The Echo from the Past

★

*'Who said, "Ay, mum's the word!"—Sexton to
willow.'*

Walter de la Mare: *Peacock Pie*

★

MRS. BRADLEY sought out Sir Adrian early on the
following morning. His grandsons had gone out
together in a punt. So much she knew because, from
the hotel garden, she had seen them go and had taken one
of the hotel launches to reach the riverside bungalows in
good time.

Sir Adrian was disconsolately digging the garden.

'Wrong time of year,' said Mrs. Bradley, disengaging
herself elegantly from her craft and leaving George to
tie up. 'Why dig now, when October might be a better
month?'

'Oh, it's you,' said Sir Adrian, without enthusiasm. 'And
what do you want now, may I ask?'

'A copy of your will. And don't look at me like that. You
have me between yourself and sudden death. Are you really
such a silly old man?'

'Do you know, I expect I am,' said Sir Adrian disarmingly.
'Say on. I am all attention.'

'But are you? I rather doubt that. I've warned you already.
I can't do more, you know.'

'You've warned me, yes. But I've brought up Derek from
babyhood.'

'A boy of seven is not a baby. You know what the
Jesuits say.'

'Give me a boy until he is seven . . . yes, you've got something there. My son was a very bad hat. You probably know that already, but Derry . . . he's like my own child.

'Not a bit of it, and don't you believe it. I know what I'm saying.'

'And what exactly are you saying?'

'I'm advising you to re-make your will, and to let both boys know that you've re-made it.'

'As . . . how?' He looked, suddenly, twenty years older than his age.

'Leave your property to them jointly, and at some date far into the future. Alternatively, leave it to a cats' home.'

'But . . . Derry is my own flesh and blood.'

'I am warning you,' said Mrs. Bradley solemnly. 'Your life means nothing to me, but I presume you wish to preserve it as long as you can. Don't be an idiot. You've done quite enough harm already. There's a good deal of sense in religious verse, you know, even if it seems trite and, from a literary point of view, deplorable.'

'How do you mean?'

Something had already happened to frighten him, Mrs. Bradley concluded. These were anything but his native woodnotes.

'I mean "he that one sin in conscience keeps when he to quiet goes, more (let us say completely and criminally reckless) is than he who sleeps with twenty mortal foes." An interesting, and, you may say, unnecessary incursion into your private and personal business.'

'No, I don't say that,' said Sir Adrian. 'Look here, have you ever played cricket?'

'When I kept wicket for Australia,' Mrs. Bradley replied, 'strong men did slow clapping. Apart from that . . .'

'I thought we were talking seriously,' said Sir Adrian. He looked worried and anxious.

'But of course we are. Cricket is the only serious subject, except, possibly, the devaluation of the pound and the chances of some remote animal winning the Greyhound Derby, that one can possibly discuss.'

'It would be nice to swim the Channel, don't you think?' asked Sir Adrian, obviously outclassed.

Mrs. Bradley gazed speculatively at him.

'Very nice,' she agreed. The conversation lapsed. Then Sir Adrian observed, defensively:

'Of course, the boys are alike.'

'So much alike,' said Mrs. Bradley earnestly, 'that I would defy you to tell one from another.' Sir Adrian was offended.

'Of course I can tell one from the other,' he said. 'One talks like a child of seven, the other like a professor of philosophy.'

'Then which of them played cricket on the day of Mr. Witt's death?' asked Mrs. Bradley remorselessly. Sir Adrian looked at her, horrified.

'You don't mean . . . ? You can't seriously tell me . . . ? That is . . . damn it, *I* don't know! I never thought of that, except that when I sent Derry—oh, I'll swear it was Derry— I'll swear it in court if necessary——'

'You'll be swearing his life away if you do. Don't lose sight of the fact that it was while this boy was absent from the field of play that the murder of Witt was accomplished. Derek . . . if you cling to your theory . . . is still the only person without an alibi.'

Sir Adrian looked haggard.

'I'd rather go to the gallows myself than have that boy accused!'

'Very possibly. But, you see, you can't. There are more than twenty witnesses (apart from spectators, too) who can testify to your innocence of that particular deed.'

'I shall say he did it under my influence.'

'Even if he did . . .' She did not add that this particular theory had already occurred to her.

'Well, even if he did?' said Sir Adrian. Mrs. Bradley smiled—a mirthless contortion which gave her the fleeting appearance of a crocodile on half-rations.

'No jury would ever believe you. They would know that you were screening the boy. Moreover, when they decided such to be the case, your true evidence, which might have helped the accused, would then tend to be disregarded. In court the truth, although often dangerous, is less so, on the whole, than lying. It is also far less tax on the memory.'

'You had better tell me what is in your mind, I think. Let's suppose, since you've chosen to raise the point, that it was Frankie, and not Derry, playing cricket . . . although how on earth they could ever have changed places has me baffled. Why, for six years, from nine to fifteen, Derry was at school. At a tutorial place, you know, where the boy was under constant supervision.'

'I presume he came home for the holidays?'

'Oh, you think they got up to their games during holidays, do you? Even when Derry went to Switzerland?'

'Both, I should say, were bored with their safe and settled existence at times. The early exchanges of identity which you seem to know must have taken place, were probably merely a way of giving rein to a sense of adventure. Then, of course . . .' She explained her theory that the boys had been blackmailed by Campbell. 'And what I want you to tell me,' she added at the end, (and she spoke gently, for Sir Adrian was looking extremely like a gaffed fish), 'is where Witt comes into all this. That he blackmailed the publican Cornish there seems no doubt, and some evidence which we have been able to gather from Mrs. Cornish suggests that Witt and Campbell could have known one another before Witt went to live at Mede and Campbell in Wetwode. Can you add to that evidence at all?'

'No,' said Sir Adrian, 'I can't. And no one was blackmailing *me*. I should very soon have handed him over to the police. *No* disgraceful secret is worth keeping at the price of being bled and losing sleep. "*Out*, damnéd spot!" is what *I'd* say, if anybody tried on me those devilish tricks.'

'And yet,' said Mrs. Bradley very thoughtfully, taking a small revolver from her skirt pocket and twiddling it absent-mindedly, 'you went to considerable trouble to remove from your vicinity a certain small boy aged seven.'

'What the devil do you mean, madam!' There was no

doubt about his reaction to her statement. His little eyes were rimmed with bright blood, his lips were drawn back. His voice was thick with the furious anger of fear. 'What do you mean, I say!'

'Francis witnessed that accident to the car, the accident in which his father and mother were killed. I've often wondered how and why that accident occurred.'

She thought for a moment (indeed, it was true) that Sir Adrian was going to launch himself at her, but a glance at her little revolver, now levelled in a business-like way, was sufficient to delay the impulse. He abandoned it, and threw himself into a chair.

'Talking through your hat,' he mumbled. Mrs. Bradley, who was wearing a sort of *fez* made of orange velvet decorated with two bloody-looking cherries which dangled over her right ear, glanced appreciatively at this monstrosity in the mirror over the fireplace and smirked complacently. 'Accidents will happen,' Sir Adrian added sullenly.

'This one was intended to happen to Francis, too, wasn't it? But when you discovered that the poor child had been rendered deaf and dumb as the result of shock (although any competent psychologist would have told you that with proper treatment he could be restored to normal fairly easily), you thought that perhaps it came to much the same thing, so long as you sent him away. Otherwise his condition might have reminded you of your frightful crime, and even you had sufficient conscience not to want that.'

'And what is supposed to have been my motive for this abominable action?' Sir Adrian sneeringly enquired. 'I presume I'm supposed to have had one.' He had regained his self-confidence, she noted.

'Yes, of course. You did it to gain the one thing you wanted . . . possession of little Derek.'

'But if the twins are so much alike that I'm now supposed not to be able to tell one of them from the other, why should I have this complete personal preference for Derry?'

'But I don't think you had,' said Mrs. Bradley. 'I think you wanted one of the boys but not both. I don't believe it mattered to you at all which boy it was. And that is why you cannot (and could not, all the time that they were changing places) distinguish one twin from the other.'

Sir Adrian sat back, relaxed.

'And you really think,' he said, 'that you could get away with all this in a court of law?'

'Certainly not. But I am warning you that one of the twins will kill you unless you re-make your will. Do you read the Sherlock Holmes stories?'

'Yes, of course. Why?'

'I don't know why you do, but, *if* you do, you will surely remember the story called *The Copper Beeches*. You do remember it, don't you?'

'Why should I?'

'It contained one point which I, personally, have found useful. Sherlock Holmes argued backwards.'

'Sounds quite unlike him. Or, no, perhaps that's wrong.'

'It may or may not be wrong. But in that story, he deduced you may remember, the characteristics of the father from those he had observed in the son.'

'I don't know what you're getting at.' He looked uneasy again.

'Oh, yes, you do. One of the twins attempted to drown Miss Higgs. (I say nothing about the deaths of Witt and Campbell). Your son was had up for manslaughter. You preceded your son and the twins. Is it too far-fetched of me to deduce that you might be capable of murder?'

'I'll murder *you*,' said Sir Adrian ferociously, 'if you dare to insinuate that I had anything to do with the deaths of my son and his wife. What makes you even suggest such a terrible thing?'

'A belated but sincere desire to speak the truth,' said Mrs. Bradley, putting away her little revolver. 'But since the truth, being the truth, is almost always incapable of proof . . . *vide* all respectable religions . . . let us confine ourselves to the uncritical care of our *moutons* and revert to the matter in hand.'

'I've lost the thread,' said Sir Adrian uncertainly. 'You were saying?'

'No, it was you. An invitation from the Queen to play croquet.'

'But you wouldn't really play cricket?' He seemed relieved by the sudden change of subject.

'Even at the expense of being hit over the heart by a body-line bowler, yes.'

'When?'

'Well, it's your cricket ground, not mine, isn't it?'

'You mean you'd play cricket at Mede? No. Look here, what's your game?'

'This time, obviously, cricket.'

'You want to come to Mede to find out what happened at the time of Witt's death, do you?'

'That, and other things. I still can't see why your grandson left the ground during what turned out to be the crucial time. That is, the time of the murder.'

'Bad luck. Bad luck. There is such a thing, you know.'

'As who should not. But bad luck, like lightning, strikes only in one direction.'

'Downwards?'

'It is your word, not mine,' said Mrs. Bradley.

'So there it is,' said Mrs. Bradley to Gavin. 'I've given him fair warning. I know he's told lies. He knew more about the boys than he admits.'

'I don't much like this cricket business, you know. Do you think he'd let *me* play?'

'I want you to play, child, and I want you to snoop. Who knows . . .' she leered hideously, 'what an unbiassed cricketer might be able to find out?'

'But I'm *not* unbiassed.'

'That is the point I was endeavouring to aim at. And, being completely biassed, you are the more likely, as any respectable historian will tell you, to arrive at some approximation of the truth. So long as you know you're biassed, neither you nor the truth will suffer. "Lord, I believe; help Thou mine unbelief" is one of the more extraordinary texts. On the surface it is meaningless. Beneath the surface, (I often think about the depths of the sea), it has rather more meaning than most of us can even begin to estimate.'

'You ought to have been a lay preacher,' said Gavin reproachfully. 'What on earth are you handing me now?'

'Arrest Derek Caux and find out, child.'

'But which of them *is* Derek Caux?'

'I know what you mean. And yet there is one simple way of finding out.'

'Yeah?'

'Yeah, certainly yeah. And, if you don't perceive what it is, I don't see why I should enlighten you.'

'Well, dash it, you're a psychologist. You've got ways and means of your own. All phoney, I suspect, but so long as you satisfy yourself you will probably satisfy me. And if you can satisfy me, you'll probably satisfy a jury. Come on, now. Out with it.'

'It has nothing to do with psychology in the sense that you mean,' said Mrs. Bradley. 'It all depends on Wetwode.'

'Wetwode?'

'*Rouge, rouge, rouge!*' shouted his hearer, on a sudden scream which took his breath away.

'I don't get it,' he said feebly.

'Not the cherry brandy, child!' continued Mrs. Bradley inexcusably. 'Throw them both into the river. But this time the witch won't swim.'

'*Oh!*' said Gavin, his handsome face clearing at last. 'Good heavens, I should have thought of it myself!'

'Why, child? Nobody else has.' But she leered upon him devotedly, as a dim-witted mother might leer upon a loved but idiot child.

'So Francis will swim,' said Gavin, looking happy. 'Any flannelled fool can make some sort of show with bat and ball, but if you can't swim, you can't, and that goes for Derek. Lord, how ridiculously simple!'

CHAPTER EIGHTEEN

The Echo of a Crime

★

*'I have tracked it clue by clue, carefully and
laboriously, with varying success for eight long years,
and at last I am in the position to say that I believe I
have my thumb upon the keynote.'*

Guy Boothby: *Doctor Nikola*

★

"Y ES, that's it,' said Gavin. 'I wonder why we never
thought of it before?'

'But I *did*,' Mrs. Bradley responded. 'What we
need now are the reports of the inquest upon the Caux
parents.'

'It must all have been according to Cocker, you know.
So far as I'm aware, nothing came up which led to the
slightest breath of suspicion. It must have passed as being
an accident pure and simple. In fact, I looked up the
records before, if you remember, and that's what it purely
and simply was.'

'According to Sir Adrian's reactions, I should say that it
was neither pure nor simple. There is no doubt that Sir
Adrian is badly shaken.'

'And you really think those boys may have planned to
take his life?'

'One, I think, has planned it.'

'Yes, but which? Why, oh, why are identical twins?'

'Let us go back a bit. Now, then: the accident . . . we'll
still call it that for the moment . . . happened ten years ago,
when the boys were seven. Two years later, owing to an
impulse on the part of Miss Higgs, or, more probably,

Derek (who was clever and bored), they met again whilst Sir Adrian was arranging for Derek's education. From that time onwards the boys kept in touch with one another, even although at first they could meet only once a year when Sir Adrian went north for the grouse-shooting.'

'So far, so good. But where does it get us? And, you know, I'm a bit worried still about this cunning and cleverness they seem to have shown, and especially this business of keeping up the fiction that Francis was still deaf and dumb.'

'I don't think there is very much difficulty. One of them ... we'll say it is Derek, just for the sake of the argument ... has a really first-class brain. We know that not only from our own observations, but from an entirely unbiassed person, Mr. Tom Donagh, who tutored him at the beginning of the summer vacation ... we'll say that Derek made the plans.'

'Granted, so far. Go on.'

'Well, child, is it straining credulity too far to believe that at first the two boys merely played a game over the deaf and dumb business? You see, there are advantages in being both beautiful and afflicted. I have no doubt whatever that in various material ways dear to the hearts of small boys, the path of Miss Higgs' charge was considerably smoothed. Who, for instance, would dream of punishing him, no matter what he did? Who would *not* dream of handing out more sweetmeats and a richer slice of cake to one on whom Nature appeared to have so little mercy? Who, having contrived to discover anything which seemed to give the little boy pleasure, would not frame and invent occasions for indulging him?'

'All right! All right! You win. But you see what all this leads to?'

'I can see one thing. Collusion. It was probably easy enough for Francis to cast off the leading strings at this end ... he had only to wait until Miss Higgs went shopping, for example; and she must frequently have gone shopping even as far as Norwich ...'

'Yes, I think that's a reasonable assumption, and we know that Francis can handle a boat. He probably miked as he pleased. But what about the other half of the sketch? How did Derek, even with his grandfather absent, contrive to sneak away out of Mede?'

'The point has arisen before. I think that whilst you again read the report of that inquest on the Caux parents, I will attach myself once more to the delightful Mr. Tom Donagh, and set him to work as a sleuth.'

'He can pump the servants, you mean. But will he agree to do that? I don't think *I* would in his place.'

'He won't need to agree, child, for that will not be what we require. All I want Mr. Donagh to do is to arrange this other cricket match and challenge Sir Adrian to bring a team against Donagh's eleven.'

'Donagh may not be able to get an eleven together.'

'Oh, nonsense! Don't be so defeatist! Surely, among my male relatives, who are legion, and the talented young policemen that *you* know, we can find sufficient players to put up a respectable game?'

'And where is it going to be played? You can't ask Sir Adrian to bat on the village green.'

'It will be played at Mede, on Sir Adrian's own perfect pitch. That, I somehow fancy, is already arranged.'

'Oh, I see!'

'And about time, too,' said Mrs. Bradley severely. 'It is the only way I can think of which is bound to succeed in getting Sir Adrian back to his own home, which at present he shows a marked disinclination to visit.'

'And then . . . ?'

'And then I shall enact the part of Mr. Witt's murderer.'

'Getting Donagh to open the house to you as we think one of the Caux boys did on the former occasion? I don't see what you'll gain from it, you know.'

'Time will show what I shall gain, child.'

'There's another thing, too, though. You know, I'm still worried about your safety. If you're right, at least two out of the three Caux people are murderers, and the other is probably an accessory. You've shown your hand quite clearly now, and are probably in serious danger. I think I'll stick on a couple of my chaps to trail you and them, and generally keep an eye on things. I don't want you pushed into the river or bashed on the head with a half-brick. Bad for my reputation.'

'Very well. I will let Sir Adrian know what you intend,' said Mrs. Bradley agreeably; for she knew that to argue with chivalrous males whose protective instinct has clouded their better judgment is worse than useless. Gavin grinned cheerfully at her.

'All right. You go ahead, then,' he said indulgently, 'and I'll get on with sorting the dirty linen of past crime.'

So efficiently did he carry out this task that at the end of a couple of days he returned with a sheaf of typed documents. Mrs. Bradley, who now had a fellow guest at the hotel in the person of her faithful and unobtrusive bodyguard, a young policeman named Willoughby, welcomed Gavin and invited him up to her hotel sitting-room, a very pleasant place which, although it was well back from it, overlooked the river.

'Any luck?' she enquired. Gavin took out the fruits of his—or rather, of two of his bright young men's—researches.

'I put Carr and Walker on to the job,' he said, 'and they went through all the old newspaper files and got out everything they could find. It's all very picturesque and interesting . . . life history of the Caux family, portraits of Sir Adrian and Derek, old photographs of Caux, his wife and the twin boys when the kids were three—that sort of thing—and a very full report of the inquest. I've read and re-read, but there doesn't seem a thing that's any good to us.'

'Were Mr. and Mrs. Caux killed instantly?'

'No, but neither recovered consciousness after the accident. Mrs. Caux died the same night, and Caux on the following morning.'

'Which hospital did they go to?'

'The Cotman and Cole, near Lymington.'

'And the boy Francis?'

'There wasn't a bed in the children's ward, so they took him to a small cottage hospital between Mede and Brockenhurst which serves several villages and seems to be staffed partly by the local W.V.S. There's a Sister-in-Charge and a couple of nurses, and the W.V.S. do cleaning, and trot about doing a sort of ambulance service for the out-lying districts.'

'Interesting. Before we get Sir Adrian to go back to Mede for this cricket match I think I'll go and stay in Brockenhurst for a bit. I like the New Forest. Or I could even go home. That might be better. How do I get to this cottage hospital from Wandles Parva? What is it called?'

'The Dedman Trust Cottage Hospital, Addersdale, Hampshire. Addersdale is marked on the Ordnance map.'

'Yes, I've seen it, I think. In fact, I've driven through it, I believe.'

'I'll pass the word to Willoughby that you're going home. You had better keep him, I think.'

'With George and Henri to look after me?'

'Well, I'd feel a whole lot easier in my mind. Sir Adrian may be a bit stupid, but apparently those nancy boys are not, and I don't trust one of the three of them.'

'Do as you please, then, child. I cannot have you losing sleep on my account.'

'Any idea of what you're going to do when you get to this cottage hospital place?'

'Yes, but I am not certain yet of the method which I shall employ.'

'Well, don't get into any trouble.' He grinned affectionately at her. 'It's about time Laura got back from New York. What do you pay her for, if she spends all her time gadding about on transatlantic liners and going to see the Niagara Falls? A secretary should be with her employer. Besides, she's a good hand in a rough-house,' he added thoughtfully. 'I wouldn't mind knowing that you had her at your back if there's likely to be any trouble.'

'For an engaged man you don't seem to over-value the

G

life and limb of your fiancee,' Mrs. Bradley remarked. 'But I shall be glad to see her again, although not for the reason you mention. I will let you know how I get on in Addersdale.'

'Yes, do. I see Malachi Thetford is back. Met him as I came along here.'

'Yes. I sent him a telegram to tell him it was safe to return. After the shocks we have been able to give Sir Adrian, Malachi's danger is past. Sir Adrian will most certainly conclude that Malachi has told us everything he knows about Campbell's body being found beneath that boat.'

'Actually, Malachi hasn't helped us much.'

'No. I wonder what Sir Adrian thought the young man had discovered?'

'Whatever it was, all possible evidence of it will be destroyed by now.'

Mrs. Bradley lost no time. By nine o'clock that night she was having dinner at her country home, the Stone House, Wandles Parva, and her delighted French *chef* and his wife, the parlourmaid, were in exuberant attendance upon her.

'And how did you get on with Malachi Thetford?' Mrs. Bradley had asked soon after her arrival whilst Celestine was unpacking her luggage.

'That one? He is a good boy, madame. He teaches Henri a new dish.'

'Really? What was that?'

'Norfolk domplings, madame. And to eat them before the meat. Most good, and of an economy unsurpassed. Most filling to the stomach if the meat is small, as, alas! in England it is! Madame should live in France for a little. It is deplorable how starved are the English.'

Mrs. Bradley declined to discuss this morbid subject which seemed to her to savour more of the outbreaks of *Pravda* than of commonsense philosophy.

'Henri should read the diaries of the Reverend Mr. Woodforde,' she observed.

'Doubtless,' said Celestine, with marked lack of interest.

'It would improve his soul, madame supposes. Me, I believe him not to possess such an appendage.'

'You believe a soul to be redundant?'

'As madame pleases.' She tossed her head, to Mrs. Bradley's delight, not understanding the last word of her employer's remark and determined not to ask for a translation.

'But we weren't talking of souls,' Mrs. Bradley pointed out, 'but of dumplings. In his diaries, Parson Woodforde describes in detail many meals, some of which I feel Henri would take pleasure in preparing. For instance: *1st Course, a Dish of Soals boiled and fryed, Couple of boiled Chicken and Tongue, Beans and Bacon, Stewed Beef and an Haunch of Venison rosted at the lower end. 2nd Course, a Couple of rost Ducks and Green Peas, a Leveret rosted, Maccaroni, Patties, Blamange, red-Currant Pye* . . . What do you think of all that?'

'One would need the stomach of an elephant,' said Celestine, sniffing. She finished the unpacking and then went off to tell her spouse to serve dinner at once, as madame was obviously suffering from lack of food because all her conversation ran on viands.

Next day Mrs. Bradley drove to Addersdale. It was off the main Southampton-Christchurch road, a tiny hamlet, but the hospital was served by crossroads which linked it with a dozen villages.

It was an early Georgian house which had not been altered except for the absence of an inside wall here and there to make what had been two rooms into a ward.

Mrs. Bradley presented her professional card, and the Sister-in-Charge came at once to greet her.

'Good afternoon, Matron,' said Mrs. Bradley briskly. 'I am, as usual, working with the Home Office over a small matter and I have reason to think that you might be able to help me.'

'Oh, yes, Doctor?'

'I wonder whether you can tell me who was in charge here ten or eleven years ago?'

'I myself would have been. I've been here nearly twenty years.'

'That's better luck than I'd hoped for. Do you remember an accident case . . . shock and bruises, I expect? It was a small boy of seven named Francis Caux. He'd been in a car smash after which his father and mother died in the Cotman and Cole Hospital, near Lymington.'

'I remember him very well, Doctor. Yes, there was a sad case, if ever I had one. Poor little chap! Such a lovely little boy! He went deaf and dumb, you know. I've often thought about him, and wondered how he got on. I did ask his grandfather to let us know, when he came to take him away, but I never heard any more about it.'

'We have reason to believe that he will make a full recovery,' said Mrs. Bradley cautiously, 'and I'm trying to obtain details of his medical history.' (What these had to do with the Home Office she would, if challenged, have found rather difficult to explain, but Sister, dazzled by the professional card which was embellished by one or two of Mrs. Bradley's formidable degrees, was not in challenging mood.)

'Well, I can't tell you *very* much, I'm afraid,' she said, 'although one thing may interest you. It was on account of the shock he'd had, poor little boy. I shall always remember it, though. His big eyes, and his piteously white little face, and his tousled hair. He sat up in bed and stretched out his arms to me and said, 'Grandy did it! Grandy did it! I saw him!'

'Now that *is* interesting,' said Mrs. Bradley very slowly indeed. 'You see what it means, Matron?'

'Indeed, yes. Delayed shock. He wasn't deaf and dumb until at least a week after he came in.'

'This is very important indeed, and the theory of delayed shock, although obviously the right one . . .' She hesitated. The Sister's evidence was so important that she was determined not to give her any lead. There was a pause. The two women, one big, blonde-grey and, by now, half-nervous, the other small, yellow and as penetrative as a gimlet, gazed at one another. Then Sister sighed and relaxed.

'I've often puzzled over whether I ought to have said anything at the time, but Doctor Smith . . . he's dead now . . . seemed satisfied that it was all due to the accident . . . but it was after his grandfather visited him that this deafness and dumbness seemed to date with Francis.'

Mrs. Bradley relaxed, too.

'Thank you very much, Matron. We are investigating a precisely similar case, you see, and a comparison is both helpful and interesting.'

'Well, I won't ask any questions, Doctor,' said Sister, with a shrewd glance. 'Perhaps I *ought* to have said something at the time, but Doctor Smith seemed satisfied, and it wasn't for me to query him.'

'Of course not. And, even if you *had* spoken (to the police, of course, you mean), it couldn't have done any good. The little boy was *undoubtedly* suffering from shock . . . for one reason or another.'

She accepted the Sister's eager offer to show her over the hospital, and departed, after tea and biscuits in the office, in an aura of general goodwill. There was one other helpful point.

'You didn't speak of this to *anybody* else at the time, Matron?'

Sister looked distressed.

'Well, I'm afraid I did. You see, I thought you meant had I mentioned it to the police. But . . .'

'No, no. It will help enormously. Confirmatory evidence, you see. I won't deceive you. As a matter of fact, I don't think I have. We are investigating murder. I know I can rely on your discretion.'

'Say no more, Doctor. I shan't say another word to a soul.'

'And the person or persons you spoke to, at the time?'

'Lady Hordle, up at the Hall. She was our Chairman of Governors.'

'No one else?'

'No one at all, Doctor. Lady Hordle advised me very strongly to hold my tongue. She had no doubt Doctor

Smith was right and she said that in any case no good could possibly come of talking about the grandfather's visit. "You'll only lose Doctor's confidence," she said, "without doing any good at all." But I felt bad about it for a long time. There wasn't any sign of anything more than superficial shock, and that came out at the time we first took him in. He was sweating and shivering and crying, and felt cold . . . well, you don't need me to tell *you* the symptoms, Doctor. But he was already beginning to get over it when his grandfather came. He'd asked me, (on the fourth day, that would have been), why his father and mother hadn't been to see him, and I broke it all to him as gently as I could. He looked solemn and a bit thoughtful, and then he said, sitting up in bed, as I told you, and stretching out his little arms to me, "Grandy did it! I saw him!" And then, after his grandfather's visit . . .'

'His grandfather, I take it, came more than once to see him?'

'Twice. The second time he took him away. And that was dreadful, too. The child clung to me . . . oh, how those hard little arms did cling around my neck! But Doctor Smith let him go. He said it might take years to get over the shock, and he did advise the grandfather to take him to a psychiatrist, but I don't know if ever he did. I called at Mede House once on my afternoon off, but the butler told me none of the family was at home. I asked him about little Francis, but he said he was being taken care of elsewhere . . . somewhere in Norfolk, he thought . . . and he didn't know anything about him.'

Mrs. Bradley went straight from the hospital to the Hall. Lady Hordle made no bones about confirming the Sister's story.

'But I advised her, very strongly, to hold her tongue,' she said. 'After all, if there was any truth in what the child had said . . . if the car had been tampered with, for example, and such cases are, unfortunately, not unknown . . . it would all have come out at the inquest. The police are *very* particular.'

Mrs. Bradley agreed. She did not add that in a head-on

collision any tampering with the steering-gear, for instance, might well be so thoroughly disguised among the resultant wreckage that even the police, for all their care, might not have been able to find out about it, particularly if there was no reason for suspecting foul play.

CHAPTER NINETEEN

The Echo from Mede

★

'Him as strikes first is my fancy.'
R. L. Stevenson: *Treasure Island*

★

GAVIN was more than satisfied; he was jubilant.

'Of course, we can't use it officially,' he said, 'but we can get on to Francis, all right.'

'He'll become deaf and dumb again if you do. Of course, there's no shadow of doubt now but that he said something about the car smash to his grandfather which caused Sir Adrian to threaten him.'

'Yes. There's no proof, which has been our difficulty all along in this case, but we ought to be able to make some sort of lever out of it. Exactly what do you hope to gain from this cricket match?'

'Either direct evidence, or complete capitulation on the part of the murderer of Witt.'

'And which of the twins *really* did it?'

'That is precisely what I want to find out.'

'You still don't know, then?'

'I still don't know. Even on psychological grounds I don't know, although by now I think I can guess.'

The next move was made by Sir Adrian three days later.

'Look here,' he said to Mrs. Bradley, meeting her in the dining-room of the hotel and seating himself without ceremony or permission at her table, 'that young fellow Donagh. Wants me to meet an eleven of his on my private ground at Mede. I suppose you put him up to it. Well, I can tell you this: you tried to call my bluff the other day. I'm

200

calling yours now. You won't, in a month of Sundays, find out anything more about Witt's death than all of us know already. I wasn't concerned, and neither was Derry, and I'll see your hand on that. And as for that other business, I've a good mind to have you up for defamation of character, and I would if we'd had any witnesses.'

'War to the knife, in fact,' said Mrs. Bradley, 'or to my little revolver.' She patted her pocket (in which the little revolver no longer lay) with gratitude and affection. Sir Adrian scowled and got up.

'You heard what I said,' he remarked.

'Have you made up your mind yet which grandson is which?' Mrs. Bradley sweetly demanded. Sir Adrian made a hoarse noise in his throat and could be heard, a moment later, in the bar parlour, calling loudly for rum and orange. Mrs. Bradley followed him in, asked for some brandy and then asked casually:

'As you have been good enough to consult me about the match with Mr. Donagh's eleven, may I take it that I am invited? You remember that I promised to play, so may I come?'

'No, you may not. If you attempt to set foot inside my grounds I'll have you thrown out. And I mean that.'

Mrs. Bradley had not expected to be *persona grata* at the match, and, in any case, it coincided with her plans that she should not be invited to attend it. It was hardly fair to expect Tom Donagh to double-cross his erstwhile employer, so the position of copper's nark, as the young gentleman in question termed it upon becoming acquainted with his duties, was entrusted to Mrs. Bradley's nephew Carey Lestrange, who had been introduced to Donagh and the rest of his side by his Christian name only, and who was so utterly unlike Mrs. Bradley in appearance that it was not anticipated that anybody, friend or foe, would suspect that any relationship between them existed. The rest of the eleven consisted of Mrs. Bradley's nephew Jonathan Bradley, masquerading under his wife's maiden name, two schoolmasters and two Sixth-form boys known to the

captain, three young policemen supplied from London by
Gavin, and the local doctor who was not required by Sir
Adrian to perform for Mede as his lawyer was present and
would act as one of the umpires. Tom Donagh had previously agreed that Sir Adrian should also appoint the second
umpire, and this man turned out to be Grandall, whom Sir
Adrian had brought over from Wetwode. Tavis came with
his friend to watch the match.

The teams were to foregather at ten on the morning of the
match, a feat made possible by the fact that Donagh's
eleven had come to Mede on the previous evening. Lestrange,
Bradley and the policemen put up at Mrs. Cornish's inn,
Donagh and his schoolmaster friends had been invited to
stay at Mede House, and the schoolboys were accommodated at Mrs. Bradley's Stone House and were run over to
Mede by car in time for the match. As Sir Adrian had
concerned himself with none of the visitors except Donagh,
(who had been compelled to cadge invitations for his
friends, who had otherwise intimated that they would not
come and play for him), these arrangements were of no
concern to the captain of the home side.

At a quarter past ten a piece of paper fluttered through
the letterbox at Mede, pushed from the inside to the outside
of the house, and was snatched up by Gavin.

'Both twins playing for Mede. Thought you'd like to
know. We are batting first. Carey.'

'Intelligent chap, your nephew,' said Gavin, going back to
sit beside Mrs. Bradley in her car which was parked outside
the Mede demesne. 'Where do we go from here?'

'I think we join the spectators.'

'But will they let us in?'

'Yes, if we present ourselves after the game has begun.
Sir Adrian has promised to throw me out, but I don't
suppose he'll notice me.'

There seemed no difficulty about gaining admission to the
ground. The public gate was at right-angles to the pavilion,
and the man in charge made no trouble about allowing
them in. He even found a bench for them to sit on.

'So far, so good,' said Gavin, regarding with a critical eye the bowling of Parrish from the eastern end of the ground. 'I say, that bloke's good.' He was more than good. With great satisfaction Mrs. Bradley saw her favourite nephew's wicket go for three runs.

'The batsman also has an eye,' she tolerantly observed. Jonathan Bradley, with good grace, walked back to the pavilion. 'Blood is thicker than water, and true citizenship even greater than cricket,' she concluded. She forbore to applaud the returning batsman for fear of making her presence known to Sir Adrian. The next man in was one of Tom Donagh's schoolmasters. He began merrily . . . so merrily, in fact, that Mrs. Bradley, distrusting so much virtuosity, left the ground immediately after his first over, and went round to the front of the house.

Here, as she had planned, Jonathan Bradley had left the front door open.

She entered the dim house noiselessly, and went straight to the stained glass window which had given Tom Donagh his first glimpse of Sir Adrian's wonderful cricket ground. The window was partly pushed up at the bottom. She raised it a little further and peered out. Then she brought a chair from the hall, climbed on to the inside sill, wriggled like a greased Indian through the aperture she had created, and dropped like a lark to the ground.

The pavilion was ahead of her and a little to her left. Its back door was open. She walked in and presented herself to the man on duty in the tea-room. He did not seem at all surprised to see her.

'Sandwich and coffee, madam?' he enquired.

Apparently anybody who came from the house was thus received, and, knowing Sir Adrian to the extent that, by this time, she did, she realized that some long time ago the men had been told to mind their own business and that of nobody else.

She turned, when she got to the changing rooms, and came back to the man.

'Have you no orders,' she asked sternly, 'concerning the

persons that may make their way through to the front of the pavilion from the house?'

'No, madam, we 'ave not. Anybody coming through from the 'ouse is the master's kettle of fish, as you might say.'

'Ah, yes, I see. Thank you so much.' She passed on, gave a glance into each of the changing rooms, and then made her way to the front of the pavilion in time to see Tom Donagh score a boundary hit. Sir Adrian was in the deep field.

'Now, I wonder,' said Mrs. Bradley to herself. Parrish, Sir Adrian's fast bowler, took balance and then projected himself. Tom turned him to leg for two. Sir Adrian was dancing with impatience. His voice came clearly across the ground.

'Smash his wicket. Smash it, I say.'

But Tom was in form. He snicked Parrish away to the off, and called. His partner happened to be Mrs. Bradley's nephew, Carey, and the batsmen ran a (this time) risky two. This left Tom Donagh facing Parrish again.

'No!' said Mrs. Bradley instinctively. But her warning was unnecessary. Tom stepped out, swirled round, and the ball (which was meant for his ribs) flew out of the ground. The small crowd cheered. Sir Adrian danced anew. He howled that Tom was playing bloody baseball, and then came over and shook his fist in Parrish's face. When the ball was returned he took it himself. His action was neat and careful. Two short strides, a long one, a cross-over step with the feet as by one who throws the javelin, and the ball, of deceptive slowness, was delivered slightly to the off. Tom, with classic timing, scored a boundary hit.

'Pretty cricket,' said the young policeman at Mrs. Bradley's side, 'but the old gentleman doesn't seem appreciative.'

Mrs. Bradley cackled.

'It's a lucky thing that the weather is fine,' she observed. 'It enables the batsmen to do themselves credit. I wonder . . .'

The young policeman nodded.

'I've often thought the weather had something to do with

it, ma'am. You see, I've been thinking it over, and it seems to me that if it hadn't been wet the day that Mr. Witt was killed, Mr. Derek Caux wouldn't now be in need of an alibi.'

'You mean . . . ?' asked Mrs. Bradley, who had nursed this idea herself and was glad to have it confirmed.

'I mean, it was because of the wet weather, it seems, that Sir Adrian ordered Mr. Derek to step indoors. If the day had been fine, he might not have told him to do it, and if Mr. Derek had stopped on the field . . . I hope I'm making it plain, ma'am?'

'You most certainly are, and I am in complete agreement with you. It was not Mr. Derek Caux who killed Mr. Witt. The only question is . . . who did it if he did not?'

'Well, ma'am, those alibis,' said the boy eagerly. 'You see, it appears to me that although they all swear by one another, hardly anybody just sits still in front of a pavilion. They go into the changing rooms, and to get a drink and to relieve themselves . . . everybody does. It didn't take more than a few seconds to hit Mr. Witt on the head, and there was no blood to worry about. It just struck me to wonder . . .'

'Whether one of Mr. Witt's own side could have done it? Yes, I know. I've wondered the same thing myself. But that throws it rather wide open. You see, when Mr. Witt was out, very soon after lunch, there were eight of his eleven in the pavilion.'

'I know, ma'am.' He sounded despondent. 'It's very far-fetched. It was just an idea I had. Ah, but that *is* pretty cricket,' he added on a brighter note as Tom carted Sir Adrian to the boundary and sent up fifty on the board.

There was faint clapping. Sir Adrian, looking murderous, walked down the pitch and cursed Tom roundly. Tom laughed and flourished his bat.

'Mr. Donagh is armed and well-prepared,' said Mrs. Bradley tolerantly. 'It will take Sir Adrian all his time to get the better of him in any way, let alone to obtain the pound of flesh of which he appears to wish to possess himself.'

Sir Adrian stalked back down the pitch and picked up

the ball which had been returned from the deep field. He tossed it up and down as he walked back to take his run. Then he turned and lumbered towards the wicket, but, instead of delivering the ball in his usual manner, he quickened his pace, rushed half-way down the pitch and discharged the ball straight at Tom Donagh's head.

There was a shout of warning and dismay from fielders and spectators alike, but Tom justified Mrs. Bradley's remarks about him by whirling his bat and catching the ball on the edge of it. The ball flew straight towards one of the Caux twins . . . which one nobody could have said. Whichever it was leapt out of the way with a high, girlish scream. The ball crashed against the stout fence with a sound of splintering wood, and Tom, putting down his bat and shaking a badly-jarred hand, went up to Sir Adrian, took him by the collar with his uninjured fingers and shook him. Then he flung him away. Sir Adrian stumbled, tripped and fell. He remained on the grass, his mouth opening and shutting. Two policemen from the opposing team came up and one of them hauled him to his feet.

'Charging him, sir?' one of them asked Tom. Tom shook his head. Gavin came up.

'Take him away,' he said. 'Attempt to cause grievous bodily harm. And I hope he doesn't get bail.'

'I don't want to charge him,' said Tom. 'He's just a bad-tempered old idiot. Let's get on with the game.'

Mrs. Bradley, meanwhile, was making her own depositions, assisted by the general confusion. Her first action was to go on to the field of play and seize the first twin she came to. This was the one who had leapt out of the way of the ball.

'I am going to toss you in the river,' she said. The youth smiled disarmingly.

'Bred and born in a briar patch, Brer Rabbit,' he observed. The rest of the game was a farce. Tom declared at three hundred and one for seven, and Sir Adrian's side, thoroughly demoralized by their captain's bad conduct and worse temper, were all skittled out for sixty-nine.

Lunch had been a meal of tropic sullenness on the part of the home team. Mrs. Bradley, who had slipped through the house and returned to her car, waited until the game was over and then pushed a message through the door. It was retrieved by the impeccable Masters and taken straight to Sir Adrian, who swore and crumpled it up. It read:

Tell Gavin ask what explanation bar tenders and refreshment stewards offer to account for loss of food between match with mental hospital and match with Bruke.'

She drove home after that, back to her own house at Wandles Parva. She knew that Gavin would find her, and that her relatives would probably drop in for a drink before returning to their various homes. Gavin, who had been previously advised of the inflammable contents of Mrs. Bradley's note to Sir Adrian, casually observed that evening, 'I spoke to those blokes. They said that they supposed one of the lunatics did a bit of pilfering. They didn't say anything about it to Sir Adrian, not knowing what his reactions might be. In any case, he never kept very much check on the food, but only on the drinks, and those weren't touched. I asked at the time, if you remember, whether they had suspected that somebody—a tramp, perhaps—had used the pavilion as his sleeping quarters, but they were pretty sure nobody had. All the same, I think I know what you mean.'

'What does she mean?' asked Carey Lestrange, who had called on his aunt after the match on his way home to Oxfordshire.

'That although two and two are not mathematically proved to make four, they not infrequently do so,' replied Mrs. Bradley.

CHAPTER TWENTY

The Echo from Wetwode

★

*'Don't be afraid of me, Marian,' was all she said: 'I
may forget myself with an old friend like Mr. Gilmore
... but I will not forget myself with Sir Percival Glyde.'*
Wilkie Collins: *The Woman in White*

★

'IT'S DIFFICULT to see how we're going to get at the whole
truth, even now,' said Gavin, when he and Mrs. Bradley
were alone. 'Thanks to the fact that the twins are identi-
cally alike, who's going to be able to say whether it was
Francis or Derek he saw at any particular time on the day
of Witt's death? I know your theory, of course. You mean
that Francis came to Mede on the day of that match against
the mental patients, mingled with their supporters, disguised with a false moustache or something obviously and
equally silly, was admitted by his brother to the pavilion
when the team and the onlookers left, and then probably
sneaked into the house after dark and slept in his brother's
bed. They were clever about it all, as usual, and Francis
wasn't spotted. He remained on and around the premises
to wait for the Bruke match, and took his opportunity of
killing Witt. Then, he simply walked out of the front door
of his grandfather's house and returned to Wetwode. You
see the snag, of course?'

'Miss Higgs, who, so far, has not told us that he was ever
away for so long. And yet she did, you know.'

'What was it, then? And anyway, I myself never thought
of connecting the lost tins of food with the presence of
Francis.'

'He has always been the hungry twin,' Mrs. Bradley rather inconsequently observed. 'But about Miss Higgs: she said, you remember, she'd had her doubts about Francis.'

'Oh, yes, she couldn't believe he would push her into the river and, (according to her) down the steps of the post-office. I suppose that means she blames Derek for her concussion and the broken leg. I don't see that it helps us very much. After all, we know now that the twins changed places.'

'It was something else she said. Don't you remember she said she had never thought Francis would stay out all night?'

'Yes, but she only meant that business with the girl who afterwards married and went to live out of the district.'

'That is what we thought at the time. We thought it automatically, as it were. But, you see, it had another significance. It could mean he was out all that night before Witt was murdered!'

'But the food, it seems, disappeared after the match against the mental hospital, and, if that's true, it would mean that Francis Caux was away from home for *two* nights. Wouldn't Miss Higgs have said so?'

'She has herself to protect, remember. She did not report the boy's absence. She concluded, I expect, just as we did, that he was . . .'

'Chasing petticoats again? Yes, I see. Well, she'll have to come across if he was away those two nights. You see, the match with the mental hospital was on a Tuesday, the following day was free, and the match with Bruke, when Witt was killed, was on Thursday. That means Francis must have spent Tuesday night and Wednesday night at Mede, and we know the dates, so now to jog Miss Higgs' memory.'

'Of course, he may only have been absent on the Tuesday night,' said Mrs. Bradley thoughtfully. 'There is no reason why Derek, accustomed to the change-over of their identities, should not have come over to Wetwode on the Wednesday night and taken his brother's place. The fact that Francis-Derek was absent all day on the Thursday may have worried

Miss Higgs, but it may not have occasioned her any surprise. You remember we were told at the beginning that Francis was a "solitary." ' '

'Ah,' said Gavin. 'I hadn't thought of that. Well, now to interview, all over again, the boy who told us about Campbell's hide-out.' The boy was available but his father was difficult.

'I don't have him drawed into any sort of a law-case.'

'He won't be. But there is one point which he can clear up for us. Won't you allow us to question him?'

'He's only twelve year of age.'

'I know. And, believe me, we won't frighten him, and he won't need to appear in court. It's simply a date I'm after.'

'I don't think he give it. Seems that ciphering isn't his strong point.'

'Nevertheless, I think you'd better let me see him. I really won't frighten him, you know. After all, he's met us once. He'll feel he knows us, and this is a case of murder. Surely nobody wants a murderer on the loose.' Gavin was determined and grave, and the man gave in.

'Can I stop along of you while you ask him?'

'Certainly. There's no objection to that.'

'On the other hand, that speak more free if I don't happen to be there.'

'Please yourself,' said Gavin in his most serious tones. 'I promise you the boy won't be mixed up in anything. It's just some confirmation I want.'

'What about?'

'Well, I might be putting my foot in it with your son if I told you that.'

The Norfolk labourer gave a slow smile. He relaxed.

'I've been a boy myself,' he said engagingly. Thereupon, having bellowed for his son, he left Mrs. Bradley and Gavin alone in the parlour, and, in less than a minute, a small, very newly-scrubbed boy sidled awkwardly in.

'Ah, you're the chap,' said Gavin. 'Look, son, about Mr. Campbell's hide-out. Remember?'

The child looked sullen.

'Blood,' said Mrs. Bradley, leering at him like Fagin at Oliver Twist. 'Blood in the lair. Do little boys like blood?'

The boy began to cry, but more because he wished to be free from persecution than because he was otherwise perturbed by the memories which her words recalled to his mind.

'Something had happened, hadn't it?' asked Gavin gently. 'And you boys said nothing because you were afraid of Mr. Campbell?'

The boy looked up at him.

'Us boys never see anything in Mr. Campbell's hide-out,' he said. 'Us stop gooing there because we find another place to go to.'

'But you did stop going there.'

'Us did. Willy Thetford say that isn't any good to go there any more.'

'So Willy didn't like the blood, either.'

'Willy, that say it isn't lucky to go there.'

'How old is Willy?'

'Thirteen.'

'Oh, yes. All right, then, laddie. That'll be all.'

The father came back and loomed over Gavin.

'What do you accuse my boy of?'

'Nothing at all. A murder was committed in Mr. Campbell's hide-out not far from here, and the boys have been accustomed to play about around there.'

The man took the boy by the collar.

'Billy, you tell the police officer and the lady all you know.'

The boy's story was what they had expected, and the date, which they left the boy to work back to without any prompting from either of them, fitted in with what was already known of the week in which Campbell had been killed. What was more, besides the traces of blood near the entrance to the hide-out, the boys had discovered the weapon, a heavy piece of reinforced concrete, possibly part of a dismantled air-raid shelter, Gavin thought, which had cut Campbell's head and made it bleed.

The boys had dropped it into the ooze at the edge of the river, having some muddle-headed theory, apparently, that to take the police to see it was to court disaster for themselves.

'A chunk of an air-raid shelter, probably off a bomb-site,' said Gavin again later. 'I said so at the time that the boy described it. It's got to be proved where it came from, and, for that, we begin in Great Yarmouth, where we know Francis Caux was staying at the time when Campbell was murdered. And we've no proof that Derek went there. In fact, we can be pretty sure that in June he could not have done so, because the only time he could stay with his brother and Miss Higgs was when Sir Adrian went off grouse-shooting in the middle of August.'

'Agreed,' said Mrs. Bradley, 'and also agreed that the twins had brought that change-over of identities to a fine art by the time the two murders were committed. But now I think we must get on the track of Sonia.'

'Sonia?'

'One of Mr. Darnwell's nieces. The one whom Mr. Campbell questioned about her altruistic but loving uncle.'

Gavin laughed. Darnwell, who now took a great interest in the subject of Campbell's death and the manner of it, gave them Sonia's permanent address and full name, and Gavin found her, after some trouble, in a touring company at the seaside. She could add little to their knowledge. Campbell had come to Darnwell's bungalow one day (when he had seen Darnwell go out) on the excuse of having run out of milk. She had let him have some, and they had conversed. He had begun to question her about Darnwell and she had refused to discuss him. Then he had become what she termed fresh, and she had turned him out.

'One more question, Miss du Bonne,' said Gavin, 'and I hope you won't mind my putting it rather crudely. Did you ever have any trouble with the boy Caux, who lived in the first of the bungalows?'

'Frankie Caux? Oh, gracious, no, poor boy! He was handsome enough, especially when he was all stripped and

that for swimming, and he used to look at me nervous . . .
you know what nice boys are like! . . . but even if he'd been
ever so, I couldn't have had anything like that from a poor
deaf and dumb. It would give me the willies. You see, I'm
sensitive, and if you're as sensitive as what I am . . .'

It did not help at all, except to indicate that whilst she had
stayed with Darnwell it was probably the real Francis Caux
with Miss Higgs, but as the date had no possible importance
Gavin felt that he had wasted his time.

'But you haven't wasted your time!' said Mrs. Bradley,
when he had faithfully reported the whole conversation. 'At
last we have an unbiassed, independent witness, who, with
any luck at all, may be able to tell one twin from the other.'

'How do you mean? If she'd slept with him, or something,
she might . . . but even then I only say she *might* . . . and even
if she did, I hardly see how, under those circumstances, she'd
be prepared to tell us how she knew the difference.'

'She's watched him swimming. You go back and find out
whether she's ever noticed any distinguishing mark. Don't
forget that he was in the dreadful accident which killed his
parents. There might be something. It's quite worth while
to try. You see, if only we were in a position to tell the twins
that we could definitely distinguish one from the other,
their great strength, like Samson's hair, would be gone. It is
only because nobody can tell them apart that they have
dared to behave as they have.'

'You said something about a sort of witchcraft trial,
didn't you? Chuck them both into the river and see which
one of them can swim,' said Gavin grinning. Mrs. Bradley
smiled mirthlessly.

'Francis will have polished up his brother's swimming by
now,' she said dryly. 'In vulgar speech, one would have to
get up very early in the morning to catch those boys out
now.'

Sonia, courteously approached once more by a sceptical
Gavin, could help very little.

'I used to watch him, yes. He was a lovely swimmer,' she
said, 'and of course he'd only wear those little bathing

trunks. But beyond he had a lovely skin, all creamy-brown and that, and no hairs on his chest, I mean, well, there was really nothing. I think he was keen on his hair, though, more than some boys, and I'm not surprised, being so pretty, all golden and that.'

'Keen on his hair?'

'Well, he always wore one of them little caps like water-polo boys.'

'The Sister at the Cottage Hospital may be able to help us now,' said Mrs. Bradley. She herself undertook the mission.

'Yes, he had to have five stitches. Doctor didn't think he would have a permanent scar, though, and, even if he did, he could have grown his hair to cover it,' said the nurse. 'It was just here.' She touched her own head above the left temple. 'I remember it well, because I thought how lucky such a lovely little boy wouldn't be disfigured for anyone to notice.'

In the meantime Inspector Cowley, charged by Gavin with the task, had set his men to work to trace the origin of the reinforced concrete with which the murder of Campbell had been committed. When Gavin informed Mrs. Bradley of this, she cackled and asked whether, now that he had returned to Mede with his grandsons, Sir Adrian proposed to stay there. Gavin, who knew her well, looked at her suspiciously. She nodded slowly. His face cleared.

'If you mean what I think you do,' he said, 'it would be all over bar the shouting, so far as the murder of Campbell was concerned. I should arrest both boys and charge them jointly with causing Campbell's death. But what makes you think . . . ?'

'That reinforced concrete lump being probably a piece from an air-raid shelter, child. Fingerprints it is too rough to take, and, anyway, it's been in thick mud, apart from the fact that those children handled it. But if we could prove that a piece of reinforced concrete found in Wetwode had actually come from Mede House, we should be fully entitled to ask those connected with both places some very awkward questions.'

'Mede wasn't in a danger area, you know,' said Gavin.

'It is not so very far from Southampton. I don't think Sir Adrian would have dreamed of running the least unnecessary risk where his favourite grandson was concerned, even if he was only at home for holidays.'

A nod was as good as a wink, and the Hampshire police, already in a strategic position for this owing to the murder of Witt, visited Sir Adrian's grounds again. The air-raid shelter had been demolished and the materials made into a rock garden. The constitution of the 'rocks' and that of the piece of masonry which had killed Campbell were identical.

'So far, so good,' said Gavin. 'We're on a straight road at last. Of course, we haven't actually *proved* that the stuff came off the rock-garden, but it's pretty good circumstantial evidence.'

CHAPTER TWENTY-ONE

The Echo of Gemini

★

'There she met Sleep, the brother of Death.'
Lang, Leaf and Myers: *The Iliad of Homer*

★

WHILST evidence appeared to be mounting against the twin brothers, Mrs. Bradley received a letter from her old school-fellow, Mabel Parkinson.

'Miss Higgs is in a state of great excitement. Sir Adrian Caux has formally notified her that he no longer requires her services, but, out of consideration of her loyalty and duty, he has bought the bungalow and put money in trust to bring her in an income of two hundred a year. She is quite overjoyed. She has seen the lawyers and there appears, in her own words, to be no catch in it. Miss Higgs is provided for.'

Mrs. Bradley, greatly intrigued, went to Wetwode to visit Mabel Parkinson, and there learned full details, including the fact that Miss Higgs had gone, the day she received the glad news, to the bungalow to live.

'She still gets about on two sticks, but she was quite determined,' she said. 'She has quite got over her prejudice about going back. And, really, Beatrice, your cheques for her maintenance have been much too generous. I want you to take some of the money back.'

'Nonsense,' said Mrs. Bradley. 'I knew you'd refuse to take any money from *her*. Besides, my chief object was not altruistic at all. I just didn't want her running away from the scene of the crime.'

'You know,' said Mabel Parkinson, gazing at Mrs. Bradley in fearful fascination, 'I'm perfectly sure you used not to be like this at school. I chiefly remember you in the gym and at cricket, and being so jolly good at maths., and English, and music, and playing up Miss Poppleweather.'

Mrs. Bradley regarded her with a sentimental leer, and remarked that both of them had watched a good many tides come in and a good many tides go out since schooldays.

'But I should never have *dreamed* you'd be good at psychology,' said Mabel, 'and interested in crime.'

Mrs. Bradley pointed out that she had been very good at Miss Poppleweather's psychology and that this, more often than not, at school had led to crime.

'But this murder of Mr. Campbell,' pursued Mabel. 'How is it all going to end?'

'Well, let's see what we've got,' said Mrs. Bradley. 'And then *you'll* be able to tell *me*.' And because she knew that, under the strangling influence of the Old School Tie (which, in their case, happened to be a blasphemous combination of gold, silver and purple) Mabel would never breathe a word of what she was told by an old school chum without having first obtained that chum's permission, she went on, 'Now, to begin with, we've twins and two murders, each murder being connected, so far as locality is concerned, with one or other of the twins.

'The murders have two points of resemblance, but the other factors are all different. The murders were each committed in the same way. They were the result of a heavy blow on the head. However, the weapons used were not the same. In the one case a sensible and in the other case an ultimately foolish weapon was used.

'The cricket bat, belonging, as it did, to the dead man, was a sensible choice. Its handle took no prints, there was no attempt to hide it, the murderer left no traces of his presence except the blood-stained bat and the corpse. It is true that he may have stolen tinned food from the cricket pavilion, but there is no proof that he did, and the tins, full or empty, have not been discovered. The murder of Witt at Mede was, in fact, almost a perfect crime. It had but one flaw. It produced a suspect, Derek Caux, who may well have had a motive for the crime, and who had no alibi for the time of Witt's death.'

'So far, so good,' said Mabel Parkinson, 'but it's *our* murder which interests *me*.'

'Let us look at it, then. Here we have a very different picture. It is true that the method was the same . . . a heavy blow on the head. But our second (in point of time, our first) murderer puts any number of unexpected touches to his crime. He moves the body from the scene of the crime and yet does not remove the traces of that crime. He hides the body underneath a boat. He even takes the extraordinary course of having staples especially made so that he can fasten the body as his disordered imagination suggests. The blacksmith who made the staples to his order can even, in some measure, describe him, and although the description would fit some thousands of men there are two persons it does *not* fit . . . but, of that, more anon.

'Between the murder at Mede and the death of Campbell here at Wetwode there is one other point of resemblance. Both the murdered men were blackmailers. In addition to this, it turns out that at one time they were acquainted with one another. Therefore, there is reason to see a connection between the murders: we have the twin brothers and the motive for getting rid of two blackmailers. We also have a criminal history almost unique, I imagine, since it runs through two generations of the Caux family for certain, and very possibly into a third.

'There are puzzling features, however, about the murders of Witt and Campbell. I spoke just now of the description given by the blacksmith of the customer who ordered the staples for fastening Campbell's body to the bottom of the dinghy, and I said that, whomever the description fitted, there were two people whom it could not possibly fit.'

'Yes, the twin brothers,' agreed Mabel Parkinson, with a vigorous nod. 'Of course, I did see that. But this is most interesting. Go on.'

'Well, that description is an insuperable obstacle in the otherwise reasonable case which could be built up against the Caux twins, and the other doubtful point is the apparently idiotic behaviour of the twin, (which ever it was), who was playing in the cricket match against Bruke, in leaving the field of play at the time of Witt's murder. But for his having done that, I don't know that the connection between the murders of Witt and Campbell would have been so decidedly noticeable.

'Then, you see, the fact that the staples were not ordered by either twin, but by someone whose general description could apply to Sir Adrian Çaux, for example, seems to dispose of any share the boys may have had in putting Campbell out of the way.'

'I'm very stupid, I expect, but I can't quite see that point.'

'Well, the natural assumption would be that Campbell was blackmailing the boys because he knew they changed places, and so were making a fool of their grandfather, who adored the one and detested the other. Sir Adrian is a conceited and bad-tempered man, and it is more than likely that he would disinherit even his beloved Derek if it were pointed out to him that all his affection and all his dislike had not availed to enable him to distinguish one twin from the other, and that while the real Francis was enjoying his favour at Mede House, the real Derek was playing havoc with village girls at Wetwode.'

'Oh, dear me, yes, of course.'

'Whereas, if Sir Adrian turned out to be the person responsible for pinning the body underneath that boat, then it must surely mean that he was aware of the boys' game of exchanging identities and had used it for his own purposes.'

'His own purposes?'

'To get rid of Campbell, while contriving to give the impression that Francis had committed the murder.'

'But that would mean. . . . Surely that might mean. . . . Oh, no one would be so wicked!'

Mrs. Bradley nodded solemnly. 'I mean what I say, and that is the conclusion to which I have come,' she said, 'and there is really nothing in Sir Adrian's reputation to give the lie to it. Remember . . . oh, of course, you don't know!

When Francis Caux was in hospital as a boy of seven, he told the nurse that his grandfather was responsible for the death of his parents in that car crash ten years ago.'

'Ten years is a long time, and there couldn't be any proof now.'

'Quite. But a guilty conscience is a terrible bedfellow. Besides, whilst he believed the boy to be deaf and dumb, Sir Adrian thought he had nothing to fear. Once he learned . . . and exactly how and when he learned it we still don't know . . . that the boy could both hear and speak, his only defence, as he saw it, was to get the boy put out of the way; that is, to take his life. He has not yet dared to kill the boy himself, but there is no doubt (in *my* mind, at any rate) that he intended Francis to suffer for the death of Campbell. Unless to incriminate Francis, what other motive could he have had in transporting Campbell's body (at such risk) to the bungalow and fastening it so that it had to remain where it was? No river current, even, could move it, and as soon as anybody attempted to use the dinghy, more particularly if he tried to lower the centre-board, the crime was bound to be discovered and the obvious suspect would be Francis Caux. Once Campbell's blackmailing exploits came to light, as they were bound to do, sooner or later, when the circumstances of his death were investigated, a motive would be provided at which few police officers would look twice before accepting it.'

'But would they hang a boy of seventeen?'

'No. But they would detain him, probably indefinitely, and the beauty of the thing, from Sir Adrian's point of view, was that, after that, nobody would believe a convicted murderer who tried to make the police or anyone else believe that his grandfather, too, was a murderer.'

'But what an abominable plot! What shall you do about it now?'

'Consult Mr. Gavin and lay all my findings before him and the local police. You see, a very strong point in my argument is that, if Francis Caux had been responsible for Campbell's death and had hidden the body, he would not have been so anxious to have it discovered. What would be the object of finding so elaborate a hiding-place if one proposed, at the first opportunity, to disclose it? It isn't as if (once Campbell, its owner, was dead) anybody but Francis himself was likely to use the dinghy. But that, of course, was one point overlooked by Sir Adrian.'

'Well,' said Gavin, impressed by Mrs. Bradley's arguments, 'there's only one thing to do now. We'll confront Sir Adrian with that blacksmith, and if the blacksmith swears to him I'll arrest him and charge him with Campbell's murder. As you say, the risk he took in going to the blacksmith at all is in character. But all this doesn't help us over the murder of Witt.'

'Oh, Francis killed Witt,' said Mrs. Bradley with great composure. 'I've never had much doubt about that. But I don't think we'll ever prove it, except by a trick which I'm very loth to play on brothers as devoted as those two.'

'Arrest Derek, because he has no alibi, you mean, and so force Francis to confess? I don't like the sound of that, either, especially as Witt seems to have been a thorough scoundrel. We've dug out most of his past, and he seems to have lived on blackmail since he caught his employer out. That man has been dead for five years . . . committed suicide because he couldn't satisfy Witt's demands any longer. So if the verdict has to stay at person or persons unknown, it won't cause *me* to lose sleep. After all, as you say, we've no evidence. Of course, if any evidence came our way, I'd be in duty bound to make use of it. That must be understood.'

'Of course, child, but I don't believe the evidence exists. Derek has no alibi; but that, in the absence of motive, would certainly not be sufficient to convict him, any more than the loss of the pavilion tinned food would convict Francis.'

'Blackmail, surely, was the motive.'

'What evidence is there that Witt ever blackmailed the boy?'

'None, among Witt's papers. I'm bound to admit that. None of the Caux names appear in anything that we've found. Of course, Derek, at any rate, is extremely intelligent. He may have found means to destroy the part of Witt's stuff which referred to himself or his family.'

'Yes, that point must be considered, but you've no reason to suppose that he did anything of the kind.'

'This sounds like special pleading.'

'I don't like murderers, but I like blackmailers even less. The majority of murders do at least take place quickly, but the blackmailer is a slow torturer.'

'We can't let that influence us, though, if any further evidence does turn up.'

'Of course not. I was merely expressing a personal opinion. Murder, unfortunately, is a human crime and a dreadful one, but torture is the work of devils, and nothing I have seen, read or heard will ever cause me to change my mind about that.'

'I'm going to see young Donagh once more, and see whether he can't think up another pointer, all the same,' said Gavin obstinately.

'He has provided us with one which we haven't used yet, but, once again, it isn't evidence.'

'I've been over and over everything Donagh has told us. *I* can't see anything else. How do you mean?'

'I mean that I want a little god to worship when it is wet,' said Mrs. Bradley solemnly. Gavin eyed her with his usual expression of mistrust, but he had so much confidence in her abilities that he scribbled her last remark down, resolved to collate it with the rest of the information at his disposal.

Mrs. Bradley went to Miss Higgs, now back in the river-side bungalow.

'Did Sir Adrian know the date when you took Francis to Great Yarmouth this year?' she asked, when, over a cup of tea, she had listened sympathetically to Miss Higgs' rapturous recountal of Sir Adrian's generosity. Miss Higgs hesitated. She flushed. Then she replied in the negative.

'Ah,' said Mrs. Bradley, rising and taking her departure without more ado. Miss Higgs cried after her, but she refused to answer or look back. When she re-joined Gavin

she observed, 'And, of course, it was Sir Adrian who tried
to murder Malachi Thetford at the regatta. We musn't
forget that. He might have murdered him for Derek's sake
but scarcely for the sake of Francis. He must have had reason
to think that Malachi had evidence that it was not Francis
who committed the crime. Of course, Malachi had no such
evidence. It is surprising what a guilty conscience will do.'

Gavin blinked at her.

'I'll take your word for all of it,' he said, 'but I don't see
the point of the little god. Oh, yes, I'm sorry! Of course I
do! The model of the man and the model of the boat when
you first came to stay in that bungalow. Then it was Derek
who asked for Herodotus on the Tuesday, but on Wednesday, when it was wet, it was Francis who decided to model
the little god. But we still don't know that it *was* Francis
who modelled the man and the boat. Otherwise, your contention that Francis, and not Derek, was at Mede on the
day before the cricket match would be acceptable.'

He grinned at her, happy again.

'I know,' said Mrs. Bradley. 'There isn't any proof of
whether Francis was at Mede to murder Witt or not. I'm
glad. I felt bound to mention the modelling again, that is all.'

Gavin got the local inspector to take out a warrant for
Sir Adrian's arrest, but only with difficulty. There would be
a lot of trouble, the local inspector pointed out, if any
mistake had been made.

'There's no mistake,' said Gavin.

But they arrived too late at Mede. Sir Adrian was dead
in his library, shot through the head. The revolver he had
used had dropped to the carpeted floor by the side of his
chair. His own prints were on it, and he had left a farewell
letter.

'Turned the boys out so that I could do this. All my
money left to Derry. Know them apart at last. Determined
to keep them both with me until I did. Higgs is a good soul.
Glad I leave her provided for. Campbell threatened Derry.
Derry told me. I had to settle that. No regrets except Derry
will share with Francis.'

'Higgs is a good soul,' repeated Mrs. Bradley slowly. 'In other words, Miss Higgs, who seems to possess more brains than those for which I have given her credit . . .'

'Tipped Sir Adrian off that she thought the game was up, I suppose,' said Gavin bitterly, baulked of his prey. He had taken along the blacksmith who had made the staples. The man gave a horrified look at the dead Sir Adrian, but identified him at once. 'And now to get hold of those confounded boys,' Gavin concluded.

'You're going to charge Francis Caux, then, with the murder of Witt?'

'You bet I am. And it's no good being sentimental about it.'

'I don't think I am,' Mrs. Bradley meekly replied. 'I see that you realize why Derek Caux has no alibi for the time of Witt's death.'

'Meant to land his brother in the soup, ultimately, I suppose.'

'The contrary, I imagine. Witt had become a menace . . . or the boys thought he had. A pity Sir Adrian did not confide in Derek. I suppose he was too deeply hurt at the trick the two of them had played on him to want to share his knowledge with his favourite . . . particularly as, for a long time, he was never sure which of them *was* his favourite. No, Derek was afraid for Francis, who was determined for Derek's sake to murder Witt, and so he did what he could to prove that if either of them appeared to be guilty, he was the one.'

The search for the boys was not a long one. They had returned to Wetwode. Among the long reeds of the Broad the two bodies were found. They were clasped together physically in death as mentally they had been clasped together in life. Their pockets were weighted with stone from Sir Adrian's garden, a macabre, symbolic touch which Gavin did not appreciate.

'Better like this,' said Mrs. Bradley, as though in benediction; and she gazed with pity not unmixed with terror at the two youths, god-like in their beauty, as they lay with their wet hair making a green-gold nimbus on the grass.

MORE VINTAGE MURDER MYSTERIES